THE *Secret* QUEST

Dear Mark and Ali,

This story is all about Ken's two sons - Tim (Bimbo) and Colin (Bollin).

Love and Blessings,

[signature]

VOLUME SEVEN

THE *Secret* QUEST

The Twith Logue Chronicles
Adventures with the Little People

KENNETH G. OLD
& PATTY OLD WEST

TATE PUBLISHING
AND ENTERPRISES, LLC

Published by Tate Publishing & Enterprises, LLC
127 E. Trade Center Terrace | Mustang, Oklahoma 73064 USA
1.888.361.9473 | www.tatepublishing.com

Tate Publishing is committed to excellence in the publishing industry. The company reflects the philosophy established by the founders, based on Psalm 68:11,
"The Lord gave the word and great was the company of those who published it."

Book design copyright © 2013 by Tate Publishing, LLC. All rights reserved.
Cover design by Rtor Maghuyop
Interior design by Jomar Ouano

Poetry excerpts from Footprints in the Dust by Kenneth G. Old
Map design by Rich and Lisa Ballou
Author photo by Karin Spanner

Published in the United States of America

ISBN: 978-1-62295-097-3
1. Juvenile Fiction / Fairy Tales & Folklore / General
2. Juvenile Fiction / Action & Adventure / General
12.11.27

DEDICATION

Ken spinning tales of the Little People
to children gathered on Sandes Hill

Dedicated to the children who first heard these stories
at the boarding school in Murree, Pakistan.

OTHER BOOKS BY KENNETH G. OLD

Walking the Way
Footprints in the Dust
A Boy and His Lunch
So Great a Cloud
Roses for a Stranger
The Wizard of Wozzle
Squidgy on the Brook
Gibbins Brook Farm
The Wizard Strikes Twice
Beyonders in Gyminge
The SnuggleWump Roars

OTHER BOOKS BY PATTY OLD WEST

Good and Faithful Servant
Once Met, Never Forgotten
The Wizard of Wozzle
Squidgy on the Brook
Gibbins Brook Farm
The Wizard Strikes Twice
Beyonders in Gyminge
The SnuggleWump Roars

To learn more about the books listed above, visit the
website: http://littlepeoplestories.tateauthor.com

EAGLE'S FLIGHT

Better grasp at a flying star
Than seize the sweet fruit on the bough.
Better than walking tall, by far,
Is to soar with the eagles now.

~

When there is a chance to choose
There are things only birds can see.
Better by far wings than shoes.
Alas, earthbound mortals are we.

~

Better a child's mind set alight
With fantasy's call to be free
Than a hundred facts put right
To maintain its captivity.

ACKNOWLEDGMENTS

Ken Old was a man of many talents. The Lord endowed him with the ability to see beyond the everyday and gave him the creative writing talent to put those dreams and visions onto paper. His unique way of looking at things opens up new vistas of imagination beyond the ordinary. It is my hope that while reading about the Little People, you can capture some of that same exciting, vibrant, carefree way of living and seeing.

Special thanks go to Margaret Spoelman, Patrick Wilburn, and Kim Dang for kindly making copies of the first chapters Gumpa sent by e-mail. After being entered into the computer, Gumpa's creative genius generated more than would fit into one book. It was split, and the two smaller stories were expanded once again. Those also became too large and had to be divided. Eventually, the initial few chapters became twelve volumes known as *The Twith Logue Chronicles*. They chronicle the adventures of the Little People as they are exiled from their homeland until they are able to return many centuries later.

It is with heartfelt gratitude and much appreciation that I acknowledge my darling daughters, Sandy Gaudette, Becky Shupe and Karin Spanner, who were instrumental in helping me with both the initial editing and final proofreading of the manuscript. My professional editor, Lindsey Marcus, willingly shared her wisdom and insight for improving the flow and readability of the story. I am most grateful for her expert guidance.

Finally, I must give credit to my dear, sweet, kind, considerate, thoughtful, and wonderful husband, Roy. At times, he must have felt like a widower once again, as I spent so many hours with my nose pressed up against my computer screen. His patient, loving support has allowed me to continue the process of sharing these delightful stories with others.

N

Ben
Armine

Scotland

Ireland

England

★
London

Wales

Atlantic
Ocean

Cornwall

Wozzle &
Gyminge   • ▪▪ Dover

Gibbins
Brook
Farm

• St. Newlyn East

English Channel

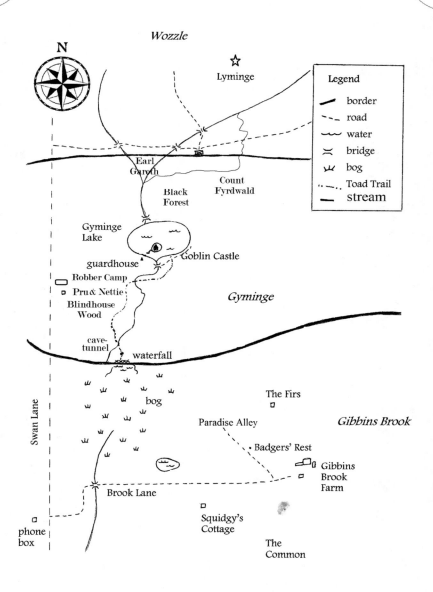

Wozzle and Gyminge—neighboring countries of Little People
The Brook (or Common)—new home
for nine of the Little People

PRINCIPAL CHARACTERS

THE LITTLE PEOPLE / TWITH LOGUE
(TWI th LOW guh)

Jock	Leader of the Twith Logue
Jordy	Jock's longtime friend
Taymar	Jock's right-hand man
Gerald	Keeper of the Lore
Stumpy / Cleemo	Oldest of the Twith
Cymbeline (CYMBAL een)	Stumpy's niece
Barney	Stumpy's nephew, youngest of the Twith
Cydlo (SID low)	A woodcutter
Elisheba (Eh LISH eh buh)	His daughter
Dr. Vyruss Tyfuss	A doctor of etymology
Scayper (SKAY purr)	A prisoner of the wizard
Pru	An elderly lady in Gyminge
Nettie	Pru's friend

THE BEYONDERS

Gumpa	An early friend of the Twith
gran'ma	His wife
Bimbo & Bollin	Their married sons / Shadow children

The Birds and Animals

Buffo	The toad, doorkeeper for the Twith
Crusty	The eagle
Loopy	Pru's wolf-dog
Sparky	The sparrow
Tuwhit (Too WHIT)	The barn owl

The Wizard and his Cronies

Griswold (GRIZ walled)	The Wizard of Wozzle
Rasputin (Rass PUH tin)	The wizard's raven
King Haymun	The king of the goblins
Mrs. Griselda Squidge	Squidgy, the old woman on the Brook
Cajjer (CAD jur)	Squidgy's cat
The SnuggleWump	Squidgy's watchguard
MoleKing / Moley	King of the moles

Places

Gyminge (GIH minge)	Land of the Little People
Wozzle (WOZ el)	The kingdom of the wizard

DAYKO'S RIME

Forget not the land that you leave
As you flee from the pain and grief.
Let Truth in your heart ever burn.
It alone can bring your Return.

The hour the Return shall begin,
The captive shall tug at her chain.
Two spheres of night only you stay;
You shall not have longer a day.

From the water the shield will come,
The sword will come forth from the stone,
The dirk from the dust will return,
And the cloth will give up the crown.

The open door's better to guard
Than one which is bolted and barred.
Though conspire the foe and his friend
Yet the dog shall win in the end.

You go through the heart of the log,
Though the way is hid in the bog.
Black and white the flag high will rise.
The Child shall lead on to the Prize.

The goblet holds no draught of wine
And yields but a drop at a time.
The king will arise in the wood.
The Rime is at last understood.

The armour the flame will withstand.
Salt wind shall blow over the land
For light in the heart of the ring
Shall end the restraint of the king.

The belt is restored from the fire.
Brides shall process to the byre.
The loss of the Lore gives grief,
Though what is that to a life?

The fall will lead straight to the wall.
Hope is restored last of all.
Two reds in the night shall be green.
All's done. I've told what I've seen.

PREFACE

Gumpa loved to tell stories to children. It gave him a chance to be a child again himself. *The Twith Logue Chronicles,* which just means "Little People Stories," are fanciful, imaginative fairy tales that he told over a period of more than fifty years to children from ages five to fifteen. He just made them up as he went along, and the children always wanted to hear more. They would ask, "Will you please read some more out of your head?" The heroes of these stories are the Little People, only half a thumb high, known as the Twith Logue or just plain Twith.

When Gumpa retired, there weren't so many children around, so he began writing the stories to send to children. The stories are a mixture of reality and fantasy, and sometimes it is hard to tell where one leaves off and the other begins. I think that sometimes he didn't even know himself. The reality part is the old Tudor farmhouse and the surrounding area known as Gibbins Brook in Kent, England. The fantasy part is the Little People—Jock and Jordy; Taymar and Gerald; Stumpy; Barney and his sister, Cymbeline; and Cydlo and his daughter, Elisheba. The adventures they have with Gumpa are where reality fades into fantasy.

So picture yourself sitting on Gumpa's knee or gathered with other children at his feet and listen as Gumpa puts you into the world of the Little People, challenging *you* to *tell the truth*. His overactive imagination will take you into strange and exciting adventures.

PROLOGUE

A prologue tells what has happened before. In the beginning, a boy named Griswold, who lived in Cornwall, studied hard to learn magic. He grew up to become a mean and cunning wizard who loves to create chaos. Anyone who uses magic has some kind of twitch. For the wizard, his twitchy right eye is a dead giveaway. It has foiled the perfect execution of more than one superior plan conceived by his brilliant mind.

The Little People do *not* use magic, and they *always tell the truth*. These tiny folk are very wise and know many things we don't. They have senses we don't have, so they can understand and talk to animals and birds. The Little People know how to halt time, so they can stop growing older whenever they want. Barney, for instance, is happy to stay a young boy. Even though they are only half a thumb high, they have managed to survive for many centuries. Winning battles doesn't always depend on how big you are. These wee folk live in the east of England in the kingdoms of Wozzle and Gyminge, just to the north of Gibbins Brook.

Over a thousand years ago, the wicked wizard decided to invade these countries and become their ruler. Changing himself to match the size of the Little People, he conquered first Wozzle and then Gyminge. Many of the Little People refused to be his subjects, so he sealed them up in bottles and stored them in the dungeons. There were others he turned into goblins, but seven of the Little People were able to escape with their valuable Book of Lore. They decided to settle on the Brook among the Beyonders. The Little People call those who live outside their land Beyonders. The adults and children you know are all Beyonders. Very few Beyonders know about the Little People, so you are privileged to be learning about them.

Mrs. Squidge, an old woman from Cornwall, arrived on the Brook, riding on her broomstick. She came to ask the wizard's help with her magic. It sometimes goes wrong. Squidgy accidentally turned a lizard into a SnuggleWump with two heads. Each head has one eye in the center that changes from red to green depending on his mood. When she settled on the Brook, she met two of the Little People and told the wizard.

For hundreds of years, the wizard has tried to catch the seven Twith who remain free. He wants their Book of Lore because he thinks it might contain a cure for his twitchy eye. Until Squidgy arrived, he did not know where to find them. Now, he makes frequent excursions into the Beyond. Once outside of Gyminge, he becomes a normal-sized man and changes back to Little People size when he returns. One of the reasons the wizard can be so sly and sneaky is that he can change himself into *almost* anything as long as it moves and has an eye that can twitch.

The wizard has already made several attacks on the seven Little People. To begin with, he captured Stumpy, the oldest of the Twith. At the same time, their precious Shadow Book was stolen. The Shadow Book contains the shadows of children who helped in the past. Both the book and Stumpy were successfully recovered, but with the wizard closing in, the Twith decided to enlist the help of Beyonder children. The children must *always tell the truth* or they will put the Little People in danger. There are now sixteen children living in the farmhouse. Five Shadow children were also called to come help.

By a sneaky maneuver, the wizard managed to capture gran'ma and took her into Gyminge. The Little People had never been able to penetrate the invisible curtain that the wizard erected around their homeland. Buffo, the toad who acts as the Twith doorkeeper, showed them the way through a waterfall. Crusty, the golden eagle, also found a way through by using the hole in the curtain that the wizard and his raven, Rasputin use. Gran'ma was rescued, along with a woodcutter, Cydlo, and his daughter,

Elisheba. They are now part of the Twith family on the Brook. The Twith were also successful in defeating the wizard's forces when he attacked the farmhouse. The tide of struggle is changing at last. No longer is the wizard clearly winning.

The Twith know that one day, they will be able to reclaim their homeland. Their ancient Seer, Dayko, left a cryptic poem called the Rime that reveals the events that must occur before that can happen. Gerald, who is the Keeper of the Lore, believes that he knows the exact day when the Return will take place. However, the unfulfilled lines in Dayko's Rime need to be resolved, and quickly.

Jock, the leader of the Twith, decides to send Bimbo and Bollin, the two Shadow brothers, and a doctor into Gyminge on a secret quest. The doctor is Dr. Vyruss Tyfuss, who was earlier taken captive by the Twith. Although he is court physician to Haymun, the goblin king, he has now promised to help the Little People on the Brook.

After the failed attack on the farmhouse, the wizard feels that the goblin king should return to Gyminge and gives him specific instructions on what he wants accomplished.

The four travelers are on a collision course heading for the same destination.

TUWHIT ON THE BOG

Tuwhit, the owl, has had a long association with the Twith. Taymar, the tallest of the Twith, cared for the orphaned owl until it was strong enough to fly away. Tuwhit chose to stay. When Gyminge was invaded and captured by the Wizard of Wozzle, Tuwhit carried Taymar to Cornwall on the orders of King Rufus. Later, the owl brought Taymar to the Brook to join the other six who had escaped.

Those six fled Gyminge on the back of Crusty, the golden eagle. From the time he burst forth from his shell in northern Scotland, Jock has been his constant companion. King Rufus appointed Jock to be the leader of the free Twith. Now they have been joined by the two who returned with the expedition team sent to rescue gran'ma, Cydlo, and his daughter, Elisheba.

The two birds are close friends and share a common goal. The Twith must be kept safe from the evil wizard and his wicked plans. They too wish to return to Gyminge and will do whatever is necessary to aid the Twith in their quest. So that the birds can be available for the Return, the ancient seer, Dayko, supplied Gerald with a rare herbal brew to allow the birds the same life capacity as the Twith themselves enjoy.

Tuwhit keeps close watch on Squidgy's cottage, where the wizard is in residence. As events unfold, he flies back to the farmhouse to keep Jock informed. He lands on the well cover, and Jock comes outside, looking at him expectantly.

"There is no sign of the wizard's raven, Rasputin. The SnuggleWump is in his usual place across the path. His eyes alternate between green and red. The six new, very odd-looking, featherless birds are perched on the ridge of the cottage roof. The wizard and Mrs. Squidge and perhaps MoleKing are inside, but the goblin king is headed across the bog towards the waterfall on the back of a licorice swirl cat. It has to be Cajjer, Mrs. Squidge's cat."

The news that King Haymun is on his way back to Gyminge does not worry Jock too much. "I doubt tha' Cajjer will go all th' way inta Gyminge. 'E wuld prefer ta fly perched on a broomstick. Bimbo 'n' Bollin will be more thun a match fur th' goblin king if thur paths shuld 'appen ta cross. E'en so, if ye cun git down ta th' bog 'n' catch up with th' two boys afore they disappear thru th' waterfall, ye shuld inform them. If, instead, ye see Crusty already ascending towards th' curtain 'round Gyminge, i' will be too late. By then 'e wuld 'ave unloaded 'is passengers a' th' waterfall. In tha' case, jus' return ta th' cottage ta continue yur vigil. Crusty will soon be back ta inform us whether thur is still a way inta Gyminge or whether i''as been sealed off as we fear."

Tuwhit asks, "Shall I bring the goblin king back to the farmhouse? It will be no problem to pick him off the cat's back."

Jock pauses a moment. "Nay. I jus' got rid o' one goblin. I do nay wan' th' mansion cluttered up with another when our space is already stretched by our own numbers."

The owl is off on his errand, thinking as he flies, *I might not bring the goblin back, but there is no reason why he and the cat as well shouldn't have a dunking for good measure. I'm not going to try to lift the cat, but I can at least give him a bad time. After all, look what they did to gran'ma!*

He doesn't get there in time to let the two boys know about the king. There is no sign of them, and Crusty is only a dot in the sky high above the waterfall, looking for the hole in the curtain. Still on his way, halfway across the bog from the croc' pond, is Cajjer, stepping daintily and warily. Mounted on him like a cowboy on a bull is the goblin king.

King Haymun used to be one of the seers in Gyminge, but he played traitor during the overthrow of King Rufus. For his treachery, the wizard rewarded him with the crown of Gyminge.

He is fat and looks rather like pictures of King Henry the VIII. The goblin king shares the northern apartments in the castle with the wizard. He enjoys being royalty; he feels it allows him to be a bully. Haymun has no clue that the wizard secretly blames him for the failed attack on the farmhouse, and is being sent back home as a means to get him out of the way. He arrived on the Brook wearing only a nightshirt and purple underpants but is returning home in borrowed clothes and shoes that don't fit. It would be better and more comfortable if they were too big, but the captain who had to give them up was taller and more slender than the overweight king. Even so, while crossing the bog, the king manages to pull his trousers up above his knees to prevent them from getting muddied.

Tuwhit circles above the bog, watching the two travelers until Cajjer halts beside the waterfall.

King Haymun is slow to dismount. *I'm not looking forward to the long, long walk on the other side. I would prefer to arrive at the castle in the dark, but it won't be tonight. The distance is just too far. I wonder if perhaps, in the wreckage of my pavilion in the woods, I can recover enough apparel to look like myself again. I need to look as a king should look. My crown, not the state crown, of course, but the one I use when I'm out traveling, should still be there somewhere. Hopefully my shoes will be there also. These are not only two sizes too small; they are three sizes too narrow as well. I'll probably only be capable of wearing slippers by the time I arrive.* He turns to say, "Thank you," to Cajjer. He doesn't really like the creature, but he has been very helpful getting him this far.

A shadow from the sky sweeps across his vision. There is a sudden eruption. Cajjer is swept sideways off balance into the waterfall pool with a tremendous splash.

The splash drenches Haymun also, and his vision is almost obscured. But he gets a momentary glimpse of the owl turning for another approach and chooses without hesitation to join the cat. Splashing around frantically, the goblin king is caught by surprise as Cajjer leaps on him. "What on earth do you think you are doing, Cajjer? Are you trying to drown me?" He has no wish to drown. He has no parents or grandparents to mourn him, no wife to weep tears over him, no children who call him Daddy. Nevertheless, he intends on being betrothed soon, and this gives him incentive. He has no weapons, but he has teeth. Flailing around in the water is not only the cat but also, attached to it, a wildly swinging tail. When, for the third time, it delivers a mighty wet smack across the king's face, Haymun grabs hold of it and sinks his teeth into it…hard.

SORE TAIL, SORE HEAD, SORE FEET

Cajjer is sensitive about his tail, and understandably so. A hungry ferret, spying the tail dangling down a rabbit hole, mistook it for a rabbit and nipped off the tip of it. Within a short space of a few days, more injury was added to insult. His tail was shortened further by Taymar wielding the Twith war axe. And someone who is supposed to be on his side is now making a breakfast of his tail, starting at the sore end. Cajjer has a choice of up or down or sideways. He shoots upwards. For a moment or so, his rear paws tread water, and then his tail emerges, acting like a boat propeller.

Haymun, initially underwater, suddenly emerges like a rocket heading skywards. His teeth, being his own, lose their grip. Had they not been his own, Cajjer might well have arrived back at the cottage with a pair of dentures locked onto his tail. Haymun lands back in the waterfall pool with a mighty splash, spitting out cat fur. Cajjer is already well across the bog, heading back to the cottage, screeching for another bandage.

Tuwhit leaves the goblin king floundering in the waterfall pool. He lazily follows the cat back to his home and perches in the ash tree to observe what happens next.

King Haymun makes his way past the torrent of falling water and now blunders through the cave-tunnel. "Ouch!" *My foot!* "Ouch!" *My other foot! I can't bear this pain any longer. I'll just go barefoot and carry the shoes for awhile.* Banging his head as the roof height diminishes, he lets out a giant yell. "Owee!" He feels blood trickling down his forehead. *Is there going to be no end to this awful day?* His yell amplifies as it echoes down the cave. It is followed by others that sound even louder.

Outside the cave-tunnel, a little to the east of the entrance, the three earlier travelers stop in their tracks. Vyruss is taken by surprise. "It's King Haymun! The last time I saw him, he was suspended from Rasputin's claws over the bog."

The two boys wonder, *What does this mean? Is there a pursuit? How has the wizard found out we are here?*

All three throw themselves down in the high summer grass. Bollin, ready for action, reacts quickly. "The king will be bound for the castle. I wonder how many are with him? Can we cause any damage to the king and his escort?" All three have swords, and Bollin raises his, ready to strike. The boy is itching for a fight, but Bimbo presses on his arm to restrain him. He whispers, "Our priority isn't fighting the wizard's forces. That isn't why we are here."

The two Shadow boys are Gumpa's sons and grew up in Pakistan. Bollin is ginger-haired, and Bimbo is blond. All their lives, they have been acquainted with the Twith and involved in their adventures. When they were about eleven years old, Jock collected their shadows and brought them back to Gerald, the scribe, to put in the Shadow Book. Growing up, they learned to talk to birds and animals. They also sort of learned the bird tunes to whistle for calling the birds when needed. They have taken more rides on Crusty's back than they can remember. When Jock calls them back from the Shadow Book, they are Twith-size and remain so. On the Brook, they are weightless, but in Gyminge, they are similar to the other Twith.

Noises in the cave-tunnel approach closer. The three burrow down closer to the ground. The king is talking out loud to himself. He is not happy. "I don't like being alone." Haymun staggers into the evening light, and sits down to rub his feet. He runs his fingers across his forehead. "Ouch! I have a big knot the size of an egg where I bumped the roof of the cave." His fingers feel sticky. He recoils as he looks at them. "That's blood on my forehead!" He is miserable. "My clothes are wet through. It takes real effort to even breathe, and it's getting more difficult all the time." The king sinks his head into his hands and groans. "How can I face the journey ahead? What am I going to do?"

Dr. Tyfuss grows concerned as he listens to the suffering king. Speaking softly, Vyruss shares his thoughts. "Boys, even though I have agreed to help you here in Gyminge, I am still the king's personal physician. It appears he is hurt, and it is my duty to tend to him." The boys nod in quiet agreement. "If he is as badly hurt as it sounds, I should accompany him back to the castle. What do you think?"

Bimbo speaks for both of them. "Yes, of course you should tend to the king. If he is as bad as you think, you should definitely accompany him back to the castle."

Vyruss walks up behind the king and touches him on the shoulder. Haymun reacts with startled surprise, and Vyruss speaks kindly. "King Haymun, I can see you are hurt. Let me examine you."

The king is skeptical. *The last time this fellow decided to treat me, he was going to cut me open with a sharp kitchen carving knife! I grabbed it from him and chased him all the way to the bog intending to use it on him instead. I ran for hours with only that one thought in my mind. However, the past is the past. All is forgiven. There is no one I would rather see! The doctor is one of my closest friends, a man of quite exceptional skills.* Correct that thought. Even in a desperate situation, that is going too far. *He might be a man of quite exceptional knowledge, but probably not skills.* He groans and allows the doctor to examine the bump on his head and then his torn and bruised feet.

Dr. Tyfuss dampens his handkerchief in the small stream nearby and washes the head wound. "Hold this to your head, sir. Come with me and bathe your feet in the stream while I see if I can catch a horse. Let me help you."

The king feels the balm of cool water on his feet and lies back, looking up at the sky. His pains are easing. He murmurs contentedly, "Is this the remedy for a man's troubles at the end of a trying day, bathing your feet in cool stream water while lying on your back? A fine man, Dr. Tyfuss. A man of integrity and vision and loyalty. The mere mention, the simple thought of a horse to ride is like hearing great music from a famous orchestra after spending years locked in a cell with a prisoner blowing a tin whistle. I always knew that I could rely on the doctor. Things are suddenly much better. If I can only get back to the castle, then…

"Oh!" An ugly thought hidden for a while at the back of his mind surfaces. The thought spoils and drowns the whole melody. The symphony fades sharply away to the repeated solitary note of a penny whistle and then nothing at all. "There's the little matter of the final orders I received before I left Mrs. Squidge's cottage. The wizard wants a garrison fort erected at the mouth of the cave-tunnel. He wants it finished within three days, and is coming to inspect it on Sunday!" He groans at the thought, but even as he groans, a flash of an idea—it must be pure inspiration—begins to percolate in his mind. "This is the location of the fort, right here. I know what I must do, how I must do it, and more importantly, *who* will do it for me!"

BOLLIN WRITES A NOTE

Two days earlier, Bimbo and Bollin had been at this exact same spot with the team sent to rescue gran'ma. Elisheba, the woodcutter's daughter who returned to the Brook with them, had to leave their two ponies behind. They have stayed close by and are munching away just a hundred paces from the mouth of the cave-tunnel. The two boys wriggle through the grass further away from the king, and watch as Vyruss entices the piebald pony closer with a handful of plucked grass.

The doctor pauses on his way back. He has not mounted the pony and puts it between himself and the king. Hidden by the horse, he bends down and tells the boys, "The king appears to be heading towards the castle as quickly as he can. He seems to have forgotten our recent differences."

Bimbo encourages him, saying, "Stay with him, but be careful. Try to keep out of trouble. Just do what he asks. We will contact you somehow. Hope you find that your woodlouses are okay. Best of luck."

Bollin asks, "Do you want me to hold the piebald while you catch the chestnut pony?"

"Thank you, but no. I'll just take the one. But what about you, Bimbo? I was supposed to help you. Are you going to be able to manage on your own?"

"Bollin will stay with me instead. We'll send a message back to Jock somehow. Don't worry. We'll be okay. You better be on your way before the king gets suspicious."

Vyruss arrived on the Brook wearing only a sheet adapted as a surgical gown, a mask, and his shoes, so there are no personal items in his knapsack. He leaves it for Bollin now that the boy will be staying in Gyminge.

Dr. Tyfuss rejoins King Haymun, who is half asleep, enjoying the coolness of the water on his tortured feet. He dreams of his forthcoming marriage and all the program arrangements required. *There's the music—the choir and the composer who will create a special wedding anthem for the occasion—the select invitees, the reception, poetry readings, the celebrations, and perhaps even a festival day involving sporting competitions. I'll declare a general holiday! A two-color wedding theme throughout the country of red and...? I know the wizard's favorite color is black, but maybe something a little more cheerful like dark purple might be acceptable on such a joyful occasion. My head is aching! I'm probably going to need surgery to fix that huge bump; it will never go away on its own.* The thought of Dr. Tyfuss performing surgery on his head jerks him back into consciousness.

Haymun sees a horse looking down at him. The horse has a mouthful of grass and buttercups and chews away in a leisurely fashion.

"I only brought one horse, sir. You ride on it, and I'll walk beside you. I'll help you get on."

"Oh, my dear fellow. You mustn't walk alongside. I insist you ride with me. As weak as I am from my severe injuries, I might slip off and do further damage to myself. Not to mention that I might get stomped on by a rampant horse who suddenly takes a strong dislike to me. Horses do that, you know. And if the horse decides to gallop away, leaving you behind, I could not possibly control him. My head is not at all clear, and I could easily misdirect the animal and find myself lost.

"Besides, my dear friend, you will get too tired with the long journey on foot. We will share the horse. It looks strong enough. Take it over to the rock, and we can both mount him from there. I will ride in front and take the reins. We will head for our camp in the forest and see what the situation is there before we go on back to the castle. I want to discuss a little project with you. I believe you might be ideally suited for it. You might consider it as a promotion. Let's be on our way. We have a long way to travel."

The horse jogs away northwards and picks up a steady pace. King Haymun is more relaxed and content. *My world has changed very much for the better since I stumbled out of the cave-tunnel just half an hour or so ago.* He is not yet interested in where the doctor has been since, from the vantage point of a raven's claws high above the bog, he last saw his physician flat on his back and in imminent danger of being sucked into the treacherous bog. However, to be charitable, perhaps the king was not able to see anything from that position. In any case, Vyruss does not intend to volunteer any information about his experiences in the Beyond.

Rasputin is flying south in a circling sweep from the castle. He has been locked inside his home territory since the wizard closed the hole in the curtain. The raven swoops down low for a closer look at the two men astride the pony. Landing on the road ahead, he waits for them to reach him.

The pony is pulled to a stop. There is a lot of news to exchange.

Bollin spots Rasputin in the far distance, long before the bird might have seen them. He nudges his brother. "Did you see Rasputin just now? The raven was circling over Blindhouse Wood and then swung back and disappeared from sight. Presumably, he is exchanging news with the goblin king."

"No, I didn't spot him, but we better keep out of sight. It will be wise for us to wait until dark before we make any move."

They retreat into the shelter of the tunnel mouth and will remain there until the light fades and it is safe to proceed unobserved by a patrolling raven.

Bollin thinks about the matter of informing Jock that he plans to stay with Bimbo instead of returning to the Brook. "Bimbo, I'll have to run hard to get back to the bog, across it, and up to the farmhouse to let Jock know I'm staying with you. It will take some time, and I'll have to do the same on the way back. But I'm pretty sure that I can get back to rejoin you before it's time to move forward. What do you think?"

"Well, I'm not sure you should go alone. Let's stash our knapsacks in the grass and run together."

While they are still considering what to do, the question is answered for them. Around the last bend of the toad trail, they see several toads hopping towards them. A couple of mothers traveling together for company are heading home with their young ones just one or two months old.

Bollin wastes no time. "Hand me a piece of paper and a pencil, bro. The toads can take a message to Jock for us." Quickly he scribbles a few words and folds the paper neatly.

He hails one of the mother toads. "Hello there. Can we talk to you for a minute?"

The mother toad says, "Make it fast. I need to get my children home."

"We want to get a note delivered to our friends on the Brook right away. Could you do that for us? Do you know Buffo?"

"Every toad on the Brook knows Buffo. He is the doorkeeper for the Little People up at the farm. I'll send the note up with his nephew as soon as I arrive home. Bingo lives close by and will be happy to perform the errand."

"Oh, thank you so much. Is there a lot of activity going on at the castle?"

"No. Everything was quiet there when we left. Goodnight."

THE DUNGEON TUNNEL

It is late evening. The boys have drifted off to sleep. No toads have come hopping by to awaken them. Bollin opens his eyes and yawns. *What day is it anyway?* "Hey, bro. Is this still Wednesday?"

Bimbo rubs the sleep from his eyes. "Yes, it is. Boy, I was much more tired than I realized."

The sun has set, but fading summer light will continue for almost another hour. They check the skies to see if Rasputin might still be around, but there is no sign of him. It is time to be moving. King Haymun and Dr. Tyfuss are long gone and will be nearing Blindhouse Wood. Rasputin is unlikely to make a further patrol this late in the day.

In the fading half light, the chestnut pony that Vyruss left behind grazes contentedly within a few yards of Bimbo and Bollin, never venturing far away. It is not saddled.

Bimbo whistles, and the pony raises its head. The boy speaks softly as he advances slowly. The pony knows and recognizes the voice instantly and responds to the call. Bimbo had driven the pair of Cydlo's ponies to the castle to rescue gran'ma. The pony knows Bollin as well. Even more recently, Bollin brought it from Cydlo's cottage to this very spot.

It will be easier to load and mount the animal from the rock near the tunnel entrance. They load the two haversacks onto the pony. Bimbo's haversack contains a flashlight with fresh batteries, two candles, and several small boxes of matches. There are Ziploc bags from gran'ma's kitchen that hopefully will be waterproof. There is a towel and a small coil of rope. There are several packets of Gumpa's raisins, yeast buns, and peanuts. It is the tools that are so heavy—the small axe for chopping kindling, a knife, and a small hand saw. All Beyonder-sized items were put through a shrinking process in the pockets or hands of Beyonder children. Barney held their hand so they could shrink.

For a while, Bollin will run steadily alongside the horse just for the exercise, and Bimbo can ride. Then they will change places. Later in the night, they will probably both ride.

Bollin was not filled in on the purpose of Bimbo's secret quest. It was intended that Bollin would merely scout the land and report his findings to Jock as soon as possible.

Bimbo tells Bollin, "I need to explain the details of the task that lies ahead of us. Are you listening?"

Bollin gives a little sigh. "Of course I am. Carry on."

"We are going to the castle on a secret quest. It will be dangerous, but we can do it. Once, long ago, there was a secret escape tunnel for the king and his family. It linked their apartments in the castle to a quarry across the lake. Cydlo pointed out the quarry to me when we were on the way to rescue gran'ma. The tunnel emerged into a cave inside the quarry. When the wizard conquered Gyminge, he wanted to enlarge the lake so it would surround the castle entirely. He had to wait until the year of the drought, and then he put his goblins to work. Cydlo heard from the workmen that the heavy excavation equipment exposed the part of the tunnel that had been underwater, breaking it apart. Goblin soldiers fully explored the whole length of the tunnel. Its entrance from the castle was inside the fireplace in the king's apartments and led into a secret hideaway room. There was great excitement not only at its discovery but even more when it looked as though someone had escaped through it only hours before. The part of the escape tunnel outside the castle was demolished completely. Those stones were used to block the portion inside the castle at the first landing beyond the hideaway room. It was sealed off by a barrier a full three paces thick. There was no need to block the end at the quarry, for it would only lead into the lake. Anyone using that tunnel would have to swim across the lake to the castle and then not get very far inside before they encountered the thick wall blocking further progress.

"Cydlo knows—I don't know how he knows, but he knows— that there is a small link tunnel off the main tunnel that leads into the dungeons. The workmen did not tell him about it, so it wasn't found. It exits into a small special cell kept for prisoners of importance. Because it is between the lake and the landing where the main tunnel is blocked, we can swim into it if we have to. The massive stone door into the link tunnel is part of the wall with no detectable hinges or handles. The Royal Sword is hidden in that stone door."

Bollin lets out a cheer. "Wow! If we retrieve that, one of the lines in Dayko's Rime will be fulfilled and the Twith will be one step closer to the Return. They have been waiting for that for such a long time."

Bimbo smiles. "You're right. Our plan is to first go to Cydlo's cottage. We will milk the cows while we are there. Cydlo has been anxious about them. Then we'll head down to the castle and check what's happening there. We can find out if the pontoon bridge has been repaired and if there is any other access to the castle. There might still be some of this season's toads around. We can ask them to help us locate the underwater access to the tunnels. We can also ask them to search in the lake for the Royal Shield. That would fulfill another line in Dayko's Rime!"

Bimbo halts the pony and swings off. "Here, Bollin. You ride for a while. You know, I'm so glad you get to go along. We can now work together. Our first goal at the lake will be to find if it is possible to swim across to the castle. Cydlo was unsure whether that can even be done. He's never heard of anyone doing it, but there's really no reason for anyone to try."

Bollin reassures his brother, "Don't worry, bro. We're both strong swimmers. We'll manage it just fine. We should expect both Rasputin and the wizard to be at the castle though, and that could present a problem. We need to be alert for an opportunity to contact Dr. Tyfuss too."

The little pony trots along the toad trail until he reaches the fork in the road. The toad trail branches off to the left. To the right is the way to Cydlo's hut and home for the chestnut. It is time now for Bimbo to climb on behind Bollin.

Leaning forward next to the animal's head, Bollin pats his shoulder. "Home, Chestnut, home."

The pace of the pony increases like any horse headed for the barn.

COLONEL TYFUSS

Several hours earlier, two similar travelers, also sharing a pony, arrived at this same point and took the left fork. The light for them was still good as they headed into Blindhouse Wood.

The king begins to feel a great deal better and mumbles happily to himself. "Getting the weight off my sore feet is such a relief. I'm no longer the man who tottered from the cave-tunnel on his last legs. It is as though he never existed and was just a figment of the imagination." He gently feels the swelling on his forehead. "To be sure, the size of this bump seems to imply that my brain is trying to squeeze out of my skull into the open. I may be vain, but by no means am I going to allow anyone to observe it raw. I'll keep my brain to myself, thank you. Eventually, it will probably go back inside my cranium. If it doesn't, I'll just get a special hat made, and a special crown.

"From the moment I stretched out on the ground and bathed my feet in the cool stream, my mind has been crystal clear. Now I need to redeem this time spent traveling. I'll take this opportunity to share with Dr. Tyfuss my vision for Gyminge. Well now, as far as I can remember, it is the same as the vision the wizard has for

Gyminge. It is always wise to keep my views the same as those of my boss. In the end, it saves a lot of trouble and can bring approval, if not rewards." The pompous king would like to believe that he has a mind as brilliant as the wizard's.

King Haymun doesn't bother to turn his head to address Vyruss. He clears his throat, and raises his voice. "My good doctor, I'm going to share with you my vision for Gyminge. Listen carefully. I am first of all going to stiffen the defenses, make the country impregnable. There are enemies all around our borders. I will strengthen the officer corps of the army, improve the training, weed out the duds, and promote the right men!

"Most especially, I have decided to strengthen the southern defenses. The trouble is coming from the south, and that will have my first attention. I will appoint a topflight officer, a man with a crystal-clear, cool mind, one who is devoted, disciplined, an adventurer, and a ruthless achiever. He must be a stop-at-nothing, devil-may-care, do-or-die kind of man." The king pauses, searching his mind for other suitable three-word phrases to describe his new officer. Nothing comes to mind, so he forges ahead. "There needs to be blue-sky thinking, a new groom in the stable before the pony is gone!"

The pony breaks into a canter at the sound of his name. The king is almost unseated, and Dr. Tyfuss with him. For a few moments, the flow of talk is interrupted while the king regains control. It is only a temporary respite for the doctor. Haymun resumes where he left off. "That brings me to the present situation. The new Commander of the Southern Zone will build a fort at this end of the toad tunnel. It's an excellent location with good drinking water available, and waste water can go straight into the bog on the other side of the border. It means all facilities will be immediately available. And the reason?" King Haymun arrogantly throws his hand sideways as though to sweep aside the instructions from the wizard he received just before departure as not worthy of mention. In actual fact, he didn't completely understand them and only agreed wholeheartedly with the wizard because that was simple common sense. Instead, he creates a whole new thread of reasoning.

"The reason is that we need to control immigration. The toads are coming in without passports. It has gone on long enough. Every other country has an up-to-date system of tracking suspicious visitors. The creatures don't understand our culture or our language. What do they contribute to the country that gives them hospitality? That's what I want to know. They are coming to Gyminge to take advantage of our social security system. What happens when a toad gets sick in Gyminge? Suppose they all catch toadpox at the same time? Our medical staff couldn't handle the influx of patients. Our health system would break down!"

Vyruss rolls his eyes. *The king is talking nonsense. The toads only come for a few months and are gone again. They have never expected anything but use of the lake as a place to spawn.*

Haymun rambles on. "Gyminge needs a better system of control, and Gyminge is going to get it. Around the clock control at the border. A security patrol of twelve men at all times. Three shifts. Separate lines for males and females. Children on their mother's passports. A limit of two hundred applicants a day. Control backed up by a cutting-edge, razor-sharp border force run by a topflight officer available to his men at any hour of the day or night!"

The goblin king is on a roll and smirks to himself. "Do you get my meaning, my good doctor? No half measures!"

Vyruss lost interest long ago and lets his mind wander. He hardly hears the king go on about using riot shields for control or how there are no sick or poor because social care in Gyminge is the finest in the civilized world.

King Haymun gulps, *Oh! I'm talking to a health professional. Well, he will soon be an ex-health professional. It's time to explain to him what his future duties will entail.* "Listen carefully, my good doctor. The first task of the Commander of the Southern Zone will be to erect an encampment at the toad tunnel so the border force can respond to this crisis. Time is critical, so it must be completed within two days!

"With exceptional foresight, I recently located the army for maneuvers in the forest. The tents and equipment for the first wave of the border force are already there. Barracks, recreational facilities, cookhouse, medical facilities…"

He swings around and eyes the doctor suspiciously. *Given my recent experience with him in the field hospital at the ambush site, I probably shouldn't have mentioned that.* "Most of the army is engaged beyond the border. There will probably need to be compulsory service to keep the army up to the strength needed here. The farmers won't like that with harvest time so close. But crisis events need crisis response! They will find me to be a man of iron."

The king pauses for breath. *The mother toads are returning to the Brook. Perhaps they would be willing to move the army field equipment. I would have to give them payment and have them sign a contract, of course. Those are details the commander can work out. Cost is no restraint. The country is completely committed, one hundred percent! The nation will make any sacrifice!*

King Haymun decides to give Vyruss some encouragement. "The Commander of the Southern Zone will have all the resources of the royal command to support him. My own total resolve will be right behind him. The tented camp we start with will later become a permanent fort. I myself will develop the plans for that once the initial crisis has been dealt with. We'll include gardens and parks and sports fields and playgrounds for the families.

"Dr. Tyfuss, I herewith and hereby at this moment relieve you from your duties as medical officer to the field forces. I am appointing you Commander of the Southern Zone with the rank of colonel. Congratulations on your promotion, Colonel Tyfuss. Your quarters at the castle will be upgraded to fit your new rank."

Vyruss blinks, gulps, and says nothing. Mass confusion clouds his brain as he tries to sort out what just happened.

The king continues. "We will soon be at the field location in the forest just ahead of us. We will review the situation there to confirm what supplies are available. Then you will accompany me to the castle. We will ensure that suitable forces will be at your command. I will come on an official visit to inspect the camp on Saturday at noon. I am confident that an officer of your abilities will have much to show me."

THE STEAM ROLLER

Dr. Tyfuss has not been asked for his opinion or his acceptance of this new assignment. He is in a state of total shock and confusion regarding his appointment as Commander of the Southern Zone. His imagination runs wild. He pictures himself as a small man in a purple nightcap holding up a red flag in front of an advancing steam roller. He's wearing more than just the purple nightcap, of course. Emblazoned on the front of his nightshirt is "Commander of the Southern Zone." When the steam roller is fifty paces away, he isn't paying too much attention. In fact, truth be known, he is really wondering whether anyone has fed his colony of woodlouses. Deep in thought, the little man is unaware the steam roller is continuing its relentless approach towards him. He hears the rattling, puffing, and chuffing right upon him and expects that at any moment, there will be a small explosion of steam that denotes the brakes have been applied. There is not. At this point, a man wearing a yellow construction helmet would be more alert. Taking immediate action, he would leap sharply out of the way, angrily shouting curses and waving wildly as the steam roller rumbles on by. However, Dr. Tyfuss classifies himself less as a man of action and more as one who contemplates—a thinker, a visionary, a lover of the arts, an opera buff, and a possible cathedral chorister. He does sing tenor, after all.

As events grow more vivid in his mind, the doctor sees himself frantically waving his red flag, but the steam roller proceeds on its stately way as though he isn't there. Flattened on the road behind, when the steam roller passes on by on its majestic course, are the red flag, the purple nightcap, and Dr. Tyfuss himself.

Shaking his head to clear the cobwebs, Vyruss forgets about the red flag and the purple nightcap. He is in shock as he realizes,

The king expects me to fulfill the duties of the new Commander of the Southern Zone! He takes in a deep breath and then another. His head spins dizzily, trying to comprehend what just occurred.

Dr. Tyfuss, the scientific thinker, is instead Colonel Tyfuss and expected to be a man of action. *Perish the thought.* Phrases he heard earlier from the king make him cringe. *Do I even know anyone like that?* Words describing the new commander crowd his befuddled brain with haunting clarity. As he reviews the entire list, he shudders. *How could those words apply to me of all people?* His mind is protesting, *Not me!*

One last thought crosses the ex-doctor's mind. *The king said my quarters at the castle will be upgraded to fit my new rank. Yes, but when am I ever going to get the opportunity to live there?*

Vyruss has a picture of himself in his mind. It is not a man with a purple nightcap and a red flag but a man low to the ground, scooting across the expanse of a limitless field with the pounding hooves of a prize red bull ever nearer behind him.

King Haymun and his newly appointed colonel reach the ambush site. The wreckage is worse than they remember. A meager group of soldiers guards the field camp. A sentry is on duty at both ends of the path that trails through the camp.

The king and his companion catch the glow of the fire before they spot the sentry. It is near midnight.

"Halt! Who goes there?"

"It is your king, you idiot."

The sentry snaps to attention. "Yes, sir, Your Royal Highness." He turns to announce, "The king has arrived!"

The whole guard is roused. Torches are lit. Salutes ripple along the line of troops standing at attention.

The king is pleased to see that all the lights are on around his pavilion. They had been smashed to smithereens just prior to the time he chased the doctor to the Brook. Some flying object wielding a long pole while dangling from the claws of an eagle had done the damage. His personal tent, demolished in the attack, still lies in ruins. His belongings have been flung far and wide.

Before anything else, King Haymun orders a search for his field crown. It requires a thorough search, but the corporal does find it and brings it to the king. The points on it are bent. The king carefully bends them back as straight as he can. Placing it on his head, he winces. "Ouch!" It bumps against the knot on his head, but he is determined to wear the symbol of his authority. As the king moves it slightly to one side, it tilts precariously. *I must avoid moving my head too quickly.* This is a replacement crown for the one he lost during the conflict at Mrs. Squidge's cottage.

King Haymun is anxious to get out of the tight captain's uniform that he borrowed. It is tight for two reasons. The king is, one might say, portly. In fact, he is plain short and fat. The captain was not. He was tall and thin. In addition to being tight to begin with, the uniform shrunk to be even tighter when the king got drenched by the waterfall. Although the clothes he finds are damp, they will certainly feel better than what he is wearing. He also locates his royal robe. With this new apparel, he begins to feel more confident about the future. He spies a pair of shoes! *What a great find. Now I can walk without hobbling.* Gathering up scattered toiletries and pieces of royal jewelry, he even begins to hum.

Colonel Tyfuss is almost dropping with exhaustion. With great weariness in his voice, he asks the king, "Do you plan to continue on to the castle tonight? Is there any possibility we could rest awhile in one of the guard tents?"

The king suddenly realizes that he has far more reason than Dr. Tyfuss to be tired. He gives instructions to the corporal. "Vacate two of the guard tents immediately. Colonel Tyfuss and I will be spending the night here. See to the care of the pony. Get two fresh horses by dawn for our journey on to the castle. You will wake us one hour after dawn. My breakfast porridge will be made with milk, not water. Be certain it is served with sugar."

The ex-doctor thinks a while. *I've always left decisive thinking to others. Now it is being required of me.* Resolutely, he gives the corporal further instructions. "Begin dismantling all tents except those the guards are using. The whole camp will be moving south tomorrow morning. Everything here will be taken down to the border. Furthermore, there will be supply wagons coming from the castle. The two boulders that completed the ambush will have to be levered out of the way. First thing tomorrow, at dawn, the whole guard, including yourself and the cook, must remove the great rocks blocking the trail so the wagons will be able to get through."

GOBLIN CASTLE

King Haymun and Colonel Tyfuss set off for the castle shortly after breakfast. Their breakfast has persuaded Vyruss, riding discreetly a few paces behind his monarch, to identify the cook carefully. *On the southern border, that goblin is going to be restricted to washing dishes or digging foundations.*

King Haymun feels that his fortunes are looking up. *I am dressed once more as a king should look. I have solved the difficulty of building the border fort by making wise decisions. I am heading home to my future bride.* As he rides, he unconsciously expresses his happiness aloud. "She is so beautiful. I will teach her how to be a good wife and mother so she will take good care of me and our children. I wonder how many we should have? Ten would be a good number. They will learn to respect their parents and be obedient. I won't stand for any nonsense. Now that she will be queen, I probably should choose a name for her that goes well with Haymun. King Haymun and Queen…? Tara. Yes, that goes well. Haymun and Tara. King Haymun and Queen Tara. Excellent!" He begins to hum and then adds words, singing softly so the colonel behind him can't make out the words.

Ta-rah-rah boom-de-ay,
I'll see my bride today,
She'll not know what to say
Just hip, hip, hip hooray!

Three days previously, Jock and his expedition team of thirteen children, one old man, and a woodcutter stormed the castle to rescue gran'ma and Cydlo's daughter. There were two birds from the Brook assisting them—Crusty the eagle and Maggie the magpie. They had left the castle in chaos. Three of the five carts carrying supplies into the castle that day were demolished. The courtyard was a shambles, full of spilled vegetables, milk, and garbage. One of Cydlo's carts scattered logs before crashing into the dining room, destroying that and a good section of the kitchen. The milk cart ended up in the lake. The portcullis mechanism was jammed by Gumpa to prevent it from dropping. Fires were started at the courtyard gate to the royal apartments and another in one of the apartments itself. The laundry was on fire from gran'ma leaving her hot iron on top of the sergeant major's trousers. Smoke billowed from the castle for hours. The team punctured the pontoon bridge, sinking it as well as the one little dinghy moored at the castle. They left no way in or out of the castle.

The leadership in the defense of the castle, at a time when it was clearly needed most, was just as clearly missing. The sergeant major will write in his report and tell everyone superior in rank to himself the true facts. "There were several scores of attackers assisted by squadrons of birds. By determined defending, only two of the prisoners escaped. The dungeons were defended stoutly against tremendous odds. The enemy did not succeed in breaking through to release any of the bottled captives. They were beaten off and forced to retreat with their wounded up the hill. The pursuit forces were called back to prepare for the next assault. They are prepared to die for their country."

He has already written the outline of his report and read it aloud to the whole gathered garrison, including cooks and cleaners so that everyone knows what actually happened. He also tells them that he plans to make recommendations for medals for valor. He won't, of course, but it will help them remember to keep the facts straight.

All the buckets in the castle were used to dip water from the lake to douse the smoldering embers of the various fires. There is an acrid smell in the air. The primary problem is the missing pontoon bridge. They are short of swimmers and have no boats. Using a bullhorn, the sergeant major ordered the guards left on land to scour the countryside for boats. A massive search of all the lakes and streams nearby was carefully made, but only one boat was found to bring to the castle lake. That lone boat makes multiple trips to and fro between the castle and the shore. The castle kitchens are closed, and meals are prepared in the field kitchen on the mainland and taken across by boat.

Sam, the sergeant major, is quite sure that neither the wizard nor the king will endure being ferried across to the castle in a small boat. He orders another search to be made as far as the borders if necessary. Eventually, a decision will have to be made whether to salvage and repair the pontoon bridge or build a permanent bridge across the lake to the castle. Whatever is done, it will be a long job.

One of the junior ranks among the goblins has an idea and a couple of suggestions. He is very nearsighted and wears large, thick spectacles. He mistakenly answered an army recruiting ad for a ditch digger and is more than halfway through his ten-year term with the maintenance squad. In seven years' service, he has risen no higher than the lowest rank in the goblin army. However, he thought he was answering an ad for a bridge builder.

Although he qualified as a civil engineer, he admits that his practical experience is limited. He approaches the sergeant major. "Sir, I have a few suggestions for a bridge."

Sam is willing to listen. "Yes?"

The young man, unmarried, has pimples all over his face, and is going prematurely bald. He is full of ideas and produces preliminary sketches. "Well, my idea is for a bridge clear of the water rather than a floating bridge. Floating bridges have problems with water-tightness. The best solution would be a suspension bridge, although there are sometimes vibration problems. A herd of cows charging across like those we saw recently could bring the bridge down if they were all going at the same speed. Another design would be a drawbridge. For additional length and security, it could be a double drawbridge. Another suggestion is a suspended span on double cantilevers." The young man, as his lack of promotion shows, is not ambitious. He does, however, seem to know his bridges.

By nature, Sam is a man of caution. He is more at home inspecting the shine on buckles and boots than in considering how best to defend a castle through its link to the mainland. However, to do nothing is dangerous and can lead to results even less desirable than making a wrong decision. He remembers, *At the last garrison parade, the wizard declared that he will richly reward initiative and enterprise among his officers.* This thought is the clincher. He tells Pimples, "We will build a double drawbridge, and you will be designer, architect, and site engineer."

A huge grin breaks across the young man's face. "Oh, thank you, sir. I'll draw up some detailed sketches right away. I won't disappoint you." He salutes sharply and turns to run to his tent to begin putting his thoughts onto paper.

THE KING RETURNS

Sam faces a great shortage of men. Nearly all of the good fighting men of the goblin army were taken over to the Brook weeks ago. Then the goblin king took most of the castle garrison to the woods for an ambush intended to trap the Twith. That camp was reported abandoned as though hit by a plague. The king and all his men just plain disappeared from the face of the planet. The men still at the castle are extremely nervous that the same fate awaits them. They spend all their spare time checking that their wills are written, writing farewell letters to their wives and children and girlfriends and thank-you letters to their grandparents and aunties and uncles for birthday gifts received and not yet acknowledged. Now Sam is short eight more of the remaining crack troops who were sent to the ambush camp on guard duty.

Rasputin returned from a morning excursion with news that the king still lives and is in Gyminge. Sam creams off the remaining garrison to get on with repairs and the new bridge project.

The quartermaster sergeant, Quartz by name, supervises all the cleanup, repair, and redecoration work going on in the castle. He is useless for anything else, and it keeps him out of Sam's way.

Carpenters and masons, painters and decorators, plumbers and plasterers, wheelwrights, ironsmiths, coppersmiths, and general blacksmiths are all at work. The castle is filled with the sound and bustle of frantic activity. Work goes on around the clock. One of the masons, claiming to be experienced in building pyramids, is put to work cleaning mortar from the loose stones. All goblin drill parades have been cancelled in favor of the repair work.

Sam temporarily promotes his bridge designer to corporal. It will give him authority to boss people around. Corporal Pimples needs vast amounts of logs, struts, braces, props, and planks from the forest. All the castle staff has been recruited to help. Medical room orderlies, the pharmacist, the stores clerks, the spare kitchen staff, the grooms, the sweepers and cleaners, the laundry workers and the gardeners, have been sent to the forest beyond the old seer's house to cut down trees.

This leaves a minimum number of soldiers left within the castle walls on simple garrison and guard duties. Only two goblins share twenty-four-hour duty on the dungeons. There are six goblins sharing twenty-four-hour duty at the castle gate. Since no one can get in without being rowed across, those goblins are relaxed. The guardhouse on the mainland also shares only six goblins, and they are now looking after the stable and horses as well.

The new corporal needs lots of ropes that can be woven into even thicker ropes. He plans a double drawbridge and each drawbridge will need to be raised and lowered. All available wagons scour the countryside, and bring in sawed or seasoned timber, ropes, and any chains that are longer than a man is tall. Sawyers working in pairs are busy sawing planks from tree trunks. Others are shaping square section logs to serve as trestle legs and props. Blacksmiths cut holes in the wood by using red-hot bars to burn through.

Pimples blossoms in his new assignment. Nervous short steps have lengthened into manly strides. Even his pimples are diminishing, and some of the bald patches on his head are showing signs of light brown fuzz. His voice has deepened, and he issues commands with authority. He knows what to do and works on designs straight out of his head, scratching marks on the ground where the men are to dig the foundations for the first great trestle. He concentrates on the landward side for the present.

This is the sight that greets King Haymun and his companion when they top the last rise from the forest. They expect the view of the castle and the lake to be a sight for sore eyes. Colonel Tyfuss blinks at all the activity.

Although not comprehending the scene before him, King Haymun recognizes there is no likely danger to himself. He rams his spurs into the side of his horse. The horse, by all reasonable standards, should have broken into a normal gallop downhill towards the guardhouse where the king would have reined him in and received a report from the sergeant major.

That this is not what happened is at least partially due to the fact that the king's spurs are borrowed spurs on borrowed boots a size smaller than what he normally wears. The king's left foot, as he drives his spurs into the horse, slips from the stirrup, and the spur gets lodged into the horse's girth band. The horse, not accustomed to such treatment, rears upright. He cannot unseat his rider because the king's foot cannot withdraw from the riding boot fast enough. The animal is back down on four legs and racing downhill as though pursued by a pack of wolves. Any other horse with sense would have put up with the pain a few moments more to wait until the spur is disentangled by helpers alongside. Not so the grey stallion! He heads for the castle lickety-split. The left stirrup swings free. On the right side, the monarch's foot is still in the stirrup but totally unbalanced. A crack horseman would probably have been able to control the horse in such circumstances, but the king is no crack horseman.

This horse does not respond to any commands to, "Stop!" "Halt!" or "Whoa!" The horse makes a break for the water, and the king holds on like grim death. His tugging at the trapped spur is, with every piercing jerk, only speeding up the horse. Turning onto the landing pier, the horse finds a great hole in the path instead of a bridge. Let it be clearly understood that even if the trestle hole had not been there, there is no way the horse could have made it across the lake in one leap.

Corporal Pimples is bent over the excavations for the trestle bridge, checking whether it is necessary to go deeper. He takes a brief glance upwards and throws himself headfirst into the hole that is handily in front of him. The men, digging closer to the lake, have been working in mud. Corporal Pimples joins them horizontally with a huge splash as a dark shadow passes overhead. The king, in a less fortunate position on the horse's back from which he cannot dislodge himself, recognizes that a bath in the lake is likely to be preferable to landing on semi-firm ground between the trestle excavation and the lake.

The horse, had it been white, could have been the inspiration for the winged horse of Greek mythology, flying without wings as few horses have ever done. It soars into the sky, over the trestle hole, over the edge of the landing pier, and out over the water.

King Haymun, driven to desperate measures and willing to lose a leg, wrenches his foot out of his riding boot. This throws him off balance. His leg swings over the saddle; he releases the reins that no longer interest him; and, curving in a beautiful arc alongside the horse, he splashes into the lake. The two splashes are almost at the same moment, although the horse's is by far the larger splash.

The king has returned to the castle.

TELL THE KING!

Colonel Tyfuss, unperturbed by the sudden unexplained departure of his companion for a suicidal gallop into the lake, allows the army to handle the crisis without attempting to intervene. He is not yet into his military uniform and does not consider himself officially on duty. Technically, until uniformed, he considers himself on leave.

The sawyers in the forest all rush to the edge of the lake when they see a horse and rider plunge in. In the initial stage of rescue, the king is treated as valuable salvage without a mind of its own. When it is brought ashore and recognized, every goblin within sight snaps to attention and salutes. Hurriedly, the king is rowed across the lake and stretchered out on a cot. Then, at the double, he is carried from the front gate of the castle to his apartment. No one dares ask about how or why the gallop and jump happened.

Returning to their work, the sawyers talk excitedly among themselves.

"What a horse!"

"What a rider!"

"What a jump!"

No one pays any attention to Corporal Pimples washing the mud off of himself in the lake. He now wonders whether the soil is strong enough to take the load of a drawbridge.

Sam releases some of the forest work crews to be the king's personal servants. They are delighted to escape the hard labor of cutting and chopping down trees and scurry around happily to provide all the king desires. They produce tubs of hot water, hot towels, shampoo, rubber ducks, and boats. One is now the court barber, another the court podiatrist, who is also the court manicurist. The court musician plays a plaintive mandolin and, because he doesn't know better, sings mournful love songs in a tenor voice.

The king, clad in a long, purple nightshirt, relaxes as he allows the court masseur to tend to his sore muscles. Pretending to be asleep, he is actually listening to the talk of the servants.

"A runaway horse!"

"Superb horsemanship!"

"A leap of at least twenty paces into the lake!"

"Alexander on Bucephalus could not have done it."

"He sacrificed himself to save Corporal Pimples and the crew working on the new bridge."

"Such bravery!"

"A leader a man could follow into the jaws of death."

King Haymun likes that last one and thinks, *A raise in pay for the masseur might be in order.* He waits for the masseur to repeat it to the valet once more, but he does not. *Time now to stir.* Pretending to be waking from his sleep, he groans and opens his eyes. He shoos everyone from the room except the valet. "I will wear my civilian clothes today, with slippers and my red robe. Where is my crown?"

The valet does not want to upset the king, but he has to tell him, "Your crown is nowhere to be seen, sir."

King Haymun regains his nervous energy. "Well, I was wearing it when the horse bolted. Search the hill and dredge the lake for it. Send swimmers and divers down. It must be found. And tell the steward I want a full breakfast."

The valet has trouble keeping a straight face as he records all that the king orders for his meal. Wheeling on his heels, he is out the door and on his way to the kitchen.

The king started off hungry from Mrs. Squidge's cottage yesterday afternoon. The porridge in the forest was burnt and not edible, so he has ordered a king-sized meal. *While the wizard is away, I am going to live as a king anywhere else in the world would live. Field rations are alright for fighting troops in a battle zone, but not for a king in his own castle.*

Colonel Tyfuss is having the two pips and a crown fixed to every military uniform he possesses. A tailor, acting as bottom sawyer of a pair sawing planks of frequently changing thickness, welcomes the orders to return to his own trade and is making the tailoring task last as long as he can. "Does the colonel want those little red tabs on his jackets also?" Of course.

The valet is downstairs, giving instructions for the king's breakfast. "His majesty wants a full breakfast, the whole lot: orange juice, hot porridge made with milk and sugar, six scrambled eggs, liver sausage, beef patties, fried beans, mushrooms, tomatoes, fried bread, grapefruit, peaches, pears, toast and Marmite, and, of course, a pot of Darjeeling tea. Nothing must be omitted."

Suddenly, the royal kitchen begins gathering momentum. Cooks and scullions run to and fro. The chaos brought about by the king's sudden and unexpected return had settled but is once again in full swing.

There is one final instruction. "Set the table for three. Colonel Tyfuss and the king's female guest will be joining him."

The head steward takes a step backwards, throws a worried glance at his fellow servants, and leaves the room hurriedly. He consults anxiously with other staff. "Who is going to tell the king that the lady he had staying in the castle is no longer here? Shall we tell him that during the fighting she escaped on the back of an eagle? Do you think it might be better to say that she suddenly disappeared in the middle of the night? Does anyone have a more likely story?"

Anyone suggesting any other tale will be appointing himself as reporter to the king. All the servants decline to bear such news. The king, in his present frail state of health, might well die of apoplexy. Even the scullion, who washes the dishes, although threatened with dismissal, refuses to put his life in jeopardy. Whether a scullion or a king, life is precious.

That leaves the army. After all, it was the army that failed to prevent the lady's departure.

The sergeant major, contacted at the guardhouse, says, "No," in clear terms. Sam intends to keep his distance from the king until the monarch recovers from the news of recent events at the castle. He can delegate the nasty job. *Anyway, my presence is required at the guardhouse until the tricky situation pertaining to the foundations for the new drawbridge is brought under control. Immediately thereafter, I will report to the king for orders.* "The quartermaster sergeant is the one dealing with castle and palace affairs. He waits upon the king at the king's pleasure. I will have him make a full report of events at the castle since the king left for the forest a little over a week ago."

The quartermaster sergeant has reached his dizzy height of rank by agreeing at all times with anyone of higher rank than himself, whether counted in terms of stripes or pips or crowns or crossed swords. Where two of higher ranks are disagreeing, Quartz always supports the man of highest rank. His wisdom has brought about steady progress. In order for his qualities and merits to be noticed, it is essential that he is frequently seen by his senior officers.

Quartz welcomes the opportunity to report to the king. He will precede his report with a clarification for the crown's benefit that things might have turned out differently had he himself not been in sickbay, suffering from the compound effects of measles, shingles, chickenpox, and whooping cough while experiencing tonsillitis and gallstones.

The chief steward knows there will be no hiding the absence of the lady at the meal. He wisely decides that bad news had better precede the serving of the meal or even the placing of it on the table in case tableware is thrown. It will be better to feed the quartermaster sergeant to the lions first. Passing through the anteroom crowded with curious servants, the steward knocks on the bedroom door. It is opened by the valet. "The quartermaster sergeant is waiting upon the king's pleasure to report on recent events at the castle."

The door closes, and after a short wait, the valet returns. "The quartermaster sergeant shall come in and report to his majesty."

The servants crowd up quietly and place their ears against the door panel. They are expecting fireworks. They will not be disappointed.

RECOVER THE LADY!

Each of the servants listening at the door of the king's bedroom is armed with a brush or a broom or a duster. When Quartz leaves, if he leaves alive, there might well be insufficient time to disappear through the anteroom door into the corridor and get lost. If that happens, they will all be busy cleaning.

Sprite, a ghostly, unseen observer, stands at the far end of the anteroom watching with interest the servants at the door. For a few moments, they are glued to the door. Then they back off as though their ears are somehow too close to the heat. Now Sprite can hear the shouting from inside himself. Even he steps back against the far wall and hopes he really is invisible.

Three days ago, the wizard gave King Haymun such a dressing-down that it left Mrs. Squidge in awe at the wizard's skill with invectives. The words are burned into the king's memory. He now reissues them as mere building blocks awaiting the plastering and painting that he supplies from his own storehouse of invectives. He searches the dregs of his own mind and throws everything at the quartermaster sergeant.

The color drains from the faces of the servants. They step back and look with horror at each other as though they have been caught eavesdropping some poignant and private farewell between a father and son. One by one, they tiptoe to the corridor door, where they walk away briskly and then break into running towards the kitchen, the pantry, and the laundry. They have heard enough. They will remain out of sight for a while, conscientiously engrossed in their duties as rarely before.

Sprite, recognizing that he cannot be seen and wishing to see what happens, remains alone in the anteroom. He expects that Quartz will soon emerge, but he does not do so. He moves closer to the door. The shouting is now much louder. *Has murder been done? If it has been done, there is little point in intervening, throwing one life after another. If it is still being done, then should a public-spirited citizen, even though unseen, interfere with the actions of his overlord the king? Are not good citizens required to accept and follow the orders of the rulers placed over them?* He shakes his head as though to clear it. *Whatever, I have no intention of interfering in state business.*

Quartz entered the bedroom ruddy in appearance, healthily overweight, and gorgeously appareled, wearing his best dress uniform. His clothes are unchanged, but his face is drained of all color. He even seems to have lost weight and bulk within the few moments he has been standing before the king.

He tried to work in a, "Yes, sir! Yes, sir!" every now and again. He does them well because he practices them in front of the mirror in his barrack cubicle.

The king, however, is in no mood for even a single "Yes, sir!"

The monarch took in his stride the news of the assault on the castle, the rescue of gran'ma, the damage to the buildings, and the destruction of the pontoon bridge...but his patience has limits and his mind explodes. *This bumbling fool tells me that my troops have allowed my future wife to fly away on the back of a bird? That is the last straw! Don't they realize how much I love the woman? That stubborn streak she has is one of her most delightful qualities. I treasure her bite and scratch marks.* It is enough to try the patience of a saint, and he has no intention of becoming a saint! The color that drained from the face of Quartz is not lost. It has transfused into the king's purple face.

Sprite wonders whether the hot lava from the erupting volcano inside will soon flow towards him. He backs away from the door, lest somehow he gets scorched himself by the king's fury. To avoid attracting attention, even though he is unseen, Sprite stands stock still and holds his breath lest the condensation betray his presence.

The king has said enough. Now is the time for action. "Take enough men, four at least, and the best horses and weapons. Take at least two of the men who brought her here. They know the way."

Quartz has never ridden a horse in his life. He is a walker and waiting for the invention of the bicycle before he tries to travel faster than a slow jog. It already exists in the Beyond, but Twith businessmen have always been slow to import fresh ideas from abroad. There is no question in his mind, however, that he might raise this matter of lack of riding experience with his king. It is not that the king would be unsympathetic. It is rather that there are no questions left in the mind of the quartermaster sergeant. There are no facts or certainties either. He doesn't even know who he is or was. His mind has stopped functioning. The blobby mass within his skull has stopped dealing with messages from his senses. It can hardly interpret what his eyes are seeing or his ears are hearing. He has to think really hard to know whether he is a boy or a girl. He has been roasted alive. His mind is only fit to be served with Yorkshire pudding, roast potatoes, gravy, carrots, and peas, followed by suet pudding and treacle.

King Haymun growls at the quartermaster sergeant, "Go and bring the lady back, or don't come back yourself! Don't you dare harm her! Advise her that the king sends greetings. He has been missing her. Do your duty. I will expect you back tomorrow morning, and you had better not be alone! Be gone!"

Quartz has been standing sharply at attention four or five paces in front of the king, his shining boots at the correct angle and his arms straight down his sides with his thumbs along the seams of his trousers. He salutes sharply. "Yes, sir!"

He turns about on his right heel, stamps down his left foot, and marches away briskly to the door. He flings it open, and without stopping to close it behind him, strides across the anteroom and is out to the corridor as though he is the lead officer in the king's birthday parade. He fights the instinct to break into a run until he is around the first corner of the corridor.

CYDLO'S HUT

Even though Bimbo and Bollin have turned off the toad trail onto the east fork before they reach the ambush site, they stay silent. They are in enemy territory. At the ambush camp, there might well be guards, and perhaps they extend south. The waning half-moon gives enough light to ride by. There is little noise save the clip-clopping of the pony's hooves. Chestnut knows the way and needs no guiding. Several times, he pauses to graze, and the boys dismount, stretch, and work their arms and shoulders to free them up. Both boys have swords unsheathed and ready to use if they should be surprised.

To the best of their knowledge, the wizard is still on the Brook, but his raven is here, and that spells danger. Rasputin patrols during daylight hours, and for this reason, the boys decide to work as much as possible during the hours of darkness. They will rest during the coming day, and when their sleep is out, they will prepare for their excursion towards the castle. They need to find the quarry to determine the line of the underwater tunnel as it used to be. They'll be looking around for any toads in the lake that they can talk to. They plan to go on foot rather than by horseback and will leave Chestnut behind at Cydlo's hut. During daylight tomorrow, they will shelter in the quarry or nearby.

The journey, in very different circumstances, is along the same path they took on foot several days ago. Bimbo's knee is well healed from the fall he took then. Bollin has gone this way a second time when he accompanied Elisheba back to the cottage to obtain her possessions before continuing on to the Brook.

As they approach the cottage, the pony's pace quickens almost to a trot. Bollin reins him back. "Steady. Steady, boy. We'll walk the last bit. No noise now!"

The boys dismount. Bimbo scouts out ahead. They do not want to fall into any kind of trap.

The first streaks of dawn are in the sky. Again, they notice the absence of birds singing their beautiful dawn chorus. The Brook is filled with the glorious sounds of birdsong at this time of the morning. The door of the cottage is latched but not bolted. Bimbo does not yet go in. He walks around the house, looking for signs of trespassing or someone inside. He sees nothing suspicious. He looks in the door of the mill below the side of the house. The stream water gurgles happily as it passes by. He sees no sign of disturbance anywhere.

Bollin holds the pony back at the edge of the clearing. The pony does not move although he can smell that he is home.

Bimbo looks in the cowshed. Although their manger is empty, clean as a whistle, the two cows stand in their usual places, waiting for a dawn milking. They stir and turn their heads. Bimbo pats their rumps and moves towards the house. The door creaks as he slowly opens it. There is no wolf-dog now to defend the house. *The house feels empty. That's good.* He makes a quick check, upstairs and down. With every step, Bimbo relaxes a bit more. There is no one here, and no one has been here. He calls out to Bollin, "It's okay. The house is empty."

His brother removes Chestnut's reins and harness, hangs them up on the stable door, and releases the pony with a grateful pat or two. The pony uses his freedom to graze. Bollin takes their two haversacks into the house. *It seems odd that I was last here only two days ago. There has certainly been a lot packed into those two busy days and nights.* He too looks around to spot signs that anything has been disturbed. Nothing has been moved. There are no footprints. Things are just as he and Elisheba left them when they headed south. "Bimbo, I'll kindle a fire to heat water while you go check on the cows."

Daisy and Belle look uncomfortable. They have not had a milking since Bollin and Elisheba were here. Their udders are full. Neither Bimbo nor Bollin have any experience milking a cow. Bimbo locates the milk pails and straddles the milking stool. He talks to Daisy in a steady, comforting monotone as he rinses the pail with the first one or two squirts of milk and then applies himself to the serious task of filling the bucket by gently stroking the teats of the udder. He sees Daisy wince. "Steady there, Daisy. I'll bet you wish Elisheba were doing this, don't you? Well, I'm trying my best. I hope I don't pinch you too bad. There. Is that better? Your turn next, Belle. This afternoon Bollin can milk you, and then you won't be so full. Good girl, Daisy. Pity you are too big to get through the toad tunnel. We would have a dozen new milkmaids wanting to milk you every day if you didn't get stuck in the bog! Who do you prefer, Daisy, my school friend Ruthie, or me? Don't answer that. There. Full to the top. How about that? My, that must feel better, doesn't it? Well done, Daisy. Well done, Bimbo."

When the two buckets are filled with rich, creamy, warm milk, Bimbo hooks their handles on the carrying yoke and puts it on his shoulders. He finds walking without spilling more difficult than the milking itself was. His walk needs a certain rhythm.

Bollin watched Elisheba light a fire using flint instead of a match. "I'm fairly sure that if tested, I could strike a spark from flint to make a flame and light a fire from tinder. But I can't be bothered with that just now. I'll just use a match instead." He already has fresh water in the pot hanging above the fire and a pan of porridge ready for heating as soon as the crackling twigs settle down to a steady blaze.

Bimbo has a suggestion. "Just in case there should be any interruption by strangers while we're resting, let's prepare our haversacks for the evening journey and hide them in the bushes."

Bollin doesn't need as much sleep as Bimbo. "I'll take the first shift and sleep beside the haversacks until noon. You go use Cydlo's bed and get some quality sleep."

"Alright, that sounds good. We can have a bite of lunch then and change places to rest until late afternoon. If it appears safe after we give the cows a last milking, we can head north towards the lake."

For their second meal, Bollin makes a stew. Much of any easily edible foodstuffs in the cottage were taken to feed the expedition team as they waited to leave Gyminge. But there are potatoes and carrots waiting to be removed from the garden and onions still in the pantry. He puts in a packet of soup for flavor. They are really hungry, something that only happens to them in Gyminge. With tummies comfortably full, they go to rest for a few hours.

Daisy and Belle return of their own accord from grazing among the buttercups at their usual time in late afternoon. They take up their places at the milking stalls. The two boys, washed and refreshed by their sleep, are ready for them. Before going to the cowshed, they scatter the embers of the fire and take a look round that everything is being left tidy.

"Come on, Bollin. You can have Daisy, and I'll have Belle. We can leave the milk in the pantry. If it goes bad, no matter. I don't feel we should just throw it away. You can have the milking stool. I'll just kneel. Come on, Belle. There, there, good girl. You know me by now, don't you? I might not be as good as Elisheba or Cydlo, but maybe I'm better than Ruthie. How are you doing, Bollin?"

They begin singing songs of their childhood in Pakistan, using the Urdu words to the tunes. They work steadily away.

"Ouch!" Something sharp sticks in Bimbo's neck.

A hand grabs his hair and pulls his head back. "Move an inch and you have taken your last breath!"

CAPTURED!

Bimbo does not move a muscle. The same thing happens to Bollin in the next stall. Neither boy has any idea who it is that has crept up on them. There is no response they can make except obedience to the orders snarled at them. The points of swords or daggers press into the backs of their necks.

Outside, there is shouting. "Bring up the horses. We've got them."

The voice behind the dagger is harsh and metallic, but it is a Gyminge voice without doubt. "Don't make a false move! Lower yourselves to the ground and stretch out face down!"

The two boys comply with the order and lower themselves carefully to the ground.

"Spread your arms out wide. Don't try no tricks. You have no value to us. If you want to stop breathing, move! You, answer my question." Bollin gets a kick in his side. "Where is the girl? What have you done with her? Where is she hidden?"

Bollin answers in Urdu. "Which girl do you mean? I know many girls."

There is no response from Bollin's questioner. Instead, Bimbo gets a kick in his side. "Where is the girl, the woodcutter's daughter, the red-haired girl? You know who I mean! Speak properly. You understand me very well."

Bimbo answers, not daring to look at his captors. He takes the cue from his brother and answers in Urdu, "The girl is staying at the home of my father."

Bimbo and Bollin often share secrets in other's company by speaking to each other in Urdu or Punjabi. Both boys realize they must try to look as though they do not understand the questions being asked of them. This might well be difficult.

The captors obviously do not understand what the boys are saying. They might understand what birds and animals say, but this is a language they cannot cope with. Muttered words flow back and forth. "Where are they from? What are these foreigners doing in Gyminge? How did they get here?"

Ropes are tied around the boys' ankles.

"Bring your hands behind your backs!"

Their wrists are tied tight, too tight. They are rolled over and for the first time face their captors.

The boys give each other a look as if to say, *Oh, yes, it is as bad as we feared.*

Hovering above them are five goblin soldiers in uniform. They are tough, professional, no-nonsense men. They have swords in their hands, and they appear prepared to use them.

The man in charge explains their problem. "We are looking for the red-haired woodsman's daughter. We left the quartermaster sergeant behind. He is an ex-cavalryman and was very anxious to come with us, but he hurt his leg in a severe fall and is unable to ride. He promised us a personal reward of his own if we succeed in bringing back the girl. It is the king's own command, and he fully expects us to be successful. We are confident. We did it before, and if she is at home, we will do so again. If the girl isn't inside, she will be hiding in the buildings somewhere. If she fled into the forest though, there will be no finding her."

Now that the occupants of the cowshed are captives, the house is quickly searched. The searchers report back, "There is no sign that the girl's bed was slept in last night. The bed is neatly made, undisturbed, and cold to the touch. The woman's clothes have been removed. There are empty hangers on the bed. The bedclothes on the man's bed are still warm."

The stable is searched. Nothing is found there; the pony is still grazing in the meadow. The grounds around the house give no indication they hold any secrets, and the goblins do not have time to waste searching them. There is no sign that the prisoners have any companions.

The goblins pull the brothers upright and point. The boys hop through the cowshed door and lean against the wall outside. They make no attempt to talk to each other.

One of the goblin soldiers pulls the milking stool up to Daisy and completes her milking with deft actions that suggest he has grown up on a farm. He does the same for Belle and then carries the two buckets of milk into the house. He brings mugs of milk out for his companions.

As they drink, they talk among themselves. "We drew a blank with the girl, but we have prisoners who should be worth something to the quartermaster sergeant."

The ranking goblin is a corporal. "I will lead on the return to the castle. You"—he points to two of the goblins—"each carry a prisoner lying face down in front of you. You will ride immediately behind me." He turns to the other two horsemen. "You follow behind with the spare horse. We'll take no chances that our captives can escape. If there is any attempt to rescue them, don't hesitate to use your swords."

Strangely, they pull the door of the cottage closed behind them.

Two horses, among the best in the castle stable, are brought over to the two boys. Two goblins hold the horses' heads steady. The other two lift Bollin and throw him face down over a saddle. Then they do the same with Bimbo. The boys feel like sacks of flour.

The corporal issues one last order. "Mount up, boys." Giving his steed a kick, he takes off at a fast-paced gallop.

The goblins swing into their saddles and follow at the same fast pace.

The prisoners are in for a very uncomfortable ride. By the time the horses arrive at the guardhouse, both Bimbo and Bollin are groaning loud enough to drown out the sound of galloping hoofs.

THE QUESTIONING

It stays light late into the evening, and there are still several hours left when the horsemen ride into the encampment at the guardhouse on the mainland. For his own safety, Sam remains over on the land side, avoiding any encounter with King Haymun. Corporal Pimples wishes the sergeant major would keep out of the way. He expects the king to come visit at any time and hopes it will be less hurried than the last time.

Quartz is also there, waiting. He has given Sam graphic stories of the dressing-down he received from the king for allowing the woman to escape. "I don't know why I should be considered responsible for her escape. I used to think I was more afraid of my father than anyone else. That was when I was young and innocent. Since I joined the army, my father has dropped to fifth, a long way behind the other four—the wizard, the king, my wife, and you—in that order. It was just today that the king moved up ahead of my wife."

Quartz and Sam are outside waiting and watching as the horsemen return from their expedition into the forest. As the riders come down to the level of the flat field in front of the castle, the corporal breaks into singing. He once sang bass soloist in the castle choir with Dr. Tyfuss singing tenor. Ever since then, he fancies himself a master musician. He tends to compose and sing arias whenever he is on horseback and out of earshot of senior officers. He sings his newly composed aria to the tune of "Twinkle, Twinkle, Little Star," which is an old Twith folk melody.

> Red is her hair, blue her eyes
> Crystal her tears when she cries
> Missed her this time, don't know how
> Never mind, we milked the cow.

Those behind him join in at suitable points with, "Yippee yippee-i-ay." At the end, they repeat their accompaniment to give the corporal enough time to compose another verse.

• The corporal sees two superior officers standing on the porch of the guardhouse. He falls silent. The procession halts in front of them.

"Corporal on special duty reporting, Sergeant Major, sir. The girl was not at the place you said. We made a very thorough search. But we picked up two prisoners for questioning."

"Take them into the guardhouse, men."

In a short while, the two boys who bumped and bounced the whole way back are gratefully on solid ground once more. They hop as best they can with tied ankles and cramping legs. The goblins that captured them prevent them from falling. Once inside the guardhouse, they slump against the back wall.

"They are foreigners, Sergeant Major, sir. They don't seem to understand our language. I think perhaps they are from China. They look different somehow. They've cut off their pigtails to disguise themselves, but it hasn't worked. They might as well have kept them. Look how brown their skins are. Look at their eyes!"

Both Bimbo and Bollin are surprised that they have been identified as Chinese, but that will serve for now. Each boy tries to narrow his eyes to look the part.

Quartz is anxious. *The king ordered me to bring back the girl. Had she been recaptured, I alone would have taken her in to the monarch and received my due praise. I don't want to have to be the one to break the news to the king that she couldn't be found.* He tries to persuade the sergeant major to do the job for him. "As senior officer, I think you should have the privilege of taking such valuable prisoners to the king."

Sam quickly comes up with an excuse. "I am unable to leave my duties at the trestle site here on the mainland." This is a poor excuse since work on construction has ceased for the day, but his rank is higher than that of Quartz, so it doesn't matter if his excuse is weak.

It is a pity that the second squad sent out to search for boats has not yet returned. They have been successful in finding several boats farther afield but have not yet returned with them. The one small rowing boat available can take an oarsman, one of the prisoners, and a goblin to guard him on each trip. Three trips are necessary before Bollin and Bimbo and Quartz are across. The main castle gates remain closed these days. The left gate has within it a small wooden door known as a picket gate used in peace time for foot traffic. The boys are led through this narrow door.

Bimbo and Bollin were inside the castle in very different circumstances only last Monday. Now they realize there is no easy way for them to escape, and a rescue attempt is almost impossible.

Quartz instructs the guards, "Blindfold the prisoners, and then undo their legs. There is a good distance for them to walk."

The ropes from their legs are fashioned into nooses and thrown over their heads. They wonder with fright, *Are they going to hang us?* The goblin guards lead their prisoners by tugging on each noose. The boys stumble over the cobbles until they are halted by a sharp pull. They wait.

The gate is slammed shut. Quartz returns and gives further orders. "Take them up to the great hall."

Again, the boys stumble forward. They climb one flight of steps and can feel they are walking on carpet. Then it is on up another flight of stairs, where they are taken along a corridor. Again, they wait. The blindfolds are removed. Guards hold the nooses. There is a sudden, sharp command. "Kneel!"

Bimbo and Bollin do not move. They look around blankly as if they do not comprehend the order given. The great hall they are in has high ceilings. The walls are decorated with shields, crests, spears, war axes, swords, and armor. There are lights around the walls to supplement the evening light through the tall windows.

Bimbo thinks, *We must be on the north side of the castle. I can see the lake stretching into the distance.*

The guards force them into a kneeling position. The king enters, wearing a purple robe and his second spare crown. His throne is on a dais at the end of the room. He turns to face them and sits down.

Quartz marches up from behind the prisoners to stand before the king and snaps to attention. "Sir, beg to report that the maiden was not located at her residence." Hurriedly, he continues, "But we arrested these two Chinese in the barn. We caught them milking the cows. I have brought them for questioning, sir!"

The king barks out his questions, "Who are you? Where are you from? What are you doing here? Where is the girl?"

Bollin smiles and tries to look friendly but insane. He answers in Urdu. "I am Bollin. I am from Gibbins Brook. I have come to try to find the sword. The girl was at my home on the Brook when I left to come here."

"What did he say?" the king demands of the quartermaster sergeant.

Quartz asks the same of the guards. The guards ask the same of the curious servants standing against the far wall. They have never seen a Chinaman before.

The king is impatient. "Isn't there anyone in the castle who can speak Chinese?"

Shoulders shrug, eyebrows raise, and heads shake back and forth.

Bollin warms to his task. At school, he memorized some Punjabi poetry about silver moonlight on the water and riverbanks and bulbuls singing in the chinar trees. He launches into a recitation, limited in its effect by the fact that his hands are tied behind his back and he can't raise them expressively. Instead, he rolls his eyes and concludes with the weeping required from the forlorn lover as he realizes his maiden of the woods and riverbank is gone forever and will not return.

Bimbo, entering into the spirit of his brother's performance, joins in weeping as the poem reaches its tragic ending and the despairing lover flings himself into the river waters.

The king realizes some action is expected of him. He instructs the quartermaster sergeant, "Take them to the dungeons! I'll see them in the morning. Be sure you have an interpreter on hand tomorrow. Don't fail! The wizard is coming on Sunday, and I leave the day after tomorrow for the southern border to prepare for his arrival. I want the woman back before I leave!"

THE DUNGEONS

The king returns to his quarters. Quartz breathes a great sigh of relief. It could have been much worse. He is not yet out of the fire, but at least the burning at the stake is put off until tomorrow.

Quartz is uneasy about this latest assignment. As he traverses the stairs he voices his thoughts aloud. "It's a pity that Dr. Tyfuss left. He is a very learned man and it's possible he might understand Chinese." The quartermaster sergeant is desperate. "Do I know of a Chinese laundry or a Chinese takeaway anywhere? No. I don't. There is a pottery on the edge of the Dark Forest. They make china. Would anyone there know the language? Rasputin is a world traveler. He might at least know a few words." Then a bright idea makes its way into his dull mind. "I need to secure the prisoners in the dungeons and then get across to see Sam. He has a talking parrot that he keeps in a cage. It probably came from China. That might give me the breakthrough I need."

Quartz marches the prisoners down to the dungeons. They are obviously not accustomed to military discipline or the parade ground. He does not bother to blindfold them. They would soon get them off when they are left alone.

The two boys shuffle along, looking around carefully at everything they see. Dividing the castle courtyard is a wall. On the north side of the wall are lawns and gardens where the wizard and the king are accustomed to walk. In the wall is a guarded gate. It has been badly burned; there is still a smell of stale burning in the air. A poorly constructed replacement gate remains unpainted. Until the king returned, it was unguarded, as Corporal Pimples needed more and more men. Now that the king is home, there is a guard on duty until daylight fades. Then it is bolted from inside by a castle servant. The guard lets them through the wall gate.

On the south side of the dividing wall are the quarters of the castle domestic servants and certain castle officers such as Sam, Quartz, and the castle steward.

The dungeon door is to the right of the laundry, where gran'ma had been held captive. The boys notice that the door which suffered damage from a flying Twith axe has been repaired. The two boys do not talk. There will be plenty of opportunity to do that when they are on their own. They go down two steps to the dungeon door, which is bolted from inside. There is a small observation window in the door.

Quartz calls out sharply. It brings a quick response.

A face peers out the window. The hinges squeal in pain as the door creaks open. A goblin head pokes out through the door only partially ajar. "Yes, Sergeant?"

"King Haymun has sent these two prisoners down for you to take care of tonight. He'll see them again in the morning. They are Chinese, so there is no point in trying to talk to them. Do you have anything for them to eat?"

The guard shakes his head. "No. I got nothing to feed them."

"Oh! Well, I'll see what there is on the mainland, but it will be some time, if I even come back at all."

Quartz thinks about the scores of glass bottles being stored in the dungeon. *I can't put the prisoners in with those. The Chinese probably eat glass for breakfast. You can't account for the appetites of foreigners. They can go in the small dungeon at the back. The prisoner already there will appreciate some company. He's been there a long time by himself.*

"You shouldn't put them in with the bottles. Will it be safe to put them with the other prisoner?"

"Yeah, that will be fine. He's chained to the floor. I won't go in with them, so once the door is locked, it will be quite safe. But you need to bring the guards back with you when you come to collect them in the morning."

The dungeon area is not well lit. There is a corridor that stretches from the dungeon door almost to the exterior wall of the castle. Two flickering torches in holders on the wall throw shadows into narrow dungeon rooms. The full length of the hallway has floor-to-ceiling iron bars to separate the prisoners from the access way. There are no solid interior walls, only thick metal bars less than a handbreadth apart.

Bimbo and Bollin can see that almost all the dungeon rooms are filled with racks upon racks of man-sized bottles lying flat. Each is sealed with a wooden plug covered with wax. There are three, perhaps four, bottles end to end stretching back towards the dim far wall almost lost to sight.

The dungeon guard has a metal ring of several large keys on his belt. He uses one to unlock a padlock on the door of the small prison cell at the end of the passageway. He stands aside as it swings open. It complains bitterly. There is no ventilation. The air smells stale and damp. There is no light inside, and the nearest torch is a third of the way down the corridor. It is almost pitch black.

The nooses are still around the boys' necks. Their goblin escorts do not remove the nooses, just release them as they push the boys into the cell. Without their hands free to help them balance, Bimbo and Bollin jostle against each other as they try to keep from falling over. Bollin trips over something bulky lying on the floor and rolls as he falls. He saves his head from cracking against the wall by hitting his shoulder instead. He holds back his exclamation of pain. Bimbo is more fortunate and manages to stay upright. He makes his way over to his brother and eases himself down beside him.

The door screeches shut, and the padlock is locked. Footsteps echo back down the corridor. The inside door clangs shut, and the bolt is thrown to secure it.

The goblin guard sits down and picks up his knitting. His wife is teaching him how to knit and has given him a project for his daughter's birthday, a doll's scarf. He mutters to himself. "Knit one, purl two. Knit one, purl two…" on and on. He wonders, *How long does a doll's scarf have to be anyway?* It will be a long night watch before his relief comes. The dungeon guard changed duty with his alternate at midnight. In better days, there had been four of them for twenty-four-hour duty. When the king took the bulk of the garrison for maneuvers in the forest, it dropped to three. When Corporal Pimples started building his bridge, the dungeon guards dropped to two. Between the pair of them, they decided on six hours on and six hours off rather than twelve hours on and twelve hours off.

THE PRISONER

Bimbo and Bollin continue to speak in Urdu to each other. They don't want to betray any confidential information and need to find out who the other prisoner is before they can talk freely. Whoever he is, the man has hardly moved. The first thing the boys want to do is get their hands free of the ropes and bring life back into their arms and hands. The brothers lean back to back. Neither makes much progress. The knots are tight and secure, and there is hardly any freedom for their wrists and fingers to work the knots loose on the other.

"Welcome, whoever you are. Come over to me. My feet are shackled, but my hands are free. I'll help you." The voice is cultured and sounds young.

Bollin answers in English, "Thank you. We are pretending to be Chinese, so we are careful what we say. We'll appreciate your help."

He bumps himself over towards the voice. As he backs into something, fingers reach out towards him. He swings his body around until his wrists are grabbed. Fingers explore and find the knots. The stranger is on his knees trying to get a firm hold on the rope. He pulls and wriggles it, but the knot is very tight. His fingers slip. He tries again and yet again. No success.

Bollin doesn't want to waste any more time. "My brother's bonds might be easier to get started. I'll move out of the way."

Bimbo moves over, and the stranger pulls and tugs on his ropes. At last, something gives. A rope slips beneath another. A steady pull, and an end drags through. A few moments of steady working and pulling and Bimbo's hands are free.

Suddenly, the pain is intense! For more than six hours, the bonds have been cutting into his wrists locked behind his back in an immovable position. The pain starts with his shoulders and elbows, his wrists, his fingers, his knuckles. He shrugs and stretches, straightens and bends, wriggles, makes fists and opens and closes his fingers. "Wow! This really hurts! Wait a moment or two, Bollin, and I'll have a go at yours. I'm just trying to get some circulation in my hands and fingers. Wowee!"

The stranger turns to Bollin. "Come back for another try." But again, he is unable to make any progress. "Move closer. Let me get my teeth into the knot." The man's head shakes Bollin's wrists to and fro as his teeth pull at one of the knots. This movement stirs the knot loose, and once the first strand is loosened, it is not long before Bollin's wrists are free and he experiences the same agony of renewed flexibility and circulation that his brother did.

The two lamps along the corridor wall give only enough light to distinguish darkness from greater darkness. There is no furniture in the room. There is a straw mattress pad on which the prisoner has been lying. It is hard to see anything at all of his appearance, except they can make out a mass of hair and a ragged beard.

The two boys, once their hands are free, seat themselves close on either side of their fellow prisoner who sits against the stone wall to the left of the door. They are slowly becoming accustomed to the smell.

Bimbo asks, "Can we be overheard?"

"Not if you speak at this level. I have to almost shout to get any attention. I think this guard—I call him Nitter—is deaf anyway."

"What do we call you? You must have a name. My name is Bimbo, and my brother's name is Bollin."

"Call me Scayper. That's what the guards call me. I'm in here because I tried to escape."

Bimbo leans forward in a gesture of friendship. "It's nice to meet you, Scayper. We want to hear as much about you as you care to tell us. However, that must wait for a while."

Bimbo's tone turns urgent. "Now listen carefully. We plan to have a busy night. We are going to break out of here. King

Haymun is supposed to see us later this morning, so we must be free before then. We'll take you with us if we can and you want to come. Are you able to walk, or will we have to carry you?"

"I can't walk very well because of these shackles. They only allow very short steps. Remove these and I think I'll be able to keep up with you. I am taken out once a day for exercise in the courtyard, so that keeps me limber. It also helps me keep track of time, and best of all, it gives me a taste of fresh air."

Bollin asks, "How can we get your leg irons loose?"

Before Scayper can answer, Bimbo says, "Never mind. We can deal with that later. The sergeant indicated he would try to bring some food from the guardhouse. We should probably wait until he comes before we make our move. We don't want him coming in while we are getting out. For now, tell us about the guards and their routines."

"There are only two dungeon guards. I am classed as a dangerous prisoner, so two other goblins come from the castle to see to my exercise. The guards have recently changed their routines. They split the day up into four equal parts. Nitter has only just come on duty. When they change over, it is already daylight. When he gets tired of knitting, he'll put his feet up on the other chair and soon be sound asleep. After all, apart from the bottles, I'm the only prisoner here, and generally, there's nothing to make a noise. The rats that run around are my friends and don't bother me, although they did at the beginning."

Bimbo leans back against the wall. "Let me tell you what we're going to be up against. Our main enemy is the Wizard of Wozzle, but as far as we know, he is on the Brook, Gibbins Brook, south of here. That's where we're from. The wizard took most of his goblin army there so that eliminates a lot of the threat. The one we have to watch out for is Rasputin, the wizard's raven. We know he is here at the castle. We also know that the wizard is coming back here on Sunday. That means we need to be back on the Brook before then."

PLANNING THE ESCAPE

Bimbo takes over naturally as leader for the escape, fulfilling the assignment he was given by Jock. Cydlo gave him key information that will help them, and Bimbo is confident they will be out before the night is through. "Show us now how you are shackled."

Scayper replies, "You will have to feel my feet. Nitter has the key to the lock fixing the chain to the floor, but he never comes in here, only the two escort guards."

The two boys feel Scayper's legs. There is a steel ring around each ankle, and the two rings are connected by a short chain. This means that even when released from the main shackle to which the chain is padlocked, Scayper can only take short, hobbled steps.

Bollin is curious. "Tell us how you came to be here."

"Long ago, I was sealed into a bottle the same as the other Twith who refused to be subject to the wizard. There was hardly any room to move inside the bottle. I don't know how long I was there. It could have been years, even hundreds of years, but one day, it was as though I woke up out of a deep sleep, wide awake and alert. I wondered how I could escape. My bottle was laying flat at the end of a lowest shelf in the main dungeon. I found that by moving my body weight slightly, I could get the bottle to move just a tiny bit. I rocked the bottle a little farther each day. It took many months, but I finally got it to the edge and onto the floor. It fell with a tremendous crash, and I was knocked unconscious. The guards recovered me, put me into another bottle, and replaced me on the shelf.

"I was determined to escape. Again, it took many months before the bottle fell. That time, I hid, but the dungeon was locked tight until the goblins eventually found me. The wizard ordered me kept in this special dungeon, shackled to the floor, until he decides what to do with me. He has never bothered to decide."

Nitter has knitted enough and puts down the doll's scarf. He takes a turn down the corridor for exercise. The three prisoners hear him approach and begin snoring loudly. Thinking they are fast asleep, he returns to his chair, lifts his feet onto the other chair, and pulls his hat down over his eyes. Like every other night, this is going to be a quiet night.

Bimbo is close to both Bollin and Scayper. He speaks softly to both of them. "First, Scayper, we pledge to take you with us. Have no worry. You can trust us. We might disappear for a short while, but we will be back. I promise. We'll not leave you here. Right, Bollin?"

Bollin affirms his brother's promise. "You can be sure we will help you escape for good."

Bimbo asks, "Do you know anything about the king's shield? The Royal Shield of King Rufus? Have you ever seen it? Do you know where it might be?"

Scayper frowns and shakes his head. "No. I've never seen it. I would think the king took it with him when he escaped."

Bimbo shrugs his shoulder. "Well, never mind about that. I think I know where it is anyway."

There is excitement in Bollin's voice. "Didn't you notice the things hanging on the wall in the king's hall where he interviewed us? I saw the great shield above the fireplace. It had the horse and the lion and the crown painted in three of the four quadrants. That's the insignia of the Twith so it must be the Royal Shield. There are other shields on the walls as well, but none of them had the Twith crest that I could see."

Bimbo nods. "Yes, I did see that, but I was told it fell into the lake when the king was wounded fighting the invaders from Wozzle. Perhaps one of the goblins found it when they were extending the lake, or perhaps the SnuggleWump found it. It doesn't matter. I'm sure that what we saw in the king's hall is the Royal Shield. Now we know where it is, that's what really matters."

Bimbo speaks to Scayper again. "Do you know anything about Dayko?"

The lad is alert and eager to share what he knows. "Yes, he was our last seer, and when Wozzle invaded us, he was killed. That was when the traitor seer, Zaydek, was also killed. It had already happened before I was brought to the castle."

Bimbo's manner grows intense. "Before Dayko died, he wrote a poem that foresaw that one day the Twith would return to Gyminge. Before that can happen, a score of special things must occur. Some of them, probably most of them, have already happened. We think the time of the Return is soon. We are not Twith Logue ourselves. We are Shadow brothers from the Beyond who are helping them. No time to explain that just now.

"In Dayko's Rime are a sword and a shield. We have come back to Gyminge to get the king's Royal Sword. I have been told where that is, and we'll have to leave you while we go get it. But when we have that, we'll come back to get you."

Bimbo leans forward to be sure Scayper doesn't miss any of what he says. "Listen, carefully, Scayper. The three of us are going to go out through the dungeon door and then through the gate to the north apartments where the king lives. Once we get there, we shall recover the shield from the king's hall and arm you with weapons of your own choosing. We'll give you a chance for some clean clothes and a cleanup, if we can. Then we'll give ourselves something to eat from the kitchen and take the king hostage. There is a lake all around the castle. There didn't used to be, I understand. There used to be a bridge of pontoon boats across to the mainland, but that has been wrecked. Can you swim?"

Bollin is worried about Scayper's strength. "He won't have to swim. I can be the one to do that."

Scayper laughs. "It's alright. I'm a strong swimmer. It suits my build."

Bimbo tends to agree with Bollin. "Well, hopefully you might not need to. Can you row?"

"Yes, of course. My arms are quite muscular."

"That's good. There will be four of us to get across to the mainland, the king and the three of us. The rowboat can only take three, so to avoid making two trips, one of us will probably have to swim. If there is no immediate danger and we can make two trips, we will. We might as well wreck the boat when we are done."

Bollin is up for that. "Can I have that job? A couple of big rocks thrown with force should put big holes in it. It will sink straight to the bottom of the lake. That will be fun."

Bimbo gives a disgusted sigh. "Okay. When we get to the guardhouse on the mainland, we'll use the hostage king to make the garrison there furnish us with three horses. We'll send all the goblins, including the king, swimming in the lake, and chase any other horses they have ahead of us into Blindhouse Wood. Then we'll go like the clappers for the waterfall that will let us out to the Beyond."

Bimbo stirs uncomfortably. "Our trouble is likely to be the raven. Rasputin will be sure to let the wizard know about us if he can. We don't want to take on the wizard and the whole goblin army from the Brook before we get back. Maybe we could douse his feathers with treacle or jam if we can catch him. We'll have to play that one by ear. We really want to be back on the Brook by Saturday evening well before the wizard starts off to come back here."

Bimbo isn't going to wait any longer. He has outlined their plans. He tells Bollin, "Come on, bro. We need to get busy."

Both boys stand up and stretch, flex their legs and arms, and do some shadow boxing into the air.

Bimbo whispers to Scayper. "Keep your eyes fixed on Nitter. If he shows any sign of interest in what is going on here, cough once and then twice to warn us. Until then, stay alert and listen for my whistle. When you hear me whistle, it means we are ready for the next phase of our plan. I want you to give a loud yell for help to call Nitter. Pretend to be badly hurt. Get him into the room somehow. Tell him we've gone missing. We'll see to the rest. Got that?"

Scayper is a bit puzzled but replies, "Yeah. Sure. I can do that." He walks over to the cell door to begin his watch on the guard.

NITTER SNOOZES

Scayper leans against the bars of his dungeon looking down the walkway. Nitter is sleeping soundly. His knitting lays forgotten. His mouth has dropped open, and he snores loudly. Occasionally, he jerks wildly, although without waking. The two torches in the wall brackets are barely alight. The vegetable oil the wicks were dipped in gives off a slightly sickly smell as they burn and smolder.

Behind Scayper, Bimbo leans his two hands against the back wall of the dungeon. It is towards the far outside wall of the castle. Bimbo knows, although it is not apparent, that there is a good distance between where he stands and the actual outer wall. He can see nothing, but he was told what to look for. Cydlo rehearsed him, although he was thinking of the entry from the other side in the link tunnel, not from the dungeon side. He searches with the tips of his fingers, poking and probing with his index finger.

He whispers to Bollin, "I think I've found something. Come here and put your hand where my finger is. Yes, just there. Now push. Did you feel something give just a little?"

"Yes, I did."

"Okay. Don't lose the spot. I'm going to try to find the other one."

He lowers himself onto both knees and begins feeling around only a couple of inches above the floor. "Sorry it's taking so long. Cydlo told me the two points are not directly above each other but offset, so I'm having a bit of trouble finding it."

Bollin isn't concerned. "No matter. If necessary, we have until dawn."

Bimbo starts again, a little higher on the wall. "It must be somewhere near here. The first king built this so he could find it if he should happen to be a prisoner in this very room. There!

I found it!" He breathes a sigh of relief. "It's offset almost a full handbreadth from the point above. It's not a round hole this time, but a slightly raised square of stone masonry no bigger than a fingernail."

He looks up at Bollin, although he can only see shadow and no detail. "Can you see where I'm pointing down here? If you have to open this by yourself, you push this with your foot while pushing the top one with your finger. Now. On the count of three, push with your finger where you are, as hard as you can. If there is any noise, just stop. One, two, three." He pushes hard with the heel of his hand while Bollin pushes above. There is a slight give, only very slight, but it is there.

Both boys push steadily. Slowly and, more importantly, silently, the whole wall, from floor to ceiling, begins moving away from them and into the link tunnel. Now they do not need to push so hard. The heavy stone door is delicately balanced. It is a brilliant display of a master stonemason's skill and ingenuity. The door swings on bronze hinges set in charcoal powder. There is never the slightest hint of a squeak. Nothing of the door protrudes out into the dungeon room. Nothing on the floor of the cell is disturbed. But the door is pushing against something, maybe a piece of furniture left inside, close to the wall. It will go no further.

Bimbo quietly asks Bollin, "Do you think there is enough space so you can squeeze through? See if you can find the tinderbox and candles. Whatever you do, don't make a sound!"

Bollin slips through easily and whispers, "I can't see any tinderbox, but I still have a small box of matches in my back pocket. The guards didn't take those. Let's not waste time. I got through. Come on after me. We'll get the door closed, and then we'll search." He is nervous that the whispers will be carried up the passageway to Nitter. However, they are making less noise than scurrying rats might make playing hide-and-seek. The dungeons have a low level of continuous sound, and Nitter is as likely to be disturbed by complete silence as he is by more noise than usual.

Scayper takes a quick look over his left shoulder at what is happening and then turns back to his watch on Nitter. From the dungeon itself, there is no sound of warning or movement.

Bollin disappears behind the door, trying to imprint whatever he is able to see on his memory before they are enveloped in darkness. He reaches behind the hinged door. A small wooden table is what blocks the door from opening completely. Lifting this with both hands, he carries it deeper into the link tunnel and sets it down without making any noise. The door opens wider, but there is not much more that can be seen.

Bimbo is through also and begins pushing the door back into place. It is almost shut but not completely closed. "Are you alright, Bollin? Do you have your matches out? Get one ready, but don't strike it until I close the door completely. Did you find any candles? The king would surely have left a supply of those to provide light."

Bollin drops to his knees. "I'll take a look. Don't close the door yet. I'm feeling around on the floor. Oh! I've got one I think. Let me check if it has a wick. Yes, it does. Okay, I'm ready. You can close the door now."

Bimbo pushes the door closed. There is a very faint click to indicate it is fully locked back into position. The darkness is complete. He tells Bollin, "Wait a minute before you light the candle. Somewhere in the door is a spy-hole." He runs his fingers back and forth at eye level and then just a little higher. "Found it!" He removes a long, cylindrical stone plug. He does not have to unscrew it but simply slides it out. Putting his eye close to the door, he looks back into the dungeon.

The stonemason builders have done well. The spy-hole position has been chosen with great care to give an open line of sight between the various vertical dungeon bars. Two bars frame either edge of the spy-hole, and in the center of its circle is the outside exit door from the main dungeon.

Bimbo is thrilled. "I can see Scayper standing at the cell door and Nitter in the far distance, sleeping soundly on his chairs. That's good! When we are ready to return, we can be sure Scayper is alone before opening the door." He replaces the plug. "Okay. You can light the candle now."

A match scratches. A flame flares. The wick flutters and then catches. A tiny flame blossoms as the match itself flickers out. It's time to look around.

THE LINK TUNNEL

The short link tunnel is narrow enough for Bimbo's outstretched fingers to touch both sides. It is about twice as long as it is wide and just high enough to stand up without bending. The entire space—walls, floor, and ceiling—is stone masonry.

Grey festoons of spiders' webs decorate the corners and droop among the stone shelves that line one wall. On them are tools, weapons, escape gear, ropes, clothes, footwear, foodstuffs, and other objects in boxes or wrapped in cloth. Lying on the floor are several candles. Bollin picks them up and lights a second one. They do not intend to be here long, but more light is helpful.

Bimbo picks up a dust-covered broadsword from a shelf and deftly removes most of the spiders' webs. "I need to retrieve the Royal Sword. Will you go over to the spy-hole and keep an eye on what's happening in the cell? We don't want Nitter showing up until we're ready to deal with him."

Bollin takes out the plug, peeks through the spy-hole, and reports, "Scayper is alone at the moment. Nitter is still snoozing away." Carefully, he replaces the plug.

An idea strikes Bimbo as he spots something on one of the shelves. "Bollin, look at these tools. They must have been here from the time of the first king. There are chisels and a hammer and some tongs, and these must be old-fashioned pliers. Will you go out to Scayper and see whether you can break the padlock fastening his shackles to the ring in the floor without making too much noise? Perhaps you could lever a couple of chisels against each other. Here are some rat-tail files." He picks up some straight, tapered metal bars that poke holes through most anything. "These might work. It will have to be done quietly, but if we can release Scayper so he can move around, he can probably get Nitter into the cell and deal with him without Nitter ever knowing what happened to us. If he could hold Nitter down 'til we get there, we could blindfold and gag him and then lock him in the dungeon when we leave. What do you think?"

Bollin, who enjoys a scrap, has a different idea. "Why don't I release Scayper as you say and bring him in here? Then you can remove his chains with the hammer and chisel without anyone hearing. I'm likely to be much stronger than Scayper. After all, he's been practically immobile for centuries and probably hasn't been getting a decent diet either. I'll take cloth for a blindfold and a gag and some rope." After a pause for thought, he says, "I'll take a knife as well, just in case. And I'll need something to lure Nitter into the cell." He looks around. "I wonder what this is?" He uncovers from its protective cloth a woman's headpiece and dusts it with his sleeve. Bollin catches his breath in surprise. "It's a queen's tiara!" It sparkles with diamonds, rubies, and emeralds as it catches the flickering changing light of the candle flames. He rewraps it in its cloth. "This should do the trick."

Bimbo nods. "I'll watch through the spy-hole so I can let you back in when you have Scayper free. Give a cough when you're ready." Carefully, he pulls out the spy-hole stone and puts his eye to the hole. Beside the far door is Nitter, still on his two chairs. He is fast asleep. It is safe for the moment. He blows out one candle and partially covers the other with a saucepan on its side. "Just to play it safe, let me have the matches. I'll wait in semidarkness until I let either you or Scayper or both of you back in."

To open the door from the inside, where secrecy is not required, there are two simple handholds to use. Bimbo takes one last look through the spy-hole. He pulls on the handholds, and the stone door swings towards him. In a moment, Bollin is through the door, and Bimbo pushes the door closed again.

It is up to Bollin now.

Bollin drops to the floor and crawls over to Scayper. He whispers, "I'm going to try and break the chain that shackles you to the floor. Can you hold really still for me?"

The prisoner nods. A large, heavy ring is set loose enough to swing and is anchored by an equally heavy U-bolt imbedded in the stone floor. To the large ring is padlocked the end ring of Scayper's chain. Bollin takes two chisels and tries to fit them both through the shank of the padlock. One will go, but not both.

I'll have to try something else.

The chain was made by a goblin blacksmith who also fitted the leg rings. He did a thorough job. Bollin gives up on the chisels and from opposite sides pushes the two rat-tail files against each other. Now he applies his strength, pulling the ends of the two bars towards each other. *I hope they don't break.* He levers them against the hasp of the padlock. *Crack!* Something breaks. He falls backwards and huddles, unmoving, on the floor.

Bimbo hears the crack from inside the link tunnel and looks anxiously towards the guard.

Nitter stirs. As he stretches and yawns, he looks up the length of the dungeons. A rat, startled by the noise, scurries across the floor down towards him, followed by another rat. He curses and aims a kick. The two creatures dart into the bottle dungeon under the rail at the bottom of the door. They knock something as they scurry, and it falls with a clatter. Nitter stretches once more, gives another yawn, and settles back on his chair with his feet up on the other one.

Bollin feels for the padlock. *Yes! The hasp is broken.* He disengages it from Scayper's shackles and asks him, "Can you crawl on all fours towards the wall?" He himself stands and takes a long look at Nitter. The man is again asleep. As he coughs towards the spy-hole, Bimbo replaces the plug.

The door slips silently open. Bimbo bends over Scayper and helps him through the opening. Bollin muffles the chains with Scayper's blanket until the lad is safely into the link tunnel. He hands back the tools, retaining for himself only the knife, the blanket, a length of rope, and the tiara.

He thinks a moment. *The door to the dungeon cell opens outwards. I need Nitter to come right into the cell.* He places the tiara in the furthest corner near the bottle dungeon. *I don't want Nitter to get his hands on the tiara and damage it. I must throw him against the stone wall, away from it.* He positions himself flat on the straw mattress, curls up, and huddles under Scayper's blanket. With his knife, he slashes the mattress and pulls out a mass of straw. He stuffs this down his shirt collar to bulk out his hair. He daren't be less hairy than Scayper. He twists one leg awkwardly under the other, so that it looks like he is hurt.

He gives an almighty groan and then another, as though he is being strangled…and waits.

THE DUNGEON DUET

Nitter almost elevates himself a foot off his two chairs like a dirigible or a balloon suddenly getting a burst of helium or hot air. He crashes back down on his chairs, out of balance. *What on earth has happened?*

He was having a nightmare. He dreamed that he had completed the knitted scarf and was taking it home. It ended up being a mile long and was coiled into one tremendous roll bigger than himself. At the same time that the center of the roll falls out of its position and the scarf unravels around him like a living creature trying to consume him, his wife tells him, "You knitted it in the wrong colors."

He groans, "Arrgh!" as he struggles to prevent the imaginary scarf from strangling him. As he rolls off onto the floor, landing with a thud, he groans again, this time in pain. He hasn't yet opened his eyes, and thinks the scarf is blindfolding him. He waves his arms, pulling at the supposed scarf around his eyes. At the same time, he tries to pull himself up off the floor, and wonders, *What am I doing down here?*

Bollin has no idea what he just set into motion or why the guard is also groaning. *That didn't work. I'll try again, louder.* Once again, he groans as loudly as he can and then groans again, as though he is being strangled twice over. Again, he waits.

Nitter shakes his head to and fro violently. Ever since he was a small boy, he has found that shaking his head wakes him up when other slower methods, like dunking his head into ice cold water, seem to have no effect at all. Unfortunately, on this particular occasion, he stands too close to the outside exit door. There are few experts at violent headshaking as a method of waking up. However, for their own good, those who are would prefer to be standing near a wooden door rather than a stone one. Fortunately for Nitter, the door that he cracks his head a real wallop on is a wooden door. Even so, it still draws blood, and it is not just a little blood. It is a lot of blood! There is no question at all that Nitter is red-blooded. He lets out a piercing scream followed by a stream of oaths and curses that somehow involve knitted scarves, snakes, blindfolds, his wife, poor pay, poor benefits, and his off-duty companion who still has three hours to go before he comes back on duty.

Bollin is confused by what's going on. *I don't understand how I have become involved in a groaning duel with Nitter. Undoubtedly, that is what is happening.* Fortunately for Bollin, he cannot understand what Nitter is yelling. Oaths and curses in Twith are not in his vocabulary. However, as far as volume is concerned, there is no need to yield victory to the guard at this early stage.

Bollin is competitive by nature and warms to the challenge. If he were standing up instead of lying flat, the contest would be more equal. Nevertheless, he is English after all, so he starts with an initial advantage. His head is largely covered by the blanket, but he uncovers his mouth and twists his head in Nitter's direction. He knows that in order to get Nitter to break his own rule of not entering the cell alone, his voice must indicate intense pain. At top volume, again in Urdu, he launches into another presentation of the Punjabi poetry about silver moonlight, even more dramatically than the first time. He concludes with the body-wrenching weeping of lost love.

Bimbo can hear both the mournful groaning of his brother and the painful scream of the guard and tells Scayper, "With all that racket, now is a good time to get on with chiseling off your leg bands. I'll check back into the dungeon when that job is done."

Nitter is now fully aware that the prisoner in the end cell is mocking him. He isn't smart enough to catch on that he wasn't the one who started this duel of the groans. He doesn't realize he actually responded to a cry given by Bollin. *I'll sort the prisoner out in a minute. I need to go wash the blood off my face under the hand pump outside. While I'm there, I'll fill a bucket with water. I hope the water is good and cold. Scayper is going to get a good dousing. I intend to splash the whole bucketful all over him.*

He unbolts the dungeon door. The rising wind flickers the oil lamps. The pump handle squeaks as he moves it up and down several times. He sticks his head under the flow of water. He shivers. "Brrr! That's good! It's freezing cold. Just what I want." He rinses himself. "Ow! That stings. I'm sure to have a bad bruise." He fills the bucket to the brim, being careful not to spill the water along the corridor to the end cell. *I want every bit of it in the bucket.* He slowly raises the bucket waist high with his left hand, places his right hand on the bottom, and proceeds to slosh the whole pail of icy cold water over the crumpled body under the blanket.

As he does, he spots, in the far corner of the cell, something bright and glittering.

THE TIARA

Several emotions, four to be exact, almost simultaneously surge through Nitter's mind. They will make or break him. He cannot choose his circumstances, but he can control his choices. Up until now, the choices he has made have not been outstanding. If asked for an example, he would quickly mention his wife. She might be beautiful, but she can't even cook a decent meal and has no idea how to clean house. He's not quite certain about her ability as a mother either.

First among his emotions this particular night is the immense satisfaction he feels as the bucket of water, thrown with great skill, is right on target. Not everyone can manage to pinpoint a target with a bucket of water when a vertical line of thick bars impedes the follow-through. The satisfaction has something to do with boyhood. All boys like to get their Wellies on and stomp in puddles. As they grow, they are also into jumping streams on their way home from school, wearing their best school shoes. They never grow out of the pleasures water can bring. They add to their skills as teenagers by spraying the dozing gardener accurately with his own garden hose. Finally, there are the buckets of cold water. These show that a man has finally emerged out of boyhood.

The second of the emotions is pain from the lump on his head. His head has caused no damage at all to the door, but flesh and blood are more sensitive to pain than wood. Probably no one, except possibly Dr. Vyruss Tyfuss, has done studies into whether wood feels pain. Wood, after all, is growing and alive for much of its career. It has limbs like humans do. It is not unreasonable to say a tree does not really enjoy a boy whacking nails into its trunk. What is fairly sure, however, is that flesh and blood enjoys pain less than a tree trunk does. In fact, the word *enjoy* is probably not the right word to use. Nitter would agree. His head is screaming with pain, and the cut is going to leave a scar.

Strand number three of Nitter's thoughts is the emotion of fear. Nitter has temporarily forgotten about the two new prisoners. He is sure they are Chinese because he mistakenly remembers they were both wearing pigtails and flip-flops. They suddenly come flooding back into his mind. But to his dismay, he can observe, by the light of the oil lamp in the passageway, that they have been replaced by empty space. He has a strong urge to run. *But where would I go? I can't swim, and the pontoon bridge is underwater.*

Nitter shakes in fear, and fantasizes that he is in a fully-lighted theater during the break between the first and second acts of *The Merry Widow*. A bell rings to signal the end of the break. Everyone returns to their seats. Slowly, the lights dim as they should. But then…they keep on dimming! Suddenly, there is total darkness. The conversation fades to silence that could be cut with a knife. People look around. It does no good. Eyes might be meeting other eyes turned towards each other, but it matters not; neither can see the other. There are no lights even behind the stage curtains. It is black there too. Nor is there any light from the vestibule. All is darkness, utter and complete darkness.

Why doesn't somebody do something?

His imagination works overtime. Someone screams. It is a woman screaming in fear. From the gallery comes another scream. Then another! Everybody begins screaming. The whole audience seems to be women, but it isn't. Nitter attempts to pull himself together and stop himself from screaming. He says to himself, "Be a man, my son! Be a man!" There is movement around him. People are trying to push past. "Oh no you don't! I was here before you got here. Get out of my way. Help! Help!"

Nitter's thoughts grow frantic. He is pushing towards where he thinks the doors are. People are slipping, stumbling, and falling all around him. He yells at them, "What are you doing?

Stand up! Can't you? Let me get out! Make way!" He tramples on them. "Out of my way!" Nitter shakes his head violently to clear his mind.

One last thought flows through his mind. When a man succeeds in thinking four things at the same time, it is very likely that one of the strands of thought will be stronger than the other three. And it is usually the one that comes last. It is so in this case. Nitter thinks about what he just saw in the cell that glitters.

The thought could have been an appreciation of beauty. The tiara is Queen Sheba's formal tiara that she wore at state banquets and on other state occasions. It has not seen the light of day for a thousand years. However, although the time frame is correct, the rest is not. To be entirely truthful, the light of a flickering oil lamp at three o'clock in the morning, in a dungeon where even the little window in the exit door is closed, cannot be called the light of day. However, the tiara is undoubtedly reflecting enough light so Nitter can see it is something valuable. It is one of the finest examples of craftsmanship of the master jewelers in Gyminge. The setting is made of silver, not gold. The silver filigree makes three quarters of a circle and rises to a peak in the front, where a large diamond displays itself amidst lesser jewels. All glitter enticingly in the half-light.

Nitter is puzzled. *I wonder where that came from? I wonder how it got there? I wonder who it belongs to? I wonder how I can get hold of that before anyone else lays claim to it?*

Now the main focus of his fourth strand of thought becomes immediate greed, lust, envy, and selfishness all rolled into one. Nitter decides, *I want that brilliant headpiece, and I'm going to have it!*

Nitter doesn't want anyone else coming in while he collects what is rightfully his. He walks back down the hallway to make absolutely sure that both tower bolts are across the door and that the small observation and inquiry window is similarly closed and bolted.

Bollin is still waiting. He is wet through, but until the door opens, he is going to stay just as he is. *I hope Bimbo and Scayper don't spoil things by coming back in too soon. I wonder whether I should utter another cry of pain to stir things up? No, I'll hold off for a while.*

He hears the guard coming back up the passage. He does not move. There is the fumbling of a key in the lock, the creak of the door opening, and footsteps coming close. Bollin sees legs striding quickly past him. He grabs, and suddenly, there is chaos with Nitter at the center of it.

As Nitter falls, he cracks his head against the wall. Fortunately for him, the contact point is on the other side from his encounter with the door. Unfortunately, all is going to be darkness for quite some time.

SCAYPER

Nitter is now bleeding from the other side of his head. The injury does not appear to be life threatening. He is unconscious, and that makes things easier for Bollin. He needs to check with Bimbo. Keeping his foot on Nitter, he coughs towards the spy-hole.

Bimbo looks out and asks, "Is everything alright? I've been concerned with all the racket going on."

"Yes, everything is okay here. Does Scayper want Nitter's clothes?"

Bimbo is away a moment. "Yes, please."

Bollin decides Scayper probably has had fewer changes of clothes than the guard, so he pulls off Nitter's army boots and socks and sets them aside. He then unbuckles the goblin's belt, strips off his shirt, and pulls off his trousers, leaving him in only his underpants. Fortunately, it is a warm midsummer night. He will not get too cold.

Bollin ties Nitter's hands behind his back, ropes his feet together, and loops both bonds to the circular shackle ring in the floor. He binds a gag around Nitter's mouth, blindfolds him, and makes him comfortable on the straw mattress. Although that may look like Bollin is being overly kind and gentle to his victim, he knows from experience that the mattress has fleas and probably bedbugs also. He flicks one or two off himself.

Bollin leaves the door from the cell to the passageway ajar. He gathers everything left over—the ring of keys, the tiara, and the clothes. *I'm glad I didn't have to use the knife in anger. Time to cough into the spy-hole again.*

Bimbo pulls the door open, and his brother slips back into the link tunnel. Bimbo pushes the stone door closed. "Well done, Bollin. We wondered what all the noise was about. You can tell us about it later when we have everything under control." He slips his hand into his pocket and returns the box of matches to his brother.

In the dungeon, there is little to show that the recent events have occurred save that the door of the last cell now swings open on its hinges and there is no one sitting guard at the door. There is still a prisoner on the straw mattress, covered by a brown blanket.

For the first time, Bollin sees Scayper as more than a shadow in the dark. Three candles are now burning.

Scayper sits on the single chair. He is delighted to be without his ankle bands. Bimbo was extremely careful cutting them off and placed protection between the band and the skin before hitting the chisel. Nevertheless, great red welts indicate where they have been.

Bimbo, who rather fancies himself as a hairstylist, found a pair of scissors and a comb. He has turned barber and is covering the floor with hair. He trims Scayper's long, dark brown hair back to his shoulders. The beard and mustache have been scissor cut as close and short as possible. Scayper is emerging as a young man, possibly in his late teens. His brown eyes show the strain of many years of imprisonment.

Bollin asks, "Do you feel like telling us a little about yourself yet?"

Scayper says, "I like wrestling and running and using a battle staff. When things are settled and I'm stronger, I'd like to test myself against the two of you." He is certainly well built and quite muscular.

Bollin thinks, *He bears a resemblance to someone I know. Possibly it's Taymar he looks like; it's not Cydlo.* Bollin is wet through. There are some clothes of the king's that are too big, but they are dry, so he changes into them, all the while looking closer at this refuge where they find themselves. He sees a few more weapons on the stone shelves. They are neatly arranged and obviously undisturbed for many, many years. He asks Bimbo, "Have you managed to retrieve the Royal Sword, yet?"

Bimbo looks back over his shoulder at his brother. He doesn't interrupt his haircutting. "No, not yet. I'm waiting until we are all tidied up and ready to move. Each of us should take a dagger or a sword. Why don't you put a few things in that small bag that Gerald might like to have back on the Brook? Most of the things should be left here, though. From its shape, that big bundle there must be the king's state crown. That should stay right where it is. We'll take the scissors and the comb. I'm just about through with Scayper." He wipes off Scayper's neck with his hands. "Now you can get out of those old clothes and into the goblin's."

Scayper is delighted to get out of his dirty clothes. Bimbo puts them to one side to leave in the dungeon cell for Nitter. Scayper has a bigger build than the guard, so the clothes are a bit tight. However, there is little flesh on his body, and his ribs show he has had little nourishment for a long while.

Bimbo looks around and asks, "Are you ready? We need to move along as soon as we recover the sword."

Each takes a last look across the shelves. The tinderbox and candles are already in the tiny leather pouch together with the scissors and the comb and one or two other items. Bollin sticks Nitter's ring of keys on his own belt. "Should we take a few of the jewels and maybe the tiara for Elisheba or Cymbeline?"

Bimbo shakes his head and turns just in time to catch Scayper as he faints and slumps to the floor. His face has gone deathly white. "We need to get him into the open air. Bollin, your old clothes are wet. Use them. Wipe his face and see if you can bring him round. We need to be going. This place is stuffy."

He faces the wall opposite from the door into the dungeon and pulls on two handles. The heavy, stone door, like the one on the other side, swings open without any noise. The old escape tunnel leading to Mad Jack's cave from behind the fireplace in the king's sitting room has a musty, damp smell.

THE ROYAL SWORD

Bimbo looks anxiously at Scayper as he pulls the door partially open. Though very pale, he is breathing steadily. He turns to Bollin. "Down there to the left, you'll find some water. Take the saucepan and see if it's clean enough to use on Scayper. I doubt it is good enough to drink. Take a candle with you."

Bimbo has the door roughly where he wants it. Directly above it in the arched masonry roof he sees what he is looking for, a deep hole big enough to take his clenched fist. He brings the chair and places it alongside the stone door but not touching it. Standing on it, he can look down at the top edge of the door. He smiles with pleasure. *It is exactly as Cydlo told me.* No one getting into the link tunnel would have any idea that within the thickness of the door itself is a cavity and a hiding place. It is designed with access only from the top so that it cannot be seen except by an observer higher than the top of the door.

Bimbo can see the scabbard of a sword. The sword is hilt down within the door. He reaches in and feeds the scabbard up out of the door and into the hole in the roof immediately overhead. This is nothing more or less than a hole intended to accommodate an object long and thin. The scabbard is secured to the hilt of the sword by a pair of fine gold chains on either side of it. The sword within the scabbard is loose and freely able to move. If the chains should slip, the sword will fall out. Bimbo is being very careful, and continues feeding the scabbard steadily up into the roof hole. *Ah! I have the hilt.*

Bollin bustles back in, brushing past his brother without pausing. His job is Scayper. The water in the saucepan has some weeds floating in it, but it is clean and it is cool. He dips the cleanest of the cloths into it and wipes Scayper's face. The lad opens his eyes and blinks. It will be only a matter of time before he rallies completely. Bollin pulls him back towards the dungeon end to give his brother room.

۰   Bimbo has the sword and scabbard above the door by a finger's width. The hilt is still not pushed up against the roof. He pushes the door open a little further to clear the way and lowers the sword beside the door until the scabbard is free from the roof. He hands it to Bollin and steps down off the chair. Shoving the chair back into the room, he pulls the door firmly shut, and walks over to Scayper. "How are you feeling?"

Bollin has the boy's head and shoulders raised, but the lad has a blank look on his face.

"Where am I? What happened?"

"You fainted, Scayper. We are in the tunnel behind your dungeon cell. As soon as you feel better, we're going to go back through, but only when you feel up to it. Wet your mouth with this water, but don't drink it. Spit it out. Are you able to sit up on the chair?"

Scayper struggles to his feet with the help of Bollin, who guides him to the chair.

"Good! You rest there while we look at the sword. We have to make sure we can get this back to the Brook safely."

The scabbard, after it has been wiped down by the wet cloth, proves to be red leather beautifully decorated with gold, although there are only traces left of any inscriptions. In a few spots, the leather itself is scuffed. At the hilt end, on either side of the scabbard, is the royal crest. The hilt is simple and straight, round for easy grasping. It is gold, but not ornate, and possibly has an inner strengthening core of bronze. The royal crest is cunningly engraved in the center of a rose flower at the tip. The handle is as long as the hilt is wide. Bimbo loosens the gold chains securing the sword and pulls the sword from the scabbard. It is made for a tall man. It is the sword of a soldier rather than solely a decorative sword of state. The blade is bronze and engraved on either side with three similar narrow decorative bands. One band is straight down the center of the blade to a short distance from its tip, and the other two lines run either side of it, a short distance from the edges of the blade. Bimbo has seen enough. He replaces the sword in its scabbard and refastens the chains.

He decides that, to avoid too much curiosity, he will wrap the sword and scabbard in one of the women's dresses. He folds a red dress around it and then wraps the sleeves around and ties them securely in a knot.

"Scayper, are you ready to move? Do you feel up to it?"

The young man gives a slight nod. He stands, shakes his head, and takes a deep breath. Taking a step forward, he leans his hand against the wall.

"Bollin, you take everything you can. What did you choose for a weapon?"

Bollin holds up a short sword.

"That'll be good. I'll take a small dagger. What do you want, Scayper?"

Scayper looks down the shelf and selects a dirk in its scabbard. He sticks it into the pocket of his goblin trousers.

Bimbo has one last set of instructions. "When we go out into the dungeon, assume Nitter can hear and that he will repeat what he hears higher up. The goblins must not know about this room, so be very quiet as we leave. We won't bother to check on Nitter but just go straight out into the courtyard. We'll have to be very careful. You go first, Bollin, then you go Scayper, and I'll come last. When we are all safely out, you lock the dungeon door. We can use the padlock to Scayper's cell if we need to. We have to get into King Haymun's apartments and secure him. After that, it will be easy. Okay. Let's go."

Bimbo takes one last look through the spy-hole. All is quiet. He replaces and pushes in hard the spy-hole cylinder. He gives the king's sword to Scayper to hold. Grabbing the handholds, he pulls the door open.

QUARTZ PAYS A CALL

Bimbo swings the stone door closed behind them and pushes on the side of the hinge that will cause it to lock shut. As he does, he kicks Nitter's empty water bucket so that the tiny click will not be noticed. *Clatter! Bang! Bang!* He pushes the wall face to be sure it is locked into position and kicks the bucket again for good measure. *Clatter! Bang! Bang!*

For a moment, their eyes need to adjust to the poor light of the dungeons after the bright light of three candles. Not a word is said.

Nitter wriggles and grunts through his gag. Bollin gives him a gentle kick to remind him to be quiet.

Someone is knocking on the door to the dungeon. "Wake up in there! Open up!"

Scayper acts. He thrusts the Royal Sword back to Bimbo. Grabbing the empty bucket, he scurries down the corridor. "Coming! Hold on! I'm coming!"

He places the bucket straight in front of the doorstep down into the dungeon, jams Nitter's cap on his head, quickly slips the two tower bolts, and sharply swings the door open against the wall.

It is the quartermaster sergeant. "I've brought some rice for…" He has no time for more.

Scayper jerks at Quartz's belt and dives his hand in behind the buckle, giving it a sharp pull. This is one of the softer places of a man's body, and though the belt doesn't give, that which it retains does.

Quartz shoots forward, off balance. His foot goes into the open bucket before him. He does the first step of what, in other times and places, might be considered a graceful minuet. His fall portrays a gentle curve.

As Quartz topples towards the floor of the dungeon corridor, the meal he prepared soars into the air. He had gone to great pains at the field kitchen across the lake to make sure the rice was cooked the way Chinese like it. He has no idea the way Chinese like their rice. Had there been a bridge back to the castle, he would have come back to the dungeon to inquire. But he knows they like soy sauce. There wasn't much soy sauce, but there was a fresh bottle of Tabasco sauce, and he decided that would give some color. He emptied that in and added a half a dozen scrambled eggs. There were no bean sprouts, unfortunately. He kept in mind that the Chinese like everything cut into tiny strips and served raw. The savory cabbages were sliced into little strips and added to the boiling rice. He thought the Chinese like a lot of pepper, so all the pepper in the kitchen had gone in whatever color it was—black, white, red, or green. It all took time, but it was worth it even though, personally, he wouldn't touch the food with chopsticks the length of flagpoles.

The quartermaster sergeant was proud of himself. "The king said to bring the prisoners back for questioning. If anything is going to persuade them to speak clearly and willingly, even though it is in Chinese, it will be this feast I've prepared for them in the middle of the night. I even had one of the loggers from the forest awakened to carve two pairs of chopsticks for the prisoners to eat with." He smiled with satisfaction.

Quartz carried the meal in a three-layer aluminum basket. He was rowed across the lake as soon as it was considered ready. The metal basket, along with the two plates and the chopsticks, were wrapped in a knotted tea towel.

It is fortunate about his rice. As it glides towards the corridor, Bollin catches the basket in one hand. He has, with his brother, hurried down the passage to assist Scayper.

Scayper needs no assistance. He has everything under control, and calmly flips the two tower bolts back into place. He lets out a long, slow, satisfied breath of pure pleasure. This is his first unassisted act using his own free will for a long, long time. The years in the dungeon roll away. He is disappointed there are not twenty more men queuing up outside, wanting to come into the dungeons with meals. Some people might think the height of enjoyment is a ride on a rollercoaster, others delight in scuba diving in the Red Sea, and still others find excitement in a high-flying bungee jump off the Royal Gorge Bridge in Colorado. Nothing approaches the purity of the joy that a flying quartermaster sergeant can provide, unless it is a flying sergeant major.

Scayper picks up the quartermaster sergeant by the back of his collar. The poor, dazed man is not capable of picking himself up. His foot is caught in the now badly dented bucket.

Like Nitter, these misadventures are matters to be grateful for. The floor could have made first contact with his head rather than contact with his hands, his tummy, and his knees at the same time. Those five points of pain could not possibly measure up to the one point of pain a headfirst landing would have created. So he should count his blessings! He doesn't!

He has a vague idea, brought about by stories his grandfather told him, that the Chinese are cannibals and that, rather than the rice and Tabasco he brought them, he himself is going to provide their next meal. As he thinks hard, he hopes he recalls his grandfather saying that the Chinese only eat other Chinese because that is the only flavor they are accustomed to. In fact, he is entirely wrong. The Chinese prefer rice, and that is the flavor they like.

To his surprise, the two Chinese are no longer speaking Chinese but laughing and joking in a language he partially understands. It has similarities to his own and bears no resemblance to Chinese.

The three boys are all hungry, and before deciding what to do with Quartz, they are going to enjoy the meal he brought. Scayper is starving, and he has images of his father carving the pork roast at a traditional Sunday dinner. He always enjoyed the tasty crackling on the pork. He had to watch to make sure his older brother didn't grab it all before he got some. He can almost smell the lovely aroma of roast potatoes, Brussels sprouts, and Yorkshire pudding. There was always plenty of gravy. Afterwards, there would be ample custard to pour over the plum pudding. His mouth waters just thinking about it.

The two boys have grown up on hot Indian curries, but they have never experienced a meal like this one! Phew! They take small helpings, but Scayper wolfs the food down as though he has not eaten for a month. His taste buds must have perished during the long years in the dungeon. There is a roaring fire in his belly, and he feels he is going to breathe out flames when he exhales. They wonder whether to make Quartz eat what is left over, but in the end, they slip it into Nitter's cell. This time, they padlock his door. The padlock for the outside door hangs on a nail near the door, and they will use that when they leave.

Quartz will travel with them.

QUARTZ TALKS

Bimbo does not want to put Quartz in with Nitter. He is sure that they will succeed in undoing each other's bonds and then raise an alarm. Better to take the quartermaster sergeant with them, and he can help ease their way to the king's apartments. Once they have the king, they are as good as home. He begins by asking the others, "What should we do with this one?"

They offer no answer, but Bollin decides to demonstrate that the blade of his sword is sharp as a razor in order to scare the quartermaster sergeant. He calmly begins shaving the hairs on his leg while fighting an imaginary enemy in hand-to-hand combat. The other two decide to compare the strike efficiency of a dagger against a dirk, thrusting downwards with grimaces calculated to put the fear of death into a bull on the rampage.

Bimbo looks up. "Let's ask a few questions before we decide. Are you married?"

"Yes." Quartz isn't being honest. He is unmarried, an orphan, and has never been in love in his life.

Bimbo waves his dagger under Quartz's chin. "Do you love your wife?"

With bulging eyes he answers, "Yes."

Bimbo moves the dagger closer to the terrified man's throat. "Do you have children?"

Quartz keeps his eye on the dagger as he replies, "Yes."

Bollin joins in. "How many?"

Quartz thinks of how many his brother has. "Fourteen."

Bollin glares at him. "Do they love their father?"

Quartz inadvertently shakes his head back and forth. "Yes."

Scayper chimes in, "Are your parents still living?"

Not daring to move his head, Quartz rolls his eyes toward the new interrogator. "Yes."

Scayper asks, "Do they love you?"

This time the head stays perfectly still lest by shaking it up and down it gets pierced by the dagger. "Yes."

If Quartz were more eloquent, he would affirm that his great-great-grandparents, dead before he was born, love him too, with immense devotion, and to lose him would break their hearts.

The three roll their eyes at each other. Bimbo turns to the other two and asks a final question of them. "Do you want to do it, or shall I?"

Quartz is suddenly galvanized into quick thinking. He knows what the "it" is they are talking about even before the quiz show host reads the question. The "it" one of them is going to do at any moment has to do with bloodletting! *I need to say something to alter their train of thought.* "You must be strangers here, but I observe you are very quick with languages. I am quite surprised. Are all Chinese as quick as you are?"

Flattery might get you nowhere, but to a flatterer of the quartermaster sergeant's skills, it is a useful weapon, and he is at the point where he is searching for the exception that proves the rule.

Quartz hurriedly continues. "I have been here for many years now and am considering becoming a tour guide to the castle and its various attractions and entertainments. Our dungeons are not the only attraction that the castle possesses." He hesitates, realizing the word *attractive* can hardly be applied to the present surroundings. They are still inside the dungeon, deciding his fate. It is only a momentary interruption. "I am very well versed with the king's apartments. We also have a very fine museum in addition to a large audience chamber. Since the wizard is away, I can even show you his apartments with some astonishing views over the lake. I wonder whether you would care to have a conducted tour around the castle, say, tomorrow morning?

There is not a passageway or an entrance or exit I do not know in this castle."

Bollin breaks in. "I'll do it. Shall I do it at the back where the guard is? It's likely to be messy."

Bimbo lowers the dagger into his lap. "No. Let's wait a moment. Let's give the man a chance. He seems willing to be helpful."

Quartz nods his head enthusiastically.

Bimbo studies their captive closely. "We have a little surprise for the king when he wakes up. How do we get to his bedroom without disturbing anyone?"

Scayper noisily tells Bollin, "I've done it before, and there is no need for a mess if you do it in the right place."

Quartz, remembering his dressing-down in the king's apartments, needs no persuasion to feel that the king would respond better to 'it' than he himself would. "There are two ways. The main door into the north apartments is the way you came through earlier. I could wake the steward and tell him I am bringing the Chinese visitors who want to talk to the king right away and confess everything. He could take us.

"The other way is to go up the stairs by the main gate and along the battlement to the wizard's apartment and then follow the balcony around to the king's apartments. The king's bedroom opens onto the balcony. On a night like this, his windows will be open. The trouble with that way is that the raven is there. His nest is near the chimney on the wall just before you get to the wizard's apartments."

Bimbo thinks carefully. "Tell me more about the guards. How many are there?"

"There are only six to guard the gate because of the work on the bridge that Corporal Pimples is building. They split into three shifts, so two are guarding the gate all the time. There are also two guards that share dungeon duty. The goblins on guard duty live near the guardhouse and come here for their shifts by rowboat."

Bimbo leans forward towards Quartz like a fellow conspirator in a plan to rob a bank. "Listen carefully. If you are found with us, the wizard or the king will have your blood. We will try to help you. We will not harm you, but for your own good, we will loosely bind and gag you. We will put you in with Nitter. You will probably hear all kinds of shouting and noises, but if you raise any kind of alarm while we are still within the castle, we shall come back into the dungeon and see to it. Do you understand?"

Quartz cannot believe his good fortune. *That black cat I saw this morning really was a good luck token.* He nods his head vigorously, and heaves a great sigh of relief. *It is certainly much better to be gagged, blindfolded, and led to the prison cell than to experience bloodletting.* Once he is locked in with Nitter, he lays his head on his folded arms. He is going to try to get some sleep.

THE RESTLESS KING

Once outside the dungeon door, Bimbo secures and locks the padlock. The first streaks of morning light are in the sky. There is no sign of movement at the gate or the small guard post beside it. The guards are sleeping; there is no bridge and nothing to guard.

Bimbo leads the way. Scayper is next, and Bollin is in the rear. Bollin has his sword drawn and ready. Scayper carries the king's sword in its red wrapping, and Bimbo has his dagger and the small pouch filled with things that might be useful.

Bimbo runs soft-footed across the courtyard to the foot of the staircase. He pauses and listens for any sound from the guards. All is quiet. He beckons Scayper to follow him and sprints up to the parapet. Scayper, also on tiptoe, does not hesitate but runs on up to join him. Still no sound from the gate. Bollin stealthily creeps across the courtyard, ears tuned for the slightest signs of movement from the goblins. He ascends to the top of the steps. Just days ago, he and Bimbo traversed this same staircase helping their wounded father down to safety.

They gather under the shadow of the turrets of the wall. Quietly, keeping well under cover and in the shadow of darkness, they scurry along the battlement towards the north wall to the wizard's apartments. As they near the chimney, they grow cautious and silently slink low to avoid being seen or heard by the raven.

Rasputin's nest is sheltered by a low rear wall. He has a good view across the lake to the north, but he has to stand up to see anyone either on the battlement wall or below in the courtyard. As the three boys creep slowly past the nest, they hardly dare breathe, but there is no sign the bird is alert or even there. They begin to breathe a little more easily now they are past Rasputin undetected. Once they get around the corner, they straighten up and walk a bit more briskly.

King Haymun cannot sleep. He has tried sucking his thumb, but it doesn't help. It is partly because of the ring on his big toe, the big toe on his *left* foot. That is the problem. It is his left foot!

As a young child, he enjoyed the teething ring his mother provided for him. When she decided it was deforming his sweet smile and his protruding teeth were beginning to frighten the neighbor's seventeen-year-old daughter, she took it away from him. This was before people realized it isn't wise to take away teething rings from children. When deprived of their teething rings, they bite people instead.

Haymun greatly missed his teething ring. There was very little, living or otherwise, that he loved more. He was a snoopy child. One day, while his mother was out, he found one of her private drawers unlocked. As he rummaged through it, he found it—his precious teething ring! He took it and hid it under his mattress. At night, he chewed on it a little and then twirled it on his right big toe. This served well both to prepare his mind for sleep and to develop the muscles on his right toe.

Teething-ring toe twirling is a habit that stayed with him into his prime years as king. He rarely now chews his ring but usually has a few moments twirling the ring around the big toe on his right foot before falling asleep. During the night, the ring dislodges itself into the bed clothes and the servant who makes the bed returns it to the bedside table where it belongs.

It is well-known that a person who is right-handed has a right foot that is bigger than the left foot. Likewise, the toes on the right foot also happen to be bigger than the toes on the left foot. No problem then, right? Wrong! King Haymun is left-handed.

He was twirling the ring on his right toe as usual when he fell asleep. In his dreams, he was riding the world's biggest rollercoaster and screaming with delight as he went around the curves and splashed down through the water. When he woke up, his bed looked as though a whirlwind had hit it. He discovered that the ring was firmly fixed onto his *left* toe. He has no clear memory of how it might have happened, but it won't come off. Worse, it looks unlikely to come off of its own accord without major surgery to either the ring or the toe itself. It is unlikely that removal of his toenail will help.

Both of the king's feet are already sore because of the borrowed shoes he was wearing when he left the Brook. Those were two sizes too small. They were not only too small to start with, but unfortunately, the previous goblin owner, a junior officer, was right-handed. Although they start life identical in size, the longer shoes are worn, the more they mold themselves to fit the feet within them. The right foot of the borrowed shoes changed more than the left foot shoe because the right foot of the first owner was bigger. However, the king's left foot is bigger.

On his way back from the Brook, the king removed his borrowed shoes as soon as he set foot on Gyminge soil. Although both feet hurt, it can be assumed his left foot hurt much worse than his right. To make bad matters worse, with every step the king takes, he is painfully reminded that after he took his shoes off, his right foot stepped on a thorn. Not only that, but he stubbed his left big toe on a sharp rock. The toe, apart from the cut it received, has still not completed the swelling process that usually goes along with a blow to the toe. A second additional factor is that the foot that slipped from the stirrup and jammed the spur into his horse, causing it to bolt down the hillside into the lake, was the king's left foot. It was his left leg, and the foot attached to it that he wrenched out of his boot in that glorious final dive into the lake.

King Haymun lays awake, hurting and feeling sorry for himself. *I understand why birds choose to fly. It saves wear and tear on their feet. Birds are wiser than people.*

THE KING GETS DRESSED

The three boys follow the balcony walkway that goes past the wizard's quarters on to the king's quarters. The wizard's apartments include several rooms stretching along the balcony. They are looking for an open window or, even better, an unlatched door. They stop and peer in through each window. At one window, the two Shadow boys grow excited as they pick out features they recognize. Bimbo whispers, "Look! This is the great hall where the king interviewed us. I can see the fireplace on the far end wall. Over on the east wall is the throne on its raised dais where the king sat. Do you see it?"

Bollin whispers back, "Yes. This is where the trophies are displayed and where I spotted the king's Royal Shield. Let's see if we can get in."

The windows and door from the balcony are firmly closed and bolted. There is no easy way in. They explore farther along the balcony, checking each door and window quietly. The door to the corridor is locked. Next to that is a large room; but all those doors and windows onto the balcony are also locked. Ahead, a window is partly open! A lace curtain drifts lazily in the casual breeze. Bimbo kneels down to see in. As the curtain blows to one side, he can see an oil lamp burning. Against the right-hand wall is a four-poster bed with its curtains pulled back to take advantage of the breeze.

Bimbo turns to look at the others and nods, affirming they have found the king. He grips the sash window and raises it as far as it will go. It screeches a warning, but he pays no heed. He quickly slips underneath and is into the room. The noise startles the king, and he struggles to sit up in bed. He has been thinking of ways to get information about his bride out of the two Chinamen in the dungeons. Suddenly, they are here upon him!

Bimbo has him by his nightshirt and swings him out of bed before he is even sitting up.

The king's feet hit the floor. He winces. "Ouch! My toe!"

Bimbo releases him and he sinks back down onto the bed.

Scayper grabs the glass of water on the table beside the bed, and gulps it down in one go. The meal Quartz prepared is having its effect. The fire in his belly is now an inferno, and the small glass of water is not enough to quench it.

Bollin says, "Hold this for me," and hands Scayper his sword. He strides across the room on an errand of his own that he wants to complete before there is any chance of an alarm being raised. He opens the door into the anteroom of the king's bedchamber. He hurries through it and opens the door into the corridor. Farther along the corridor is the door into the great hall. He knows what he is after and intends to get it. He pulls a chair across to the fireplace to stand on. The shield is not as heavy as he expected. It lifts easily off the hooks on which it rests. As it tilts forward, he grabs hold of it on both sides and steadies it almost vertically. Slowly and carefully, he lowers it to waist height and steps backward down off the chair. Holding it upright in front of himself, he carries it back to the king's bedroom.

"Scayper, do you recognize this? Is this the king's Royal Shield?"

Scayper looks carefully. "I haven't seen it before that I can remember, but those are the king's royal arms engraved on it, so it must be the king's. Why else would it be a trophy of the wizard?"

Bimbo does not want to take back the wrong shield. Paying no attention to the king's discomfort, he pulls the king to his feet. His face is only a handbreadth away from Haymun. "Tell me about this shield. Speak softly and speak clearly. The Chinese have great skills in making men talk. Their persuasion never fails, and maybe I'll need to use it on you!"

The king cannot understand how the Chinese have suddenly gained such mastery of his own language, but he is not about to ask questions. He is quite anxious to answer them though. He is too frightened to tell lies. It requires careful thought for a good lie, and the truth does not threaten him just now. Something else does, and it is the least likeable of the three with ginger hair. The king's voice quavers, "When the wizard invaded Gyminge, there was fierce fighting between his men and the troops of King Rufus at Fowler's Bridge. He had turned himself into a toad and was sitting in the lake, watching the fighting. The king was wounded, and a bird brought him back to the castle. As they flew overhead, the king's shield fell into the lake beside the wizard, nearly hitting him. It took little effort to recover it, and it has been one of our principal trophies ever since."

Bimbo is satisfied the shield is the right one to take back. Time is ticking away. "We need to be moving. Get yourself dressed. You're coming with us! Don't waste any time or we'll take you as you are. Put on your shoes!"

This is easier said than done. Neither foot is going to fit comfortably into a shoe. The right foot can be forced into a slipper, but the left one is not going to do so with that confounded toe ring attached. "I can't go anywhere. I'm sick. I have a fever. Feel my head. Look at my feet. I can hardly walk."

"Bollin, maybe you would like to encourage the prisoner to hurry up. Would you like to use my dagger, or would you prefer to use your sword? Shall I stamp on his toe? Or maybe we should let Scayper repay a few debts. Would you like to have a go, Scayper? You have a dirk; it looks quite sharp, and that might be better suited. I think we need to help the king get that ring off his toe."

Scayper is enthusiastic to encourage the king to move along. His dirk is already out and stabbing its point into the mattress. His tummy is on fire, and he needs to get something more to drink soon. He wants to be moving.

King Haymun suddenly forgets his fever and his feet and is into his clothes and his cloak and his crown as though his bed is on fire and he is still in it. *I'll just wear one slipper and hop when I need to.*

"Now show us the way down to the kitchen."

There is a back staircase down to the kitchen from the king's dining room. The three help themselves to fruit and milk and bread. Scayper drinks great quantities of water. The king has absolutely no appetite, although he is offered food and is warned he will be going a long way before he can return home. In the end, he slips an apple into his pocket. Bollin looks around for something that squirts. He picks up a plastic container of tomato ketchup. For good measure, he also grabs a full bottle of dishwashing liquid from the shelf above the sink.

RASPUTIN ATTACKS!

King Haymun finds it extremely difficult to negotiate the stairs as the four make their way back up to his dining room. The former prisoners decide to take time to snatch a short rest in the king's bedroom. They do not bother to bind the king. Instead, he is on his stomach on the floor with two pairs of feet on his shoulders and legs. This has not been helpful as far as his toe ring is concerned. His foot hurts worse than before, but he is exhausted from the trek to kitchen and back and drops off into an uneasy sleep.

The three boys are awake first. Bimbo gives the king a little kick to wake him and jerks him to his feet. "Bollin, give me that cord from the king's bathrobe. I'm going to tie it around his waist so he can't run off." Bimbo ties it in a loose slipknot and gives the king a shove. "Get going. We're leaving the castle, and you are going with us."

The sun is already well above the horizon. It is going to be a clear, warm day. Haymun is in front as they walk along the castle parapet and can only hop slowly. He doesn't want Bimbo to pull on the cord around his tummy, and he doesn't want to get ahead either, which will have the same effect. He just wants that cord to sag in the middle like the main cable on a suspension bridge and never feel a tug. *I'm glad that little Scot is not one of my captors!* He saw Jock in action during the battle at Squidgy's cottage on the Brook and is terrified of him. Haymun is convinced that the Scots are even worse than the Chinese.

Bimbo wonders, *Should we cause some damage as a memorial to our visit?* However, he decides, *If we are coming back soon, it would be the Twith who will have to repair it.* So he doesn't.

As they move, Bimbo holds the Royal Shield and the short sword as well as Haymun's bathrobe cord. Bollin is next, ready to take on Rasputin. Scayper, thirsting for some action, is in the rear, carrying the Royal Sword and everything else to leave Bollin's hands free. The bird is sure to be up.

Sure enough! As Haymun turns the corner by the wizard's bedroom, the raven, with a squawk of surprise, flutters into the air from his nest to get a closer look. He sees a rope around Haymun's tummy and three strangers following. Rasputin is no coward. Like the wizard, he is willing to risk everything to defend his turf. Beating his wings rapidly, he attacks. He comes in fast, claws aimed at Bimbo, who is the one holding the king captive. As a scare tactic, he caws loudly.

Bimbo dives out of the way, tugging on the rope as he does so. Haymun is pulled off balance and tumbles to the floor. The king yells, "Arrgh!" as his left big toe gets banged against the stones.

Bollin fires a salvo of liquid from both hips. Two jets shoot out like laser lights into the sky. Rasputin gets a burst of tomato ketchup in his left eye. Ketchup is enjoyable when served on fried egg, potatoes, and sausages but less tasty on strawberry trifle and downright offensive in the eye. Because of its color, it is used by actors and actresses to give the impression of blood on the victim. It is in the nature of ravens that they do not like the sight or sound or smell of blood. Many ravens who have been to too many dramas actually believe that blood smells like tomato ketchup.

Into the right eye goes a stream of dishwashing liquid. It is not even the thin kind but a thick, green goo. It takes a firm and accurate hand to eject a squirt strong enough and fast enough to catch an attacking raven amidships bang-on in his right eye when he is coming at you like a bullet. Bollin has that hand! Technically, it is not really amidships but half a thumb to the left of amidships.

Rasputin now flies on instruments. When airplanes suddenly fly into a thick cloud, instruments take over. The pilot puts his feet up on the handles, leans back, and gets out his little packet of chewing gum and his book of funnies. The airplane doesn't even hiccup. Inside its innards, little gadgets click and whirr, and the passengers don't spill even a drop of their milk or orange juice. The word for the instruments inside a bird when this happens is spelled *i-n-s-t-i-n-c-t*, and the designers of airplanes can't even get close with what they design.

Take a bird suddenly struck blind while it's flying. The airplane in the thick cloud keeps on going straight. It doesn't alter its course an inch. It could be flying straight into another airplane coming the other way with the same problem. Too bad! The bird, however, thinks. That's the difference. A bird thinks things through. It will go in horizontal but come out heading for the moon or else heading back the way it came in. A bird is more likely to get through a dark cloud than an airplane.

Rasputin is temporarily blinded by red gunk in his left eye and green goo in his right eye. The solution is simple. He needs to wash his eyes. The raven first zooms upwards to avoid collision with anything ahead of him and, in the process of increasing height, recalls that directly behind, to the north, is a lake where a whole squadron of flying fish doing acrobatics could take off and make crash landings in complete safety. The maneuver he makes is known as a loop followed by rolling off the loop at the top into a screaming, full-fledged crash dive.

There is something else here to consider also. Dishwashing liquid is designed to be sticky. It is hard to know why this should be so. Tomato ketchup, for instance, is not as sticky. When dishwashing soap is squirted onto a plate, it sticks to the plate in a green, slimy blob. It must be soaked in water in order to get it to dissolve. It will just mess up the plate if it gets put back in the rack without being immersed in water. Husbands sometimes try this, and they get it in the neck. It is rubbing the blob with water that cleans the plate, not the blob itself. That's the way the stuff is designed.

The raven is not merely squirted with a jet of high class dishwashing liquid but soaked in it from beak to tail feather. When Bollin gives a squirt, make no mistake, he gives a *squirt*! The bird's feathers are stuck together. He is not going to fly any better than a heavy object dropped from an airplane flying on automatic pilot within a dark cloud. He will likely drop like a stone.

Rasputin could be mistaken for a flying SnuggleWump. One eye is red; the other is green. The green side is totally gummed up while the red side is partially functional only because tomato ketchup is less sticky. The raven tries to make all parts of his flying apparatus work, but there is something partly working on one side only and nothing at all working on the other. It is not only his eyes; his feathers are coated with the same sticky substance as his green eye. They are stuck together and will not allow proper navigation. There is no way he is going to drop like a stone. A stone drops straight down. What was at the bottom when the stone started falling is still going to be at the bottom when it hits the water.

Not so with the raven. As he dives, his descent is in the form of a corkscrew. His right wing is glued down to his side and only his left wing is flapping, which creates a clockwise, spiraling spin. Rasputin goes into a screaming corkscrew dive almost but not quite vertically. The fright of being so out of control causes him to caw like a banshee on All Saints' night in Dublin. It could be said that, for the raven, this is his lucky day. He is fortunate to hit the water at the deepest part of the lake. Totally submerged but moving fast, he leaves a trail of green soapsuds and bubbles, indicating to observers on the wall of the castle the direction and extent of his journey underwater.

To be helpful, Bollin pushes Rasputin's nest on the chimney slab off into the lake so that the bird will have something to hold on to if he ever comes back in this direction. It seems unlikely for a while. The soap bubbles show it is possible to swim in a straight line under water with your eyes closed. It is the bird's instinct at work again.

Rasputin needs to come up for air. The tomato ketchup is virtually all gone before he surfaces. He changes course into a steady circuit of the lake instead of a straight line. The bedraggled bird is on his third circuit, doing the crawl. The lake is full of soapsuds that confuse the fish even while giving them a once-in-a-lifetime chance to wash themselves in soapy water. The raven swims several more times around the lake, attempting to rinse the dishwashing goo off his feathers, but they are still sticky. He is tired from so much swimming. He dislikes swimming as an exercise. It is not natural. Webbed feet belong on toads and frogs and platypuses, not on birds. Birds are designed to fly. That is why they have feathers. Certain birds, like ducks and mallards, can enjoy swimming if they like. He doesn't.

Rasputin spots some floating debris that he thinks he recognizes. He takes a turn around it. He is aghast and caws out loud. "Oh yes! I recognize it alright! It is my nest! That just isn't cricket! These people are not fighting a civilized war between soldiers but as ruthless schoolboys playing rugby. Destroying birds' nests is unacceptable! It's deplorable, just plain barbarism! Don't the Chinese eat bird's nests? It's a wonder they didn't eat mine."

The raven's steady splashing stroke gradually removes most of the dishwashing liquid from the black feathers. As he swims, he is not only washing out the dishwashing liquid, but venting his feelings. "The enemy is not the Twith I know here in Gyminge. They must belong to the bunch on the Brook, but they have to be new reinforcements brought in from somewhere else. I have never seen any of those three among the seven I do know. This is not a good sign."

Rasputin recalls a recent conversation with King Haymun. "The king told me that he has two Chinese prisoners in the dungeon. Now three more have captured the king and attacked me. I better get back to the Brook right away. The wizard needs to know the Twith are massing foreign forces inside his own country. Already, the enemy has captured the king, taken over the castle and it is no longer secure."

The raven tried earlier to go through the opening in the curtain but found it sealed off. He is not happy about the only other option available. "I'm not looking forward to having to take the way the goblins go, through the cave-tunnel to the waterfall. It will be dark in that tunnel. I don't know why I should be afraid of the dark, but I am. Besides that, my feathers will get soaked going through the waterfall, and it will be nearly impossible to fly. I'll end up walking the rest of the way to the cottage, and I'm certainly not looking forward to that."

Rasputin changes course towards the shore. He gives his feathers a final frantic rinsing before he steps ashore. "As soon as I am dry and my feathers are working properly, I'll head south."

HERBIE

Three soldiers have just crossed the lake in a rowboat to exchange their shifts. Only one goblin soldier emerges from the picket gate. It is Herbie on his way to relieve Nitter. He likes the six o'clock shift because it gets him out of having to help get the kids ready for school. There are six of them at home, and they are all of school age!

At the door to the dungeon, Herbie is surprised to see the padlock on the door. *What on earth is Nitter doing locking the dungeon before I have even come on duty? Where is the key to get in? Come to think of it, where is Nitter?*

A strange goblin, someone he hasn't seen before, is coming with the ring of keys. The strange goblin is Scayper, of course. He unlocks the padlock without saying a word and releases the holding clasp. Suddenly, with a mighty shove, he pushes the relief goblin down the steps and inside.

Herbie can be forgiven for believing that the man, coming at him with a dirk in his right hand raised to strike, is breathing fire. Scayper is breathing out deep breaths drawn not from his lungs but even deeper down from his belly. Those breaths are not really singeing Herbie's hair and clothes, but they are close to the temperature where it could happen.

Stepping in behind the aggressive goblin are two others who are not goblins. They are no less aggressive. The one with ginger hair carries a short, raised sword and a huge shield. The other carries a red dress, and is pulling a rope tied around the tummy of his king who half falls into the dungeon last of all.

Bollin quickly closes the dungeon door so any noise will not reach the guards at the gate.

In falling, King Haymun does not step into the bucket that is bent and deformed and laying under the chair. Instead, the ring on his left toe catches against the edge of the step and flicks itself horizontal. This is not intentional and feels like a knife slicing through meat cooked to a turn and hot from the oven. He lets out an unearthly scream as he feels his teething ring cut into his flesh. He hops on the spot like a performing bear on a hot plate. That would be cruel, however. He actually hops like a Cornish festival reveler at a May Day folk dance.

Herbie has trouble comprehending the events that erupted so suddenly around him. He sees the predicament of his king and wonders if this is some new kind of torture. He would possibly have tackled someone the size and shape and character of Nitter, whom he tends to bully. But this man with the fiery breath is an entirely different matter. He looks as though he would enjoy turning someone into a crisp roast dinner.

Herbie is terrified, and fears for his life. He takes his family responsibilities seriously. He spends much of his off-duty time out in the allotment patch growing vegetables. It is also a good excuse to get away from the children for a while. His wife wishes he would grow something other than parsnips. Herbie feels it is unwise to abandon a gift you are good at to pursue other notable produce such as potatoes or carrots. He might be a complete failure, and his children could starve. Mrs. Herbie has tried every which way she knows to make parsnips appetizing to growing children. She has perfected parsnip soufflé, parsnip and treacle pudding, parsnip trifle, and parsnip jam, but it is getting harder by the day to raise their enthusiasm for the vegetable.

The thought of how his wife will bring up all the children without him hardly crosses his mind. After all, she has done quite well thus far. The thought of how his wife will grieve at his graveside is also absent from his thinking. She possibly will, but it is unlikely. She is an independent-minded woman who argues that marriage is of equals, not master and servant. But he is concerned that the first thing the children will do when he is no longer around will be to go pull up all his precious parsnips.

Beyond parsnips, his thinking is much more basic. *My own life is also precious.* He wonders what he might have that he could bargain with, but the only thing that comes to mind is his lunch. He decides that even the fire breather would turn down parsnip sandwiches.

Herbie looks towards his king. Although he is presently a captive, he is watching and will remember the valor of his troops in combat. However, he doesn't consider this real combat and drops to his knees clasping his hands as though in prayer. He cries with passion in his voice, "Remember my children."

Scayper advances towards Herbie, who hurriedly gets up off his knees and retreats. In a series of backward moves, Herbie ends up against the rear wall of the dungeon. Scayper unlocks the padlock to the small cell. Inside the dark cell lie two motionless, blindfolded, and gagged forms sharing the mattress pad. They are not asleep. Even if they had been dead, the scream of the king would have roused them. They pretend to be asleep, hoping that whatever is going on will pass them by.

Herbie obeys the nod of Scayper's head and scuttles into the cell. He wonders, *Is there any place to sit? I better wait for a while before I start to claim a piece of the mattress and blanket.*

Scayper locks the padlock. There was a time he wondered about life and whether it was worth carrying on. He can hardly remember when he has enjoyed himself so much. With a big smile on his face, he snaps the padlock shut and walks back down the passageway.

THE CASTLE GATE

Only two goblins leave for the far shore. The rowboat goes off without Nitter. If he wants to waste time on the changeover, the other goblins do not; they want to get on home.

The two replacement guards at the gate settle down for their shift. They like to sit in the area between the jammed portcullis and the great castle gates behind them. The jammed portcullis leaves its spikes just below arch level and does not obstruct their view.

The two brothers congratulate themselves on their relationship to the sergeant major who has arranged this duty for them. Their mother is Sam's sister. You don't have to be smart in this world. It's relationships that matter, not brains!

Above their heads is the roof of the archway between the portcullis and the main gates. Several round holes along the center line in the roof are known as murder holes. Through these holes, missiles are fired and stones dropped on invaders who penetrate the portcullis and attack the gates. Boiling oil is intended to be followed by flaming torches.

The shift is eight hours before there is a change. They will remain on duty until 2:00 p.m. Ted and Bill get out the cards. They are into Crazy Eights and Old Maid, and because they are brothers, they rarely get angry when the other cheats. Being goblins, they feel that this is the most fun and the best way to play the game.

An anguished voice from a far distance somewhere above surprises them. It is barely audible. "Help."

They look around, and then they look up. A limp hand hangs over the edge of the middle murder hole, a man's hand. The fingers move weakly and then stop moving. "Help!" It is hardly more than a croak, but it is followed by a groan!

Ted looks at Bill. "Who's up there? There are no guards on the battlements these days. The servants left in the castle are only the king's personal servants. Why should one of those be up there?"

Bill shrugs his shoulders. "I don't know. But it must be one of them. None of the outside day staff has yet come on duty. I suppose it could possibly be the king himself. In case it is, we better go check it out."

Once more, they hear a groan, a dying gasp more than a cry for help.

"We better hurry!" They memorize the cards face up on the table; you can't trust anybody these days, especially your own brother. They slip back the bolts of the picket gate, raise the latch, push the door open, and step over the sill of the door into the castle courtyard.

They turn to their right and quickly climb the stairs to the parapet of the castle wall. They are within a few steps from the top when a ginger-haired boy, not a goblin, steps into their sight at the head of the steps wielding a short sword. He has an angry look on his face and is obviously not interested in playing a Happy Families game of cards with them. In fact, he looks intent on making some families very unhappy.

Ted wishes Bill were in front. Bill is glad it is Ted, not himself who is ahead. To be sure that he doesn't get too close to the front, he turns and takes a step back down the stairs. He only takes one step. Ahead of him at the foot of the steps is another foreigner. This one has dark brown hair. Standing beside him is a third stranger with blond hair, who has their king linked to him by a cord.

Bimbo turns to Scayper. "It's your turn now."

Scayper not only has the king's shield, but he also holds the king's sword. He pulls the sword from its scabbard and hands the leather scabbard to Bimbo. Both the shield and the sword are large for him to manage, but the sword makes a satisfying *SWISH* as he sweeps the air with it. He also pierces an imaginary enemy by thrusting up the staircase towards Ted and Bill as he places his foot on the first step ready to approach his weaponless victims.

In a way, Ted and Bill are glad their two swords have been left propped against the wall near the card table. No matter how valiant they might be, what can they do when superior forces of the enemy hold both ends of the staircase where they are standing? If they had swords in their hands, they would have no choice but to sacrifice themselves trying to rescue their king. *Long live the king!*

They have rarely seen such a ruthless face as the one on the boy above them who now takes a step down towards them and then another. He is coming at them with the clear intent to hack them into tiny pieces no bigger than a golf ball, and they are defenseless. Not a weapon between them. *This is just not cricket!*

Ted is in the more dangerous situation. It is true that the boy below has the bigger sword, but at least he is not yet climbing the steps. Ted sticks up his right hand, twists the first two fingers together, and cries "Fainitz!" He knows he is speaking for his brother also. Ted is unsure whether either enemy boy wielding a sword knows what *Fainitz* means, but it is a signal known to boys and goblins all over England. He hopes it is the same in China. Since the upper boy halts and both boys lower their swords with frustrated looks, he knows with a great sense of relief that he is understood. The enemy cannot now hurt them, and they are safe.

Fainitz is a word that has the same meaning in any language. It means, "I surrender. You have beaten me. I take no further part in the struggle. I am a prisoner of war. You cannot harm me now that I am your prisoner."

Goblins do not feel themselves bound by the signal but often pretend to accept it. The boys have no choice but to accept it completely. It is the universal word binding on all boys.

Bollin motions Bill and Ted down the steps. They can see he is reluctant and feels himself cheated of his prey. Scayper stands to one side, his sword still raised and his shield defensive lest the prisoners play any tricks.

Bimbo, the king with him, is over at the dungeon door, opening it.

Bill and Ted march briskly towards the dungeon. They are prisoners of war, soldiers caught on the field of battle. They have their pride even if they are vanquished. They display a stiff upper lip. Sometimes you win, and sometimes you lose. They wonder whether they should salute the victors as they enter into captivity, but since their caps are resting on the handles of their swords and they do not salute when they are not wearing a cap, they decide not to do so. Instead, Bill has one last request: "Beg to speak, sir!"

"Yes, what is it. Be quick."

"If you would be so kind, may we please have our playing cards? They're on the table inside the door. They'll help us pass the time away. Thank you, sir."

Bollin gathers the cards, collects a pair hidden in the hinge of one of the folding chairs and several others stuck in the underside of the tabletop. He takes a last look around, and puts them in Bill's outstretched hand.

Once more, Scayper adds to the content of the last cell in the dungeon block. There is less and less blanket and mattress per prisoner.

A MATTER OF STRATEGY

Bimbo, Bollin, and Scayper sit beneath the portcullis, dangling their feet above the water and considering their best strategy. They are in sight of the goblins on the far shore. Because they want to talk freely, they have blindfolded King Haymun and put him in the far corner, facing the closed picket gate. They talk in whispers.

Bimbo is confident. "The castle is ours. We can defend it easily. Shall we stay here, liberate all the Twith in bottles, and develop a complete defense of the castle before the wizard returns? We have the king as hostage. The wizard made a serious mistake. Nearly all his troops are on the Brook. He has hardly anyone left defending Gyminge."

Scayper isn't sure they could defend the castle. "Is the situation any different now than when King Rufus was in total command of the country? Yet he was defeated when the wizard and his Wozzle army first attacked."

Bollin also decides against this course, although it seems attractive. "The wizard will be sure to bring all his troops back from the Brook and then block the toad trail through the cave-tunnel. He can just wait until he is ready for his next move. Perhaps he would attack, perhaps just starve out the castle defenders. Everything would be back in the wizard's hands, and he would be even stronger than before."

Bimbo agrees. "You are right. The bottled prisoners appear to be in no danger from the wizard if they are left as they are. Dayko's Rime does not suggest that freeing them is one of the events he predicted for the Return. We'll do better to make our way as fast as we can back to the Brook so that the Return the seer foresaw can take place as soon as possible."

Bollin goes to the picket gate to question Haymun. Removing the blindfold, he says, "Answer my question, and don't you dare lie. Where is Dr. Vyruss Tyfuss?"

The king is accustomed to lying. He will lie now if there is more advantage in lying than telling the truth. However, he has a strange feeling deep in his stomach that this boy knows by instinct when a lie is being told. He can think of no convenient lie that would persuade the boy to stop that awful shaving the hairs on his leg with the edge of his sword blade. He licks his dry lips, wondering how the boy knows the doctor but not daring to ask. "Dr. Tyfuss has been relieved of his duties as my physician and as field medical officer. He has been appointed Commander of the Southern Zone with the promoted rank of colonel."

"Carry on, and don't leave anything out."

The other two have also come across and are squatting on their haunches, looking at the king intently.

Again, the king licks his lips. *I hope I don't get in trouble with the wizard telling what I know.* "The wizard ordered me to build a defense post at the entrance to the toad tunnel. It is on the Gyminge side, of course, and will also serve as immigration control. He insists it must be completed in three days. That is by this coming Sunday. He plans to inspect it on that day, and I was going down to check on progress and inspect it tomorrow. Colonel Tyfuss has taken troops from here and also the men still assigned to guard the ambush site in the forest. The tents there are probably still being moved. That is why there are few wagons left for our work on the bridge and why there are so few men working on the bridge."

Bimbo knows his father is interested in bridges. He might be particularly interested in what is going to replace the pontoon bridge. "What kind of bridge is being built? I want all the details, so tell me everything you know."

King Haymun has no idea what kind of bridge it is. To say so is not going to satisfy this curious boy. "Corporal Pimples is over there by the guardhouse." He points across the lake. "He is both the bridge designer and the man responsible for building it. If you wish, we could have him come over and you could talk to him about the design."

"No. That won't be necessary. We'll go across and see him."

King Haymun's earnest desire is to be left behind in the dungeon with Nitter and Herbie and the others. His toe throbs with screaming pain. His left foot is bare, and he is sure that sooner or later, one of these young men is going to step on his teething ring. They are not being careful where they walk.

ACROSS THE LAKE

Bimbo and Bollin are surprised and pleased to see that there is now a flotilla of rowboats moored at the castle gate. They will be needed when work on the new bridge begins at the castle end. The destruction of the pontoon bridge at the beginning of the week continues to be a considerable inconvenience.

Bimbo and Bollin need two boats to get ashore. They remove the oars from the others, drop them in the lake, and push the boats away from the landing. Bimbo rows one boat holding Scayper and the king. As Scayper guards the king, he runs his thumb along the sharp edge of his dirk. The poor king's eyes bulge in terror. Immediately ahead of them is Bollin. In his boat are their trophies: the short sword he has been using, the king's sword wrapped in the red dress, the shield, and the pouch he filled with useful items. The dagger is still with Bimbo.

The day is clear and fine. Like yesterday, it looks like it will be a warm day. They pass through the line of suds where the bottom of the lake becomes murky and obscured. In the distance, a bird rises from the shore of the lake, ascends with difficulty, and takes a steady course towards the south to Blindhouse Wood. He soon disappears from view.

Bimbo calls to Bollin, "Look! There's Rasputin. I wonder why he didn't first take another turn over the castle to see what is happening. I guess he's in too much of a hurry. He must be heading off to report to the wizard. If so, we can expect trouble later on. The cave-tunnel will be the test for us. We need to get there as soon as we can. It will be wise though, to remain hidden at the southern edge of Blindhouse Wood until nightfall. We can continue on to the border during the night to avoid being seen by Rasputin or anyone else."

As he rows, Bimbo tries to imagine how the wizard will react and what he will do. He expresses his thoughts to Scayper. "If the raven has to go through the tunnel instead of through some new hole in the curtain arranged for him by the wizard, it will be several hours before the wizard can get back to the castle. The bird really knows very little. He can only take news that the king is captive within the castle. It is possible he will also tell the wizard that the castle has been taken over by foreigners. He will have heard about the Chinese prisoners from the king.

"The wizard is likely to just overfly the woods on his way to the castle. He isn't likely to pursue us until after he finds out what has happened here. We probably won't have any problems in the forest. Pursuit is difficult there except on foot. But we could encounter trouble as we come out into the open and approach the cave-tunnel. We need to throw the wizard off the scent. But how can we do that?"

Bimbo considers taking another captive. *Corporal Pimples is the key designer of the bridge. It is still in the early stages of construction, and removing him will delay the work, perhaps indefinitely.* However, Bimbo drops that idea. *It will be in the best interest of the Twith on the Brook to have some kind of easy access into the castle completed as soon as possible. Better to leave him to get on with the job.*

As the two boats approach the shore, all kinds of activity can be seen. There are scores of men busy digging, lifting, carrying, sawing, and banging. There is no one on parade or performing drill. All the activity is directed to hastening the preparation for the bridge. Few are yet engaged on erection of the trestle. The timbers first need to be cut to length, roughly shaped, and joints made. It will be tested for fit on the ground before assembly in the air.

Corporal Pimples is at hand on the shore to greet the two boats. He has seen the little vessels approaching, but because he is extremely nearsighted, he was unable to clearly identify the king or observe the cord around his waist. Others with him are seeing more clearly and inform the corporal.

As they approach the muddy shore, Bollin calls out to the men running to help. He has dropped his oars and is standing up in the boat. "Move back twenty paces, all of you. Stand well back. The king is going to order it. Back. Back farther!"

Scayper gently prompts the king with a short tug on the cord and a nudge with his dirk. "You heard him. Order it."

Haymun calls out from the other boat. "M-m-m-move back twenty paces, all of you. Stand well back. I order you. Back, back farther." His sore toe causes him to stutter. Scayper has him on his feet and is assisting him out of the boat. The king wants to get ashore without injuring his toe further and moves slowly, being extremely cautious.

The dozen or so startled men, including Sam and Corporal Pimples among them, count their steps backwards. Two of them, less cautious than the others, step backwards into the trench for the trestle and disappear. From choice rather than from injury, they stay disappeared.

When Scayper has the king ashore at last, Bimbo jumps on shore, drops his oars in the water, and pushes them and the boat out into the lake. He reaches into Bollin's boat to get the king's sword. Unwrapping it, he removes it from the scabbard and advances towards the men as though he is about to take them all on singlehandedly. They step further backwards. He motions with his sword. "Keep well back! Listen carefully, and don't make a single false move. Sit down, all of you. SIT DOWN, I said!"

Everyone within hearing sits down without bothering to check whether the place he sits is wet or dry, clean or muddy. Even the king decides, *My left foot hurts beyond bearing. I'm going to sit down too.* He also doesn't check the best place to sit, and there is a good-sized muddy splash.

It is not the splash, but the fact that the king sat down that causes a ripple effect all the way up the hill and into the forest. Workmen there see those nearer the lake sitting down as though they have been ordered to take a ten-minute tea break from their labor. They have not heard any orders but do not wish to be singled out as the only ones left standing disobeying them. Even those up trees, trimming limbs and branches, find somewhere to sit and try to keep their balance without swinging their legs.

Those peeking out from within the guardhouse are out of sight but sit down as though the boy with the sword is close enough to strike.

"You, sergeant! Yes. You! Come over here! I have some questions and orders. Stop! Stop right there! How many horses are there in the stable?"

Sam looks nervously towards the king as he answers, "There are maybe ten." He has been avoiding the king because he doesn't want to answer questions about how it came to pass that the king's bride-to-be escaped or was taken away from the castle during the king's absence.

The king is not thinking about Elisheba as much as he is about his toe, and what the wizard will say, and whether he will still be on the throne when it is all over. It does occur to him, however, *Nothing went wrong with my being king until the time I went hunting in the forest and saw the woodcutter's mute daughter. Since then, nothing has gone right. I'll sort it out with her once we are married.*

Bimbo tells the sergeant major, "I want every horse, *every horse*, in the stable brought here, saddled and ready for a journey. No matter if they are lame, I want *all* of them! You have five minutes. You stay here but get it done."

Sam looks around. He sees the stable sergeant. "You heard what the boy said. Take as many men as you need and get back here in five minutes. Bring *all* the horses, the boy said. Run!"

Scayper thinks that the king might move them even faster. He gives a little prod with his finger in the king's back.

The king thinks it is the dirk. He yells "Run! Didn't you hear? Run!"

ONE TO ONE HUNDRED

Bollin and the others stand waiting for the horses. More and more men find they are conscripted as grooms and stable boys. They run to the stable in response to shouts. Bimbo nods to Bollin to take Scayper's place behind the king and takes Scayper off to one side so that they cannot be overheard.

Scayper nods as they talk. He points north across the lake in the direction of the Dark Forest. He must be describing something within or beyond it. Scayper confirms, "Yes, I am an experienced horseman. I've been riding horses all my life."

They return to Bollin but motion him to remain where he is. "Bollin, we will all leave together, and then I'll send Scayper on ahead to make sure there are no traps set up for us. He knows the Dark Forest well and long ago lived just beyond it. He says that beyond Count Fyrdwald's castle is a small cottage on the far edge of the forest and then beyond that is Up-Horton where Earl Gareth used to live. He'll be there well before we are, and we'll meet him later. We'll take the king with us."

Bimbo turns to the king. "Do you know Count Fyrdwald's castle in the Dark Forest?"

The king nods.

"Do you know the way through the Dark Forest to Up-Horton?"

The king nods again.

"Do you know the way beyond that to Lyminge Castle?"

The king nods again with a hint of a grin on his face. He will not be unhappy to postpone an encounter with the wizard who is in the opposite direction.

Sam has not moved from where he was positioned by Bimbo, but his hearing is very keen. He listens intently, trying to store in his mind everything he hears so he can report to the wizard later.

The boys hear horses approaching and turn to look. Ten horses are being brought, each one led by a groomsman. They are saddled and harnessed.

Bimbo motions to the groomsmen. "Take the horses to that gathering point on the right. You!" He points to Corporal Pimples. "Bring me a long length of rope. No, two lengths of rope. The rest of you," he swings his arm in an arc, "retreat a further twenty paces. Go!"

There is plenty of rope nearby; it is needed in the bridge work. Corporal Pimples brings two coils.

Scayper takes them. He knows horses well and is clear what he is doing. He separates the horses, selecting the three best for himself and the two boys. The other seven he divides into two groups and passes the ropes through their reins. The remainder of the two coils he drops onto the pommel of the saddle of the horse he has chosen for himself, a mare he calls Black Beauty. She is larger than any of the other horses, jet-black, beautifully groomed and the outstanding animal among a fine group.

Scayper leads a horse to where Bollin stands behind the king. The king has a bedroom slipper on his right foot, and his swollen left foot is bare. Three groomsmen succeed in helping the king mount. His feet will be forward of the stirrups and free from any contact with them.

Bollin mounts the horse, sits behind the king, and gathers the reins in his left hand. Bimbo has given him the dagger and he wants his right hand free to use it. In the saddle bag is the pouch and the folded red dress. He is now ready to move off.

Next, Scayper sees to Bimbo. The boy mounts while Scayper holds the reins of both horses. Bimbo will carry the shield strapped on his arm and the king's sword in its scabbard on his belt as his weapon. Bimbo takes the reins.

The groomsmen are dismissed to join their fellow goblins.

Scayper slips Bollin's short broadsword beneath the girth band and to the side of the saddle of his own horse and swings up easily into the saddle. He is more at ease on a horse than the two boys. Handing the ropes of his seven horses to Bimbo to hold for a while, he borrows the king's sword. Wheeling his horse to face the goblin soldiers, he waves the king's sword around his head. He lets out a bloodcurdling war cry that he has neither uttered nor heard since his capture. His horse—the best and proudest of them all, a true war horse—rises on her two hind legs and neighs. "I am going to count to one hundred. When I start, run for your lives! After I reach one hundred, I shall be after you. Expect no mercy! Long live the king! One…two…three…"

The other horses neigh and stamp and jostle. Both boys are hard put to hold the animals in check. The first to break and run for their lives are the groomsmen and stable boys, but they are first by only a split second. The most fortunate and least active are those sitting in the trees on the edge of the forest. They climb higher and yet higher.

The whole plain before them is full of men fleeing into the sunrise as though only the first to reach the sun or beyond is likely to survive the consequences of this demon counting to one hundred. Before he counts to ten, even the slowest is over the east brook.

The two men hiding in the trestle trench suddenly realize they are being deserted by their friends and that they are likely to be the first to whom Scayper pays attention. Neither wants to be the father of orphaned children. Out of the hole they scramble and, without looking where their friends have gone, dive into the lake. They swim as far as they can underwater and come up among the soap suds, blowing green lather. There they float on their backs and pretend to be bubbles.

By the time Scayper reaches twenty, the bulk of the fleeing goblins are beyond the quarry. Only a few are smart enough to break south and run to hide in the trees. Snatching a look back, the slowest ones see the lonely parade ground without a pedestrian upon it. To them, it is like seeing Alexander the Great mounted on Bucephalus with a raised sword ready to charge. Scayper patiently continues, counting out to a hundred. "Seventy, seventy-one, seventy-two…"

Among the runners is the sergeant major, who, unfortunately, was one of the nearest to Scayper when he started counting. It means all the others got a better head start. Since all the other forces are stationed on the Brook, Sam is the senior ranking officer. He is certain that the horseman behind him has never been an officer or a gentleman and not even a non-commissioned officer like himself. Therefore, he probably has it in for all officers with a rank above private. This thought gives him an extra touch of speed. He pulls at his various markings of rank like the stripes on his sleeves as he runs. By the time the runners reach the quarry, he is ahead of and lower in rank than Corporal Pimples.

"Ninety-eight, ninety-nine…one hundred!" Scayper gallops halfheartedly a hundred strides in pursuit of the fleeing goblins, yelling and swinging the sword around his head.

One goblin falls out of a tree and is either unable to move or doesn't want to be seen moving. No one comes to his aid.

Scayper retrieves the horse ropes and returns the sword to Bimbo. He nudges the mare into action, his seven horses in a jostling group behind him. He leads the canter around the lake towards the Dark Forest. Within the shelter of the forest, Scayper will release the seven horses. Once around and beyond the spur running down to the lake, he breaks into a gallop. They want to be well out of sight, hidden in the trees before the goblins return to the castle and guardhouse.

FYRDWALD'S CASTLE

As they journey around the lake, they are seen by pedestrians on the road. Bimbo is content that the king be seen and recognized. Haymun still wears his crown. The fact that he rides in front of Bollin makes it plain that he is captive. The people they pass look at the four men on three horses and are startled but indicate neither joy nor sadness. Those on the left of the king observe his bare foot and assume he is wearing a teething ring on each of his big toes. They wonder whether this is a new fashion at the castle. No, it is not. They cannot understand what is happening, but the king is not a popular figure. They blot out of their minds what they see and continue on their journeys as though they have seen nothing.

The horsemen gallop along the lake road that is west of the castle. Scayper, with his seven spare horses trotting behind him, is still leading. He knows the Dark Forest far better than the forest to the south that the two boys are acquainted with. The Twith lad has grown up in this part of the country and used to hunt in the forest. In the middle of the forest is Count Fyrdwald's castle with paths radiating in all directions.

Bimbo moves up alongside. As they travel, they discuss their next move carefully. It will be wise before changing direction to gallop north past the castle. The goblin garrison will see them and report it to the wizard later. Their plan is to work their way unseen around to the southern edge of Blindhouse Wood. They will rest there until dark and then head for the cave-tunnel. If necessary, they will fight their way through onto the Brook and arrive before dawn tomorrow. There is a long journey ahead before that.

Suddenly, Scayper spots danger, real danger, on the road ahead. Coming towards them is a group of goblin cavalry, equipped with lances, pennants flying, returning to Goblin Castle from the Dark Forest.

Scayper, spurring into the lead, reins his horse to a halt while they are still thirty paces distant. He raises his hand, indicating for them to stop. He does not hesitate. "Halt. In the name of the king, HALT!"

Bollin rides up beside Scayper. King Haymun can be clearly seen by the soldiers facing them.

Scayper continues. "In the name of the king, turn 'round and escort us to Fyrdwald's castle. When you arrive, halt outside the main gate of the castle and do not enter."

Bollin prods Haymun in the side with his finger. The king knows full well what that means and speaks out. "Do as you are commanded. I, your king, and commander-in-chief, so order you!"

The animals the cavalrymen ride are large black horses, well-groomed with coats shining like silk. They are some of the best, the pride of the whole cavalry. If they are going to be the king's escort, then they will look their best doing it. There is no hesitation or question. They turn and reform into pairs. There are five pairs, their lances vertical, and their backs straight as ramrods.

They break into a slow canter. Behind them, twenty paces behind, are Bollin and the king and then Bimbo. Scayper, no longer needing to show the way through the forest, drops back to the rear. There is nothing to cause any concern behind them.

It is not long before they reach the castle. The horsemen in front rein to a halt. They remain in formation, waiting for orders from their king. The gates of Fyrdwald's castle are open.

Scayper hands the ropes of his horses to Bimbo and rides around to face the escort. "Drop your lances on the ground. Do it! Now!" He selects the least impressive rider. "You! Move over to the left and dismount." He has made a good choice if he is looking for the least able and least intelligent of all the riders. The young soldier failed all his O levels at school with the lowest marks ever recorded. He is also flatfooted and failed his physicals because he is overweight. However, Dumdum is the nephew of the cavalry sergeant. So, if he survives, in time he is bound to rise high in rank in the Gyminge cavalry. A man has to look after his own kith and kin. It is a goblin tradition.

Scayper is content to carefully work through his orders to the remaining horsemen one by one. In a regular sequence from front to back, they dismount, walk their horses over to Dumdum, hand him the reins, and then sprint into the castle. The soldiers and staff within the castle stand in the entrance gate. They dare not venture a step beyond by clear orders from the king who begins to stammer as he relays the orders Scayper gives, and Bollin reminds him that he needs to give also.

Dumdum now holds ten reins. He is the only goblin outside the castle entrance apart from King Haymun. It makes him nervous. He assists Bimbo, who remains mounted, to thread rope through the reins of his ten horses, not daring to miss a single one. He tries to keep clear of the reach of Bimbo's sword. The horses are well trained and accustomed to remaining stationary for long periods of time. When the last one is joined in with the others, Bimbo nods him towards the castle gate. He is off like a flash.

Bollin nudges his horse towards the castle gate and reins up short of it. All those standing in the entrance back away into the castle courtyard. The king recites the orders Bollin whispers to him. He is very clear about what is going to happen to the first man who emerges from the gate after it has been closed. "You will be assigned to clean out the Gyminge castle stable singlehandedly for a minimum of one hundred years before any leave application, even for twenty-four hours, will be considered. Is that understood?" Not getting any response, he shouts, "IS THAT UNDERSTOOD?"

Heads nod vigorously. It is understood, and so is the next order. The gate is pushed closed, and the great locking bar falls into place with a thud. The portcullis outside, unused for centuries, drops from above and crashes down into the dirt, twisted and awkward. It will be a long while before that gets raised. Until it is, the garrison is locked inside and unable to pursue the king and his captors.

Scayper takes from Bimbo the ropes, securing the seventeen riderless horses. He is not at all perturbed by the difficulty of keeping that many horses under control. He clicks with his tongue to reassure them that everything is going to be okay. Motioning to the other two to follow him, he takes the north path away from the castle.

RASPUTIN HEADS FOR THE BROOK

Rasputin is thankful that the soapy goo in his feathers finally washed out. He is clear in his mind that he must get to the wizard without delay. He sees the forest ahead, but is slower to gain height than usual and doesn't try to fly high over Blindhouse Wood. The raven is content to be just above the treetops. However high he chooses to go, he will only have to descend later.

In the far distance across the fields, he sees a tent city beginning to develop. Only a few tents have been erected so far. There are several wagons along the toad trail between Blindhouse Wood and the border, loaded with equipment from the forest ambush camp. Even more wagons, empty, are on their journey back for a second load.

I better have a word with Colonel Tyfuss. The wizard is sure to want news of progress.

As he arrives and glides in for a landing, the colonel is addressing his troops and work crews. Yesterday, all they had succeeded in doing was arriving and setting up their tents for the night. The colonel has experience observing woodlouse colonies. He intends to use the principles a woodlouse leader does and develop a goblin encampment as similar in design as he can to that of a woodlouse housing colony.

That is the long-term plan. In the short-term, it is much more simple. Get something up, anything, and in place by tomorrow noon. That is when King Haymun is coming to inspect the finished product. When the king finishes his inspection, it will be too late for him to return to the castle. He will undoubtedly plan to spend the night, and that fixes the priorities for the work today. The important things to be taken care of are the king's pavilion, the royal cookhouse, the royal bathhouse, the royal sickroom, and the accommodations for the king's horse and the king's servants.

After these priorities are seen to, Vyruss wants to get on with the immigration center for the toads. He is not sure this will ever work. The toads believe they were here first, so they have a right to travel along the toad trail and no one, simply no one, is going to stop them. One toad probably weighs as much as ten or fifteen goblins. They are unlikely to be willing to answer questions about where they are going or what they plan to do or whether they are carrying any banned substances. He does not plan to stay in Gyminge long enough to find out. *If I were planning to stay, I would apply for a transfer to the northern zone and a posting to Lyminge Castle in Wozzle.*

The tents are being placed well to the west of the cave-tunnel. He wants to keep the residences well away from any possible demonstrations by angry female toads! The creatures will emerge from the tunnel through an open gate into a large field. They will pass through the field to another gate that is always kept open. Once through that, they are on their way north to have their babies. Nothing could be simpler. As long as the gates are left open, there should be no problems. If it becomes necessary to close either or both gates, Vyruss hopes that it is not during the baby toad season from February to June, and that he is somewhere else at the time.

Vyruss has acquired a sergeant from the castle garrison. When Rasputin arrives, he hands the urgent tasks over to the sergeant and turns to the raven.

Rasputin tells the colonel, "I am going to see the wizard. Since there is no opening now in the curtain, it means that I must go through the toad tunnel to the waterfall. I've never been that way before, and I'm sure the journey isn't going to be easy. The tunnel is bound to be very dark."

Vyruss extends an offer. "I can send a goblin ahead of you as far as the waterfall with a lighted torch to help you on the way."

The raven is grateful. "Thank you. That would be helpful." He shares his news from the castle. "At least three non-Twith are holding the king captive. There must be many more since the whole castle is in their hands. The king told me they are Chinese, and they certainly look Chinese." Rasputin has never seen any Chinese to assist that opinion. However, he is sure that when he does meet some other Chinamen, they will look like the captors of the king that he has seen.

The raven also tends to exaggerate. "The castle is probably swarming with them." Rasputin is not so hot on geography, but he has gathered the idea from somewhere that Chinese, like bees, travel in swarms. "They are heavily armed with a completely new range of weapons in addition to swords and shields. When I left, the Chinese were squirting soapsuds into the lake to help clean the water and spraying blood on the walls to show they mean business if anyone tries to stop them. They were definitely speaking a dialect of Chinese and chewing bamboo shoots while they were doing so."

Vyruss can make little sense of the events at the castle as described from the bird's point of view. He does not know that what Rasputin saw was seen through ketchup and dishwashing liquid. *It does seem as though there are major problems at the castle. I am glad to be well away from there. I don't understand why the Chinese on the other side of the world have suddenly become interested in what is happening at Goblin Castle. I suspect that Bimbo and Bollin might be involved somehow, but I can't fathom where their Chinese allies suddenly came from.*

It could be considered remarkable that Rasputin has made it this far given all he has recently been through. However, now is when things begin to go even further awry. It is unfortunate for the raven that the goblin chosen to help light the way through the tunnel and on to the waterfall is the ex-cook from the ambush site. He burned the porridge served to the king and Dr. Tyfuss. Given a bare flame, he is likely to burn down his own tent around his ears, and any others too if they happen to be nearby. He is untidy and erratic in his actions and behavior. He is the despair of the barrack tent because he leaves things in a mess. For inspections, he just hides everything under his bed out of the way. All soldiers know that inspecting corporals and sergeants look under the bed before they ever look at what is on the bed or in the bed. He is always in trouble. So it is this time.

Rasputin would have done far better on his own without a light. Things go alright on the journey through the tunnel. He follows the goblin until they get to the end near the waterfall. There should have been no reason at all for his feathers to touch the bare flame of the torch the goblin in front of him is carrying.

The cook has completed his mission. He will now return to camp. He is in a hurry because he is afraid of the dark and fears that the torch will go out before he gets back through the tunnel. This goblin has problems that go back to his early childhood!

Rasputin has to get past him to continue on his journey to the Brook. There is no way around it. They have to pass each other and wish each other a safe journey. It never gets to that.

The accident-prone cook not only manages to set alight the folded left wing feathers of the raven, but in completing his own turn, he then sets fire to Rasputin's tail feathers.

Rasputin hops quickly to the bank overlooking the waterfall and dives downwards into the pool at the foot of it. He batters any stillness out of the waters. The waterfall cascading into the pool nearly drowns him. The falling water splashes over him and puts out the fires on both his tail and his wing. Unfortunately, Rasputin did not succeed in completely washing out all the dishwashing liquid in his feathers in spite of his strenuous efforts back at the lake. The tremendous *swoosh!* washes out the remainder of the awful green goo. This compounds his problem. He is blinded in a bubble bath of immense proportions as the waterfall stirs up every bubble of lather the dishwashing liquid possesses. He is completely immersed in bubbles. It is uncomfortable for children when they get soap in their eyes. It is even less comfortable for a raven that doesn't have a mother standing nearby with a towel to wipe the suds away.

Rasputin struggles his way to the slit in the curtain and enlarges to Beyonder-size as he passes through. He is half blinded by soapsuds, and it is impossible to see the horizon, but he takes off across the bog by walking on water without webbed feet. The raven's left wing and his tail feathers are no longer the length they used to be. Until his right wing feathers are trimmed back to about the same length as the left wing feathers to give him some balance, he is not going to fly in horizontal or vertical circles but in wiggly-wobbly orbits somewhere in-between. Nevertheless, he attempts to take off and fly to Squidgy's cottage. He cannot accomplish it and spirals downwards. It is his lucky day after all. He crash-lands in the middle of the croc' pond. It could have been somewhere harder. This washes the soap out of his eyes, and at last, he can see again, although he cannot see clearly under the water because the weeds festoon his face as they get torn out by their roots.

The one duck on the pond, a mallard, missed by inches by the raven who is not as happy as he should be, ferries himself rapidly to the middle of the pond. By using one leg only, he goes furiously round in circles. He quacks madly. There are days, even for mallards, when you can't really understand what is going on. This is one of those days again.

RASPUTIN AT THE COTTAGE

Rasputin decides to walk the last portion of the way from the croc' pond. He dislikes walking almost as much as he dislikes swimming, but the thought of flying in and around trees in circles and ovals at odd angles is more than he can handle at this time. He claws off as many of the water weeds as he can.

Starting from daybreak, his day has not gone well. *Surely it can only improve,* he thinks. Through the trees, he sees the familiar, friendly eyes of the SnuggleWump. They are red, but the bird is sure the SnuggleWump's annoyance is not directed at him.

Rasputin is not feeling cheerful, and his greeting to the creature lying right across his path is only casual. "Hi."

The SnuggleWump is not really angry. He is in pain. He only has two of his original four ears left—his inside left ear and his inside right ear. Creatures with one head have the capacity for only half the number of problems he has. If he had earaches in his remaining ears, then he would put up with it by explaining to himself it is from the draft or the prevailing wind or something like bugs in his ears. However, these are not the ears that hurt. The ears that hurt are the two that are missing. Each head has taken a careful look at the other head to make sure the pain is coming from the ear that is missing, and the SnuggleWump is convinced that this is so.

He told Mrs. Squidge, who told the wizard, who says the problem is that the SnuggleWump has a split personality. In his opinion, the ears that really hurt are the two that the animal still has, but his split brain is sending messages to the wrong head. The SnuggleWump wonders, *What else is likely to go wrong if the wizard is right and I really do have a split personality?* Right now, he has too many problems in his heads to want to talk, so he answers the raven with his own casual, "Hi."

On the ridge of the cottage roof are the six titchy pterodactyls. The teros are relaxed, just waiting. Mrs. Squidge told them very firmly that they are not to follow her to the post office. One day, they had followed her as far as the end of Brook Lane. They were spotted by the garbage collector who reversed wildly back down the lane and ended up in the brook. When the driver of the library van saw them, she swerved into the telegraph pole at Greenfields and had to be cut out of her cab by the fire brigade.

Rasputin doesn't bother to greet them. *They deserted me at the kitchen window in the battle at the farmhouse. If they had done their duty like I did, I wouldn't be in this state now. From now on, I'm just going to ignore them.*

Just two days ago, Cajjer was also in the waterfall pool, although he would hardly recognize it now with all the suds. It was there that the goblin king severely bit his tail. It is once again wrapped in a bandage. He is lying on the porch, thinking. *Things had been so much better before the wizard and his raven discovered us on the Brook. I don't wish to go back to Cornwall though. I don't like the dog Squidgy's sister has at their home in St. Newlyn East. Just a little peace and quiet is all that I crave.* He watches the sorry black raven—face draped with weeds, wings and tail wet, bedraggled and singed—hop up the steps of the cottage porch.

Rasputin spots the cat and croaks, "Hi," halfheartedly.

Cajjer thinks, *Oh, oh! Trouble again!* and only meows, "Hi," to be polite. He does not stop licking his paws. *If I had never met this raven in the first place, things would have been a lot better for me. I would still have a regular tip to my tail.*

The raven knocks with his beak on the door and caws weakly. He is not in the best of shape, but the mail must go through. He has a message to deliver.

A black-and-white-striped duckbilled platypus answers the door.

Rasputin gulps and, for a moment, wonders, *Am I at the right house?* He looks at Cajjer to make sure. *Yes, that's definitely Mrs. Squidge's cat.* He looks back at the animal holding the door ajar. *This is impossible. What is it, bird or beast or fish with legs?* He looks at its feet. *Webbed feet! It's a duck. Ducks have webbed feet. But ducks only have one pair of legs, and they have feathers. This bird doesn't have feathers and has four legs. There is no way this animal can be a bird.*

"Come on in, Rasputin. Mrs. Squidge is up at the post office. She'll be back by lunchtime. The wizard is in a meeting. I can give him a call."

Strangely, Rasputin feels a huge sense of relief and then puzzlement. *The creature knows me! How can it know me?* With some doubt in his mind, he goes in. *This animal is much bigger than I am. If the creature should turn nasty, where can I fly? I'm not in good flying shape anyway.*

"Sit down somewhere, Rasputin. You probably don't recognize me."

That is an understatement. Rasputin is absolutely sure that never before in his life has he seen the creature in front of him. In fact, he would swear an oath to that effect in front of a magistrate if called upon to do so. He could truthfully say, "I do solemnly swear that never before have I met, seen, encountered, or even imagined the accused standing in the box opposite. I have absolutely no acquaintance with him and decline to be liable for his debts or misbehavior. If he was caught speeding, I was not in the car at the time."

"I'm Moley, king of the moles. We used to play Scrabble together, and you said *onomatopoeia* wasn't a word. Remember that? Do you remember me now?"

Rasputin remembers very well playing Scrabble with a mole, but he doesn't recall Moley looking like this. "What happened,

Moley? Did the wizard do this to you? What did you do to make him so mad? I didn't even know he could do things like this. Phew! That's really something." The bird begins to feel insecure. *If the wizard does this to a harmless mole, what is he likely to do to a raven who lets him down and doesn't come back to report after a fight at the farmhouse?*

"No, it wasn't the wizard. It was Mrs. Squidge's yeast buns. While the fighting was going on at the farmhouse, I was here in the cottage and got hungry. I found some yeast buns in the pantry. No one told me it was the buns that turned the chickens up at Gibbins Brook Farm into titchy teros. If they had, I wouldn't have touched them with a ten-foot pole. But no one told me. I woke up looking like this, and so far, no one has thought of any way to change me back. I suppose it is better than looking like and being a tero. I hate heights. Give me the ground every time.

"Even the wizard doesn't know what to do. I was really comfortable being a mole. I liked being a mole. No one knows what to do with me now, whether to say, 'Hello,' or, 'Good-bye.' Well, I'm glad you're back. I've missed having someone to play Scrabble with. The wizard says I am not to go outside until the Summer Games on the Brook begin. He's training me to be a weightlifter."

Suddenly, life begins to feel a little better for Rasputin. *After all, I am still a raven. Maybe I can't fly straight until the wizard gives me a feather trim. Maybe I have been squirted with green goo and burned. Maybe I do have a broken beak. But I am still a raven. I once thought how nice it would be to be a swan or an eagle or even a canary or a chicken with all your food provided for you. Not anymore! Being a raven is just fine with me. I hope the wizard will continue to see it that way as well.*

THE FERRET FADES

The wizard is out of touch with the real world and what has been happening at home in Gyminge. He has been busy at Squidgy's cottage, plotting against the Twith at Gibbins Brook Farm. He prides himself that he never gives up once he sets himself a target. He is completely focused on outwitting the Twith and getting his hands on their Book of Lore.

Griswold also prides himself on his gift of handling with exceptional brilliance a number of different problems all at the same time. He congratulates himself, "I can be relaxed about how things are back at the castle. I've left things in good, capable hands. After all, I took care of the problems that began to appear. No birds from the Brook will get into Gyminge through the curtain again. Foresight is the test of a true leader.

"Although things have gone a little awry on the Brook recently, I'm putting the finishing touches to a plan of such brilliance and simplicity that the successful result is inevitable. Then it will be time to return home in triumph." He considers, "Is there a suitable place on the mainland in front of the pontoon bridge to build a victor's triumphal arch? It would provide a grand entry for when I return in triumph from conquering the Twith. After all, the Romans did that when they came home from abroad after a victory. I personally prefer Vespasian to Julius Caesar. There is a better ending to Vespasian's story. My own triumph is not going to be any less."

The wizard is determined by hook or by crook to get the Book of Lore. He is sure it is in the farmhouse. He believes it holds the cure for the Magician's Twitch, a malady from which he suffers. Like the Roman emperors he thinks about, he is ambitious and wants to control more and more of the world around him. But that is not possible until the twitch in his right eye is cured.

When he left the castle a day or so earlier with the SnuggleWump, he didn't have time to check how things were at the castle. He would have done well to have made time! He thought everything was going his way. A week ago, he had successfully captured gran'ma from the farmhouse and seen her installed in the castle laundry ironing goblins' uniforms. Several days later, the free Twith split their forces, and he launched his perfectly planned attack on the farmhouse. The SnuggleWump was his secret weapon for the battle. He was certain that the Book of Lore would soon be in his grasp. It didn't happen.

The wizard accepts the setback of defeat as no fault of his. "The fact that the attack on the farmhouse did not go as well as planned is once more due to the failures of my troops to live up to the genius of their commander. Ah well. No use crying over spilt milk. Napoleon had the same problems, or was it Wellington?"

And he shrugs off the rescue of gran'ma. "Despite the fact that in some strange way, the rescue expedition succeeded in rescuing my captive, it might well have been for the best. All of my enemies are now back at the farmhouse; Gyminge is free of intruders."

He shifts his focus to the future. "A good leader makes his own luck by good planning! The final strike against the farmhouse that I'm preparing will deal with the enemy once and for all. And it won't leave a big mess in the countryside at home."

He chuckles at his superb skills in strategy. "I have also taken the necessary measures to sort things out so an escape from Gyminge can't happen again. I closed all exits and blocked all entrances except for the toad passage that does not respond to my magic. Under my direct instructions, the goblin king is taking care of that so it too will no longer present a problem. By Sunday, the new defense fort will be complete. After that, I will relax, put my feet up, enjoy the view, and see how the escaped Twith handle the problem of reentry."

The wizard is mourning the loss of his right-hand helper, Rasputin. He thinks the raven was lost in the battle at the farmhouse, and believes the bird is dead. He recognizes that with Rasputin gone, he needs help in the Beyond. But he is a little short of possible replacements. He is currently in conference with Jacko and considers, *Could I possibly train this ferret as a helper? I'm not so sure. Rasputin had no motive except to serve and be found faithful, an ideal set of qualities for an assistant. Jacko's only motive is to benefit himself from anything he does. The more I have to work with this sneaky ferret, the more I appreciate and miss Rasputin.*

The wizard is about to be happily surprised.

Moley lumbers up the flight of stairs and bangs on the wizard's bedroom door.

It interrupts the ferret, who is negotiating for a job as personal assistant to the Wizard of Wozzle. He is in the process of setting out the wages and hours of work and holidays he expects from an employer who will benefit from his services. He is due to be disappointed.

Griswold rises and moves to open the door.

"Excuse me, sir. An unexpected visitor to see you. He's waiting downstairs."

"I'll be right there. We're finished here, Jacko. We'll talk again later." He waits at the bedroom door until the ferret is on his way downstairs and steps back into the bedroom, closing the door behind the creature that he is finding increasingly unpleasant. He has no idea who is visiting the cottage at this time, but he welcomes the interruption as a break from negotiations with Jacko. The wizard opens the window to ventilate the room. It reeks from the strong odor of the ferret. He changes his dressing gown, which also smells of ferret, thinks about the teros on the roof, and closes the window again.

As he descends the stairs, he sees and recognizes a rather fragile raven with a familiar broken beak. He is delighted to see that the bird is alive. A great burden rolls off his shoulders. *I won't have to consider hiring Jacko after all.* He can see that the raven is not well. Before Rasputin can utter a word, the wizard puts up his hand. "Don't try to talk, my good fellow, until I have seen to your needs. I have been unable to sleep because of worrying about you." This is a lie, of course. He fetches a kitchen towel and dries the bird's wings. Seeing the burned feathers, he spreads out and compares the feathers on both wings. "This will require surgery or at least a trim."

Rasputin attempts to speak, but the wizard stops him. "No, not yet. There'll be time for talk later. Let me see to your balance. You can't fly like this. You must have had great difficulty getting back here."

The raven nods.

The wizard's world is now suddenly much brighter. Sunlight is streaming into the room instead of dark shadows. He forgets he has a bad arm and even takes the steps upstairs two at a time. He brings down his scissors and a comb. He also brings the soothing ointment from his toilet kit that he uses when he cuts himself shaving.

"Not a word, Rasputin, my lad. First, we have to make you comfortable." He pushes aside the tablecloth on the dining room table, and perches the raven on the arm of the rocking chair so that his burned left wing feathers are spread out on the table. He trims the burned feathers slightly to produce an even, rounded edge to the wing. With a wet finger, the wizard traces the edge onto the table. Now the bird turns around on the arm of the chair. The magician trims the right wing feathers to match closely the shape of the left wing, all the while chatting cheerfully to the raven as a dentist might talk to an unwilling child. A balancing trim is given to the tail feathers. A final polishing of the bird's plumage with Mrs. Squidge's fine silk tablecloth—she is not yet back from the post office—a little salve in the right spots and Rasputin starts to feel much better.

"Thanks, boss. That really helped."

"Would you like to take a trial flight to see if I got your wings even?"

"No, not yet. There are urgent matters I need to share first."

The wizard is curious. "Did you get your feathers burned at the farmhouse?"

"It did happen earlier there, but this time, it was while I was in Gyminge."

"Oh? What were you doing there?"

THE WIZARD
GETS THE NEWS

Rasputin breaks the news to the wizard without looking for a gentle way to do so. The words tumble out of his beak in a torrent that leaves the wizard struggling to make sense of what he hears. "Eastern magicians found a way to breach the curtain. The Chinese have invaded Gyminge, and the castle is in their hands. They swarmed in their hordes over the southern walls of the castle under cover of darkness. Most of them are invisible. Those that are visible are Twith-size. They have narrow eyes and wear pigtails and speak in a strange dialect."

The wizard thinks, *It's probably one of the local languages in the area near the Great Wall of China. They must have used the Great Wall to practice climbing.*

Rasputin continues, "Apart from swords and shields, they have fantastic new weapons, highly accurate rocket-powered squirt guns. They fire a venomous mix of blood and green goo huge distances. The lake around the castle is a sea of soapsuds.

"King Haymun is in their hands and is being tortured in the dungeons. His screams are awful! There are few goblin forces anywhere near the castle. Colonel Tyfuss has most of the men defending the entrance into Gyminge at the toad tunnel. He is also masterminding the construction of the defense fort and passport control at that same spot."

It is all a bit much for the wizard to digest. His questions are directed more to himself than Rasputin. He really isn't expecting any comment from the bird. "The Chinese! Why the Chinese? What do the Chinese have against me? I stole jewels from the Raja in Kashmir, but that isn't in China. Perhaps I should have visited China when I was in Kashmir. And magicians? I don't even know any Chinese magicians. Does it mean the battle is going to be magic against magic instead of magic against truth? That is likely to prove more difficult. What have I heard about Chinese magic? How powerful is it? Why are they attacking Gyminge? Are they really Twith, or are all Chinese only Twith-size? Could they be soldiers recruited by the farmhouse Gang of Seven? Is this some fiendish alliance against me? Maybe they are immigrants coming over the Channel, hidden in delivery trucks. In that case, they could be shrunk Beyonders. There are millions of Chinese, hundreds of millions. Is there going to be any stopping them? What about the culture they bring with them? We like roast potatoes, fish and chips, not panda patties, rice, and raw red cabbage cut into narrow strips."

The wizard prides himself on his capacity to absorb difficulties and then respond against them. Already, his mind is fertile and active. *First things first. Plans for a final strike against the farmhouse must be put off for the time being. One thing at a time! My first priority must be to bring Gyminge under my total control. I did it once before. I will do it again! I will be ruthless.*

He shares his strategy with Rasputin. "Tonight, as soon as it is dark, the counterattack against the Chinese will begin. All the troops on the Brook will move out from Mole Hall and across the bog back to the waterfall. Not a single goblin will remain on the Brook by dawn tomorrow.

"Cajjer can show them the way. He found his way with King Haymun and returned without difficulty. On second thought, the cat might not be reliable crossing the bog in the dark. I will need to provide the men with lights. I can prepare lamps to guide them across the bog. Come to think of it, I will plant the lamps myself. If there is a problem finding the way, I can always change myself into a toad and sniff the way across.

"I will give the orders to the goblin officers in Mole Hall. Their instructions for a forced night march to Goblin Castle must be crystal clear, without any chance of misunderstanding. The enemy at the farmhouse must not be aware of their temporary departure." The wizard is pleased with the crisp, clear way his mind works. *It is the mark of a leader. Weak subordinates and a strong leader make for harmony, quick decisions, and success.*

His mind turns back to the goblin king. "Haymun should have been working on the completion of the defense fort at the border. What is he doing being tortured in the castle dungeons? Did the Chinese go into Gyminge along the toad trail as well as through the curtain? Was that where they captured the king?" Here, he expects an answer from Rasputin. "Rasputin, when you said, 'Colonel Tyfuss,' did you mean *Dr.* Tyfuss?"

Rasputin nods his head. "Yes, it's the same man."

"Well, he's the king's physician. How on earth did the doctor get the job of constructing the defense fort? That work must also stop for the time being. This is a crisis! It's an invasion! Every man will be needed to recapture the castle."

The wizard ticks off a list of things he must do before he departs. This is one of his gifts. "I will not take Mrs. Squidge, her cat, the ferret, the SnuggleWump, the teros, or Moley with me. I have no idea how they would react when surrounded by hordes of invisible screaming Chinese soldiers. The invaders are probably wearing decorated dressing gowns and conical hats, and have long, drooping mustaches. They are likely wielding heavy two-handed backswords, and shooting off fireworks. All of them will turn tail and run when they come up against my troops who are men with steel wills and iron courage."

MRS. SQUIDGE MAKES TEA

Mrs. Squidge comes bustling in from the post office. "I have a letter from my sister Frijji, but there was nothing for you, Griswold." She is delighted to see the raven, although he is somewhat lacking the confidence he once had. She replaces her treasured silk tablecloth with a dish towel and restores the tablecloth to its rightful position. "The Wizard has been missing you so much! We were afraid you were lost in the battle at the farmhouse. Would you like a cup of tea?" She notices that the wizard is pale and unsteady. "I'll get you a cup too, my dear Griswold. I'll have some as well. A cup of tea will do us all good."

The deformed Moley agrees and tries in his fumbling, bumbling way to be useful by setting the table. Unfortunately, he spills the milk all over the lovely silk tablecloth. While trying to wipe it up, he tips over the sugar bowl and spills sugar all over the milk.

Griswold pays no attention. His mind is on other things. "My dear Mrs. Squidge, I wonder whether you could prepare something for Rasputin and me to eat to go along with our tea. We need to return to Gyminge later this afternoon for a short while to deal with a problem that has arisen there. It would be good if we didn't need to worry about food. An anchovy sandwich or two would suit very nicely."

Mrs. Squidge says, "I could send some yeast buns with you to eat on the way."

The wizard is quick to reply, "No, that won't be necessary. We won't bother to take any buns with us. Thank you just the same. A little snack to eat before we leave is all we need."

The wizard wonders about the best way to get back to the castle. *Should I fly through the curtain or go through the waterfall? Rasputin's injured wing might prevent him from flying high enough to follow me through the curtain. So that's out.*

"Rasputin, my lad. You are the only creature on earth that I can trust absolutely. You and I are going to Gyminge. We'll need to go by way of the waterfall. Once we are through the waterfall and the cave-tunnel, I want you to drop down to Colonel Tyfuss and give him some instructions for me. I want to fly directly from the border to the castle without stopping. I must find and repair the curtain where the Chinese have torn it to shreds. I will strengthen the curtain at least three times with an even stronger spell, the strongest one I know. That will provide a test for the Chinese magicians. If they can get through a strengthened curtain, I will know I have a real fight on my hands."

Mrs. Squidge rings the bell sitting on her dish and plate dresser. She could just as easily have yelled, "Grub's up! Come 'n' get it," but she knows that the wizard is accustomed to a dinner gong when he is at home. She doesn't have a gong, so the bell is a good substitute. It makes her feel as though she is gentry.

Mrs. Squidge doesn't have anchovies, but she has plenty of parsnips, so she slices them thin, arranges them neatly on the buttered bread, and spreads them thick with blackberry and apple jam. The jam is beginning to ferment, so the sandwiches are quite colorful. They are also nourishing, even if not particularly tasty. The wizard grimaces with pain at the first bite of his sandwich but decides he is hungry and continues eating. Moley likes parsnips and is ready to finish off any sandwiches left over. As they eat, Griswold shares Rasputin's news. At the same time, he mentally designs bog lamps using parsnip ends and mustard. He also plans ahead. *It will be possibly two or three days before I return. Then I will launch the great final attack on the farmhouse Twith.*

Mrs. Squidge has read her letter and shares her news. "My younger sister, Frijji—such a sweet child—has written to ask whether she might come for a visit. We are orphans, and there is a close bond between us. How do you feel about that, my dear Griswold? I don't wish to interrupt any of your plans." She realizes that with the departure of King Haymun, there is a guest room vacant, so it should not affect the plans of her earlier most eminent guest. "You are certainly free to leave your things in your room until you return."

Moley, sitting up at the table with them, wriggles uncomfortably. *How is a sweet Beyonder child going to respond to a zebra-striped mix between a duck and an otter? However, I am also a guest and must not raise such an awkward question. It is up to my hostess to sort out such problems.*

The wizard is courteous. He too is a guest utilizing Mrs. Squidge's generous hospitality. "Of course the young lady should come to visit you. Perhaps she wants some romantic advice. With your wide experience of courtship and marriage, who could be better to ask? If she should need a man's viewpoint on romantic affairs, then I am a man of the world with much experience. No doubt I would be able to throw light on her problems."

Mrs. Squidge wriggles uncomfortably in her chair. *I'm not sure it's such a good idea for Frijji to come visit after all. If Griswold showers her with his charms, she might lure him back to Cornwall. I don't want that to happen!*

THE GREEN BUBBLE

The wizard is fond of repeating to himself, "Time is of the essence." He learned this from his father in his early days while learning to crawl. He has never forgotten it, although in his childhood he was unsure of its meaning. He thought it meant something like jam on bread or sauce on chips. Over the years, it has come to mean that occasionally he needs to hurry. Even in a land like Gyminge, where time is a servant and not a master and sometimes a hundred years is like an evening gone, it is necessary to move quickly. This is such a time. He must get to Gyminge without delay.

He makes his visit to Mole Hall and throws everyone there into complete chaos. The fuss will not settle until the last goblins depart later in the day. He is insistent. "There will be a full inspection of troops and barracks before departure. Even the wastepaper baskets must be left empty. Everything must be tidy and in good order for the return when it happens. Is that clear?" He gives the officers their orders. "You will leave as soon as night falls. Be sure your men take their weapons."

This remark does not reassure them. The wizard does not know that there are no weapons left after the failure at the farmhouse.

"Do any of you know how to speak Chinese?" Heads shake back and forth. "Well, that's a pity."

The wizard gives Sergeant Major Agamemnon his special instructions. "On the way across the bog to the waterfall, keep the parsnip lamps on your right. The safe path will be to the left. Leave them in position for your return in a few days' time. On your return, of course, keep the lamps to your left. Is that understood? Be sure your men know or they will all end up in the bog as sludge. You are to ensure there is not a single fighting man left behind on the Brook. You are to be the last man across the bog. Is that clear?"

It is all too clear to the sergeant major. The safety of the entire garrison has just been put on his shoulders. He can only nod and utter a reluctant, "Yes, sir," to the wizard.

After the meeting with his troops, the wizard's next task is to prepare the parsnip lamps inspired by Mrs. Squidge's sandwiches. He uses every parsnip remaining in her pantry. There are a hundred or more, and he cuts four inches off the tip of each one. The flat end of each parsnip tip, after he plants it in the bog, will be painted with English mustard. The wizard will cast a special spell into the mustard so that the parsnip tips will glow yellow in the dark. The heat that causes the parsnips to glow will flow down to the tips so that they will burn the hands of anyone who tries to remove them. The wizard smirks. *The farmhouse has bird spies watching the cottage. If they try to remove the lights I plant in the bog, they will only try it once.*

There are basically two kinds of mustard in the world. French mustard is mild and gentle like a maiden gathering posies of wild flowers in the hedgerows for her sick grandmother. English mustard, on the other hand, is the nearest thing to fire without flames invented by man. It is an inferno hidden and unleashed in an innocent bite of bread and bacon. Sir Francis Drake chose to sail around the world rather than go back home to be kissed by Katie Killigrew, who loved the stuff.

The wizard puts all the parsnip tips, his toothbrush, and a new jar of Mrs. Squidge's English mustard into a plastic shopping bag. He wonders, *How best can I disguise what I am doing from the birds that are sure to be watching from above?* He decides, *It's all too simple.* He tells Rasputin, "Take a turn or two outside to see whether your feathers need a further trim. When you come back, we'll leave for Gyminge."

Rasputin's wings are surprisingly good. They will need no further balancing. While Rasputin flutters and practices, he looks to see who is around.

In the meantime, the wizard warns Mrs. Squidge, "Don't be surprised at what is about to happen. Everything is under control." He stands in the middle of the living room, away from the furniture, and concentrates. Breathing heavily, he folds his arms in front of him. Changing himself into some other creature is relatively easy for him. However, that is not what he is doing. Instead, he is fashioning a bubble around himself, a circular bubble. It is slowly forming, starting at his feet and building up. He has not tried this particular method of hiding before and wonders why he has not. He realizes he doesn't have his hat on and stops the bubble as it reaches his shoulder.

"Mrs. Squidge, would you be good enough to pass me my hat and call Rasputin in? I do thank you so much for your hospitality. I doubt there is a better cook than yourself in the whole of Sellindge. Your buns have been particularly enjoyable." He staunchly declined her offer of her yeast buns, and could barely manage to swallow her moldy sandwiches, so of course his flattering remarks are nothing more than a pack of lies. "Is there anything I can bring you as a gift from Gyminge when I return?" He doesn't wait for an answer. He has no intention of bringing anything for her. "Look after Moley for me, will you? He is going to be our star performer at the Summer Games on the Brook."

Turning to Moley, he says, "Don't neglect to keep practicing your weightlifting, my friend. I shall expect to see a distinct improvement when I return."

The raven returns. "Ah, there you are, Rasputin. Sit on my shoulder, will you?"

The wizard has a final word for Squidgy. "Good-bye, Mrs. Squidge. When you can no longer see us, will you kindly open the door, go outside, and distract attention while we leave? Please make sure your friends on the roof make no fuss and that the SnuggleWump doesn't even stir. We must be on our way. Time is of the essence."

The bubble continues to grow upwards until it is higher than the tip of the wizard's hat. It stops growing and closes over into itself to make a roof. The wizard and the raven are enclosed within a transparent bubble. The wizard does not wish to be seen and identified, so he turns the bubble green. It is the color of a tarpaulin or perhaps the green scum on the face of the bog. *That provides perfect camouflage.* A sneer of approval flits across his face. *The Chinese are up against a different kind of enemy now! They have been fighting apprentices. They are now about to meet the master!*

Mrs. Squidge, losing sight of the wizard and the raven beneath their green canopy, opens the door. She goes out onto the porch, waving her garden rake, which, these days, is replacing her twig broom. That was lost over Paris the night of the farmhouse attack. *I'll ask Frijji to bring a replacement broom if I decide to let her come up from Cornwall.* She waves the rake at the rabbits who scamper away from her carrot tops into their burrows. The burrows have been rebuilt into a completely new network once the extensions to the cottage by Weasel and Mink, contractors, were completed. Unknown to Mrs. Squidge and the wizard, they now completely encircle the cottage and provide the rabbits with improved spying positions.

The green bubble moves outside onto the porch and down the steps. The rabbits do not see the bubble, but Tuwhit and Sparky almost fall off their branches with surprise. For several days, things have been quiet at the cottage, and the birds have even been wondering whether the wizard had gone back to Gyminge by sneaking out in some way without their seeing him. Then this morning, Rasputin arrived, and he was walking, not flying. The pair of watchers couldn't fathom what happened to him. As far as they know, their Twith friends have not been in action against the raven since he fled to Gyminge during the battle at the farmhouse.

Sparky remains to continue the watch at the cottage. Tuwhit follows the green bubble up the path towards the croc' pond. *The wizard is surely up to something, but what?*

LIGHTS ON THE BOG

From within the bubble, there is no difficulty seeing outside. The wizard carries the bag with the parsnip tips. As they walk from the cottage towards the pond at the edge of the bog, Rasputin shares further news from Gyminge.

"When the Twith rescued your captive, gran'ma, they sank every pontoon in the bridge by slashing great holes in each one. Without instructions from you for guidance, no attempt was made by the goblins at the castle to salvage the pontoon bridge. Instead, Corporal Pimples designed a new type himself. It is a double drawbridge in which half the span can be lowered from the landward side and the other half from the castle side. The men are working flat-out, but there hasn't been much progress so far. It still is no further than the mainland guardhouse."

The wizard ponders what the raven has just told him. "I'm not sure that I want possible enemies to be able to raise or lower one half of the bridge while I only have control over the other half. But I can see advantages also. In the present situation, where the Chinese hold the castle while I am limited to the mainland, it could prevent them from sallying forth on raids to pillage and destroy the countryside." This is a borrowed phrase he heard from others. "I don't know how pillage—which I guess is the process of making, selling, and eating pills—gets involved in the fighting between myself and the Chinese invaders. I'll ask Dr. Tyfuss to explain the process. Or I can look it up in the dictionary when I get home."

While the pair talks, they reach the north side of the croc' pond. The wizard, looking around to see whether they are observed, spots the barn owl parked on a lower limb of the tree where the eagle nests. He smiles to himself. "Look, Rasputin. See that owl up there? We can see him, but he can't see us. He has no idea what's going on. Let's give him something to see, shall we?" Crossing his arms again, the wizard concentrates. As he does, the bubble expands in length to six paces.

Tuwhit cannot believe his eyes. *What on earth is going on? What made the bubble expand like that?*

Griswold lifts Rasputin off his shoulder and sets him down on the bog, "As we cross the bog, Rasputin, you follow a step or two behind me. I want you to use this toothbrush and paint the top of each parsnip tip with a good plaster of English mustard. You must be careful not to run out of mustard, but we don't want any left over when the last of the parsnip tips is planted in the bog. Just enough, neither more nor less, must go on each parsnip."

This is where the wizard's genius becomes apparent. Ever since he was a boy, he has counted things. It began with counting how many steps from home to the shops and to school, how many broken paving slabs, how many curbstones to the corner, how many stairs up to bed, how many pencils in the jar, how many chocolates in the box. As he grew, he continued counting. Even while talking to his friends, he would be counting lamp posts, or panes of glass in windows, or the spots on a Dalmatian dog. All the while, he was storing the information in his head.

Less than a fortnight ago, he went ahead of gran'ma across the bog. It took four hundred and eighty six paces, neither more nor less. He has one hundred and seven parsnip tips, which his mind counted automatically as he cut them. That means almost exactly four and a half paces between each parsnip lamp with none at either end.

The wizard will pace the correct spacing distance for the parsnip lamps across the bog and plant them along the right-hand side of the toad trail. The raven will paint the tops.

Suddenly, there is a snag! The mustard lid is tight. It was obviously never intended by the suppliers to be opened. They do this deliberately with all sorts of things, although jam and pickles are the favorites. Mustard isn't far behind. The wizard fails to open the lid, although he tries many times. Each time, his hand slips, and it gets red and sore. He considers whether he needs to change himself into the strongest man in the world in order to open it. He tries one last time. The lid at last gives and opens with a *Blurp*! The wizard decides, *Once I am resettled in Gyminge, I will turn my gifts to designing a mustard jar lid that can be opened by anyone who is only normally healthy and will not require special training.*

Now that the jar is open, the wizard casts the spell to make the mustard glow brightly. With a start, he realizes that he will have to hold it to avoid having it spill. Ravens are not particularly well adapted by nature to walk on a bog while holding a jar of mustard and painting the top of a parsnip tip with a toothbrush all at the same time. In fact, it is impossible, and it is surprising the wizard did not think of it sooner. It would help if birds had arms. The wizard might have done well to bring Moley along to help. With his additional pair of webbed feet and bodybuilding physique, he might have been designer made for this particular task, especially if he also had a pouch like a kangaroo to hold the jar in.

The wizard decides that at every twenty-seven parsnips, he will check that exactly one quarter of the bottle of mustard has been used each time. He looks at the bottle and mentally divides its contents not into four parts but into eight parts descending down the bottle. This way he can have a further spot check that the right quantity of mustard is being used every thirteen and a half parsnips.

Off they start. A rhythm soon develops. The wizard knows the way; he's been this way before. He is also able to pick up a faint whiff of toad smell, although the mustard also smells. The path leads on towards the center of the bog and then veers right to go northeast towards Blindhouse Wood in the distance. In his right hand he holds one of the two handles of the plastic bag. In that same palm, he carries the open jar of mustard. The lid is in his pocket. His left hand dives into his bag, removes a parsnip tip, and every four and a half paces, the tip is stuck into the right-hand side of the trail. Every second parsnip tip goes next to his right foot, exactly nine paces apart.

The wizard then holds back the mustard jar to the bird, high enough to keep the bottom of the plastic bag of parsnip tips from getting wet. This means that Rasputin has to stretch high to get the toothbrush into the jar, and he splatters the mustard over the trouser legs and shoes in front of him as he pulls the brush out of the jar. As the wizard becomes more and more covered with mustard, the smell increases. He realizes a problem is developing, which is not only that his trousers are turning yellow and beginning to smolder. The mustard will never last as far as the waterfall, and the goblins will end up in the middle of the bog without lamps for the last quarter of their journey. There will most assuredly be panic and chaos for the goblins if that should happen!

His brilliant mind recognizes the problem and deals with it promptly. Instead of holding one handle of the plastic bag, he buttons up his coat and hangs the handle of the bag on a high button. He realizes, *It would be even easier for Rasputin if I walk backwards across the bog. But if I do so, one of three things is likely to happen that will mess up progress. My nose and my eyes happen to be fixed to the front of my face, not to the back. It is possible I will lose my way and end up sinking in the bog. Another danger is that by walking backwards, I could trip and fall and spill the mustard. Or the length of my pace will change because I will take shorter steps walking backwards than forwards. And that would mean that once again, the goblins will be left in the middle of the bog without a light. I'll just continue forward and turn around each time I plant a parsnip.*

The speed of progress slows. At each parsnip light, the wizard stops, turns, and leans down with the jar. Rasputin stands on one leg, which begins to sink a little into the bog. He dips onto the toothbrush just enough mustard to paint the parsnip. All surplus mustard he shakes back into the jar. After painting, he holds the toothbrush in his beak until it is needed again and hops after the wizard, who waits exactly four and a half paces ahead.

Overhead, Tuwhit occasionally swings back and forth over the bubble. He observes the stop-go-stop movement of the green bubble beneath him that leaves a string of little yellow discs precisely four and a half Beyonder paces apart. He decides that when the bubble has finished its journey and there is nothing more to report, he will carry one of the little discs back to Jock at the farmhouse.

The journey takes longer than the wizard expected. His trousers are spattered with yellow. So is Rasputin. The mustard is only just going to last out, and he has to be very careful. His parsnip tips are lasting better. There will be enough to see them to the end of the journey across the bog and still leave one left over.

Ahead at last is the waterfall. The last parsnip tip is placed in the bog as the splashing of the waterfall hits the bubble. The wizard retrieves his toothbrush, paints the remaining parsnip tip, removes the heat spell from it, replaces it in the plastic bag, rinses the toothbrush and puts it into his pocket. The jar of mustard is rinsed out into the pool. The pool itself will now shine as a guide to the goblins later.

The wizard steps through the Gyminge curtain onto the stone platform to the left of the waterfall. There is the shock of a change of size, but he expects it. Rasputin follows. The same shock hits the bird. He doesn't like this size-changing, but he is glad to be shrunk back to his regular size again. It is more comfortable. He doesn't like the enlargements that are necessary whenever he goes into the Beyond. The bubble vanishes as soon as it is no longer needed.

Tuwhit can no longer see the bubble and nothing of whomever or whatever might have been under the bubble, moving it along. Taking flight, he glides down to the bog and plucks a parsnip tip with his claws. His claws start to burn with fire, and he flies hotfooted for the farmhouse.

All is quiet on the bog once more.

Smoldering Hair

The wizard has thought ahead. It is a gift that has stood him in good stead time and time again. It is one of his mottos. He uses it in his lectures on leadership to the goblin officers. "Think ahead! A leader must always be one move ahead of his enemies. Otherwise, he does not survive and ends up peeling potatoes and onions in the enemy cookhouse. Onions are worse than potatoes." In this present instance, his thinking ahead means that he saved one of the parsnip lamps to light his way through the cave-tunnel.

Rasputin remembers his difficult experience at this location earlier in the day. *I am not anxious to return the way that I came, but I have no choice. My master is trying to help me by providing a light.*

The light under the overhanging foliage is shaded and half dark, a kind of twilight. The wizard smiles. *This will provide a good test for the lamp.* He removes the remaining parsnip from the bag. Thinking ahead again, he had temporarily reversed the heat spell so that it wouldn't burn the bag. Now he uses a special spell to make it glow brighter than before by focusing all the heat into the light so none flows down to the tip. It is as though there is a light bulb within the parsnip powered by a strong battery. The yellow light is like a sunflower caught in sunshine. It is a brilliant success. *Superb, Griswold, superb!* He puts his hand a little above the glowing light, and can feel heat rising up from the top. In fact, it is hot enough that he jerks his hand up away from it.

Griswold crumples the plastic bag into a ball and briefly wonders whether he should just toss it away. *No. I better not. I punished one of my soldiers for littering up the countryside. I made him eat a plastic bag in front of all his friends after he had thrown it away on the Brook. Keep the countryside clean, that's my motto!* He stuffs the bag into his pocket.

He pauses a moment at the entrance to the cave-tunnel and turns to look back down at the curtain beyond the waterfall. *Now that I am through, I don't want any other Beyonders blundering into Gyminge as they explore the bog for plants. Marsh orchids might be rare and fascinating, but I don't want collectors barging into my country.* He recites his curtain spell so that the opening in front of the waterfall will close. He knows that because of the toads, he cannot close it completely, but anything bigger than a toad is not going to get through. *The toads will be dealt with at the other end if the new colonel, Dr. Tyfuss, has done his job properly and the passport gates are in place.*

Rasputin follows the wizard into the cave-tunnel. In the far distance, the opening shows as a small, round, white light.

"Come along, Rasputin. It's good to be home. Can't you smell the air? Keep close to me, my boy. There are some low spots in the roof."

As they walk, he thinks to himself, *Because time is of the essence, I need to travel fast. I will change into uhhh...what? A bat is definitely out. It will have to be a bird of some sort though.* He likes to use different bird disguises. *A swallow is good for speed. If I needed carrying capacity, a vulture would be best. For endurance, I would choose a Canada goose. Hummingbirds are pretty little creatures and packed full with energy.* They appeal to his enjoyment of beauty. He saw them when he was in Central City in Colorado. *A hummingbird is small enough and fast enough not to be seen if a Chinaman should blink his eye.*

The thought of a Chinaman, not one Chinaman but hundreds of Chinamen, makes up his mind for him. *Chinese fishermen use cormorants for fishing. I will be a cormorant although I will dispense with the ring around its neck that keeps it from swallowing fish. Quite possibly cormorants, because of their long association with Chinese fishermen, will have acquired some fluency in the language. Perhaps*

200

not speaking it but possibly understanding it. Some knowledge of the language could prove very useful. He smiles one of his twisted smiles to himself.

Turning to Rasputin, he says, "Here are the instructions I want you to give to Colonel Tyfuss for me. Tell him that work on the defense fort is to be suspended. His troops will lead the counterattack. He is to send all of them at battle readiness to the castle within an hour of receiving these orders. They are to march through the night. To get there, they will need to fight in the fields, in the towns, and in the streets. They must fight even on the beaches." There are no beaches in Gyminge; the country is landlocked. The wizard is getting carried away by his own words.

Just now, he feels unappreciated. *I wish there were a larger audience than one single raven. What I'm saying is almost poetry, and it is being wasted on a bird that has never read anything more elevating than the comic strips in the Sunday newspaper. I can imagine the Duke of Wellington, or even the Emperor Octavius facing Attila the Hun, or Hannibal crossing the Alps making such a rallying call to his men.* With an effort, he pulls himself back to reality.

"Alert Colonel Tyfuss that the Brook goblins are on their way. He is to organize them into squads before they head for the castle. He will know when the last goblin from the Brook is through because Sergeant Major Agamemnon is going last. Be sure to let him know that. Before moving them on, he is to feed them. The goblins have already received their instructions and will need no further instructions from the colonel, only food and drink. The colonel alone shall remain where he is. If there are severe casualties, we will send for him. Is that all clearly understood, Rasputin? As soon as you finish delivering my message, hightail it for the castle.

"I will go on ahead. I have decided to be a cormorant so that the Chinese will not be suspicious when I arrive. I will reconnoiter among them before resuming my identity as the Wizard of Wozzle, commander-in-chief. Then I will contact my troops. By the time you arrive, I will probably be leading the castle garrison in the defense of their positions. We will hold on to every foot of ground against the surging mass of humanity attacking from several directions. We will never surrender!" The wizard feels another speech coming on and fights back the temptation. He will save that one for the officers when they arrive.

They make good progress passing through the tunnel. The sloping roof knocks his hat off so the wizard carries it in one hand while holding the parsnip lamp in the other. He tries to give some light to the raven following him. He is not concentrating on what he is doing. Instead, he allows his mind to focus on the question of dealing with invisible Chinese swordsmen soon to be coming at him. *How will I cope with invisible men? No problem. I will place one of my curtains a yard or so in front of my troops. Every time the curtain bulges as a Mongolian runs into it from the other side, my men will whack the bulge with a brick or a bludgeon. I must warn them to hold on tight to their brick, otherwise it is liable to bounce back and whack them instead.*

"Ouch!" Just as Haymun had done previously, the wizard whacks his head on the roof of the tunnel, and a trickle of blood begins to work its way down his face. He groans and leans against the side of the tunnel. He wasn't paying attention to where he was going, and now he is not paying attention to the parsnip lamp. It is in the same hand he raises to feel the bump on his head. Horse hair is probably more flammable than human hair, which is why horses become frantic when their stable catches on fire. Even so, they hardly become more frantic than the wizard when his grey-white, long hair begins to smolder as it touches the hot mustard on the lamp.

There is always a pleasant breeze with a slight hyacinth smell blowing through the toad tunnel towards the Brook. This creates a draft and increases the smoldering of the wizard's hair. The smell changes rapidly from hyacinths to a bonfire on Guy Fawkes night in England, or one on Midsummer's Eve in Estonia, or the residue from a Fourth of July celebration in America. The wizard beats frantically at his shoulder, where the smoldering is most active.

Rasputin caws because he doesn't know what else to do.

THE WIZARD'S BUMP

The wizard never loses his presence of mind. Well, maybe not never, but at least only for a moment or two. He knows that in the absence of water, he needs to smother the fire. If he had a wet blanket, that would be best of all. He doesn't have a wet blanket or even a dry one. Anyway, a dry one might burn. His only option is to try his hat, especially since it is his hair that is alight.

The ceiling of the cave is not high enough for the wizard to get his hat on. He kneels, grabs the brim, and pulls the entire hat down over his head, including his eyes. Unfortunately, his hair is longer than his hat can reach. Because the hat is down over his eyes, he can't see where he is going. Even worse, it is jammed on so tight that it won't come off. The bump on his head is above the brim and continues to grow. His hat is well made, strong and durable. The brim has never, throughout its long existence, been stretched with such force. It reaches the end of its stretching and becomes like a band of steel stretched around the trunk of a young oak tree ten years ago. The wizard fails to pull the hat off. He also fails to stamp out the smoldering hair below the brim. That hair now begins to burn the back of his neck.

The lesson here for youngsters is that a boy's hair is intended to be cut short, both back and sides. If the wizard had kept to this simple rule, he might still have burned his scalp, but eventually, the hat would have successfully controlled the burning.

I'm not having any success. I need some other solution. He stretches out on the floor of the tunnel. "Rasputin, my lad, tug at the peak of my hat. See if you can pull it off, or at least tear it so I can then see through the top of it." It is all in vain. There is only one recourse left. Because the wizard's ears are large and lower than his eyes, there is still a way forward for him. He can still hear.

Rasputin picks up the parsnip lamp. To leave it in the tunnel might well turn the whole place into an inferno. Crying, "Follow me, sir," he hops towards the exit. He caws constantly. The wizard, reeling and bumping along the wall, tries to follow the sound ahead of him. He could do with two pairs of hands. He keeps tugging at his hat to get it off while smacking the back of his neck where the hair smolders. At the same time he tries to protect his face from collision with both sides of the wall as he totters along towards the daylight.

Rasputin leads him straight from the cave-tunnel to the stream where King Haymun rested such a short while before. The wizard trips as he reaches it, and his head goes under as he falls forward. Steam rises from the water. Dampening a hat, as any man caught in a monsoon knows, shrinks the brim considerably.

It is at the stream that Colonel Tyfuss finds them. He pulls the hapless wizard from the pool and hurries back to his tent for scissors. Returning, he snips away at the rapidly shrinking hat band squeezing the wizards head. In trying to relieve the intense pressure, he has to be careful to avoid the immense bump still enlarging on the wizard's head. Once the hat is removed, it allows the bump to increase further in size.

The stretcher squad rolls the dazed magician onto their stretcher. Unfortunately, the four men are of uneven height. Three of them are short. The fourth, ironically nicknamed Shorty, is approximately half as tall again as any of the other three, and is stronger than all of them combined. Shorty is a professional weightlifter. While others sleep, he practices lifting weights and doing pushups. The stretcher crew runs at the double. Dr. Tyfuss races ahead to get the surgery ready and is not able to look back, lest he himself go head over heels. If he had looked back, he would see an uneven contest among the stretcher carriers. Shorty is the left-hand front man. It would have been better if he were in the rear, where he could at least see what is happening. As it is, the left-hand rear man has to hold his handle at neck level to avoid being lifted off the ground by Shorty. The two men on the right, according to rules and training, carry their side at standard Red Cross / St John's Brigade height.

As he runs, Dr. Tyfuss thinks about doing emergency surgery. *This is a crisis! I'll have to turn my own tent into a field hospital. I can see in my mind's eye the hordes of medical consultants that wish to view the results of my surgical skills. As the patient turns his head, they will sneak envious glances at the skin graft on the back of his head. A graft stitched like a skilled seamstress, a perfect circle the size of a cup or a saucer, depending on what is handy to guide me when I reach for my surgical knife. Even a grandmother with 20/20 eyesight could not improve on my stitching. There is some benefit*, the doctor acknowledges silently to himself, *to having a mother who treated her son as a girl when he was growing up and made him do embroidery.* This is a secret that he carefully guards.

What knives do I have? It is a pity I don't have the one I was planning to use on King Haymun. That was an ideal size. Dr. Tyfuss knows virtually nothing about medicine and nothing at all about surgery. His doctorate is only on the lifestyle and habits of the woodlouse, and not in medicine, but he doesn't let that stop him. He has learned a good deal since he was appointed in error as the king's physician. He dispenses what he doesn't know with flair. He can make confident choices for patients based not upon the ingredients of medicines but the shape and size of pills and how they match the shape and size of the patient. Wherever possible, he chooses the color and taste of medicines to match the patient's hair and eyes and clothing. He has many patients who would have gotten better even without his help. They are the ones who swear by him and the medicines he prescribes.

The wizard hangs on desperately to the slanted stretcher. It is hopeless. Shorty, with his longer legs, races ahead of the other men. The man behind Shorty falls, and the wizard falls sideways, at high speed, off the stretcher to the right. It takes three falls before the wizard finally chooses to walk. He wisely decides, *I will consider my bump as a wound sustained in the heat of battle. I will leave it untended and untreated.* He ignores the doctor's advice to the contrary. "No, my good man. I must be on my way. I cannot afford any delay. Courage and noble cause must override pain!" Silently, he screams, *Owee!*

THE BORDER DEFENSE FORT

The wizard stiffens his upper lip and questions his area commander. "What signs of the Chinese invaders have you observed, Dr. Tyfuss? Was their entry through the toad tunnel?"

Vyruss shakes his head. "Rasputin told me they captured King Haymun, but they didn't get in this way. I haven't seen any Chinese at all. I know that all men from the Far East wear flip-flops. They have pigtails and long, trailing mustaches. Their women wear kimonos and have tiny feet. There are probably few women among the invading force though. But army boots would disguise the size of their feet. I'm sure I would have recognized any Chinese at once if they had come by here.

"I was surprised to hear about King Haymun. The last I saw of him, he was firmly in control of events at Goblin Castle. My troops have been fully engaged on their construction duties. I'm not allowing anything to deflect them from their task."

The wizard's eye twitches furiously. "Your orders are changed. All your forces, with the exception of yourself and the cooks, are posted back to Goblin Castle immediately. All the construction troops need to move out at battle readiness within an hour. Tell them to expect a forced march clear through the night. If necessary, they must fight their way through to Blindhouse Wood and beyond. They will fight in the fields and in the villages, in the forests and in the pastures. If there are severe casualties, I will send for you, but not until you are needed. Meanwhile, you, my good doctor, will remain responsible for defending the border to the last man."

Dr. Tyfuss is good at simple arithmetic. He shudders. *That means I have to defend the border with no troops and only two cooks to help me! That's suicide! I'm not sure I like the idea.*

The wizard continues his instructions to the Commander of the Southern Zone. "The Brook goblins are coming as soon as it is dark enough for them to cross the bog unseen. I don't want the enemy at the farmhouse to know that my strike force of troops is leaving the Brook. An army marches on its stomach and the troops will need to be fed. You and the camp cooks shall see to that. There will be seven hundred and fifty men arriving. As soon as the men have eaten, they must move out. So there will be no mistake, the last man to arrive will be Sergeant Major Agamemnon. He already has his orders and will need no further instructions from you. As soon as he leaves for the castle, the cooks too shall leave for the castle.

"There is one further order. Before the last squad of goblins, the cooks, and the sergeant major leave, they are to block the end of the cave-tunnel with rocks for a length of four full paces into the tunnel. Don't give a thought to the toads. Even if they think they have a right to pass through, this is a crisis. A crisis needs crisis measures. Gyminge has been invaded, and Gyminge will strike back. All access to the kingdom is closed indefinitely. Should the troops need to return to the Brook at some later time by way of the cave-tunnel, they can remove the obstruction at that time. But for now, Gyminge will be sealed off from the Beyond. If I, the commander-in-chief, wish to get rid of the Chinese, I will lift the curtain to let them go. No problem there. Meanwhile, no one, absolutely no one, is going to enter or leave Gyminge until the Chinese have been dealt with using all the powers at my command.

"Is that all clearly understood, Dr. Tyfuss?"

"Yes, sir!" Although his answer is affirmative, he is not at all happy with the situation. *I will not be sorry to see the wizard go. Some people create ripples. When the wizard visits, the dam breaks.*

The colonel blows his whistle. The sergeant and corporal appear and stand at attention. The colonel is aware that the wizard is listening, but he has learned to give instructions crisply. He snaps out a few sharp commands. "Have your men parade in battle dress and boots in five minutes! They are to be armed for hand-to-hand combat. That means swords, daggers, and dirks, not just bows and arrows. Be sharp about it! This includes the men in sick bay. Issue weapons to the cooks also."

Vyruss knows that neither man understands what he is supposed to do, but as good officers, they pretend to know at once, and disappear, running. They'll be back later to check once the wizard and the raven disappear.

"Sir, would you like the cooks to prepare a snack for you before you leave? Or they could make sandwiches to take with you."

"No. We must be on our way without delay. Get busy preparing the food for the troops from the Brook. Time is of the essence."

The sun is already slipping below the horizon.

The wizard admits to Rasputin, "The invasion of Gyminge by hordes of Chinese seems to have no connection at this time with the seven escaped Twith. It's much more likely to be illegal immigrants who want to take advantage of the social security system I have established for the good of my people. I can see an epidemic of yellow fever, and that would be a whole new and possibly more serious crisis. I need to rid Gyminge of these invaders without delay."

He scowls with disgust. "This is deflecting me from my main goal of getting my hands on the Book of Lore. I am convinced that it is hidden somewhere in the farmhouse at Gibbins Brook Farm. It's sure to contain the solution for the Magician's Twitch I'm plagued with. If I can't get it from the house, I'll need to trick the Twith into bringing it out into the open. Then it will be easier to gain possession of it.

"You know, Rasputin, I was about to launch a daring and ambitious scheme for the Summer Games on the Brook. Your unexpected arrival, my loyal and faithful friend, interrupted my train of thought. Your news of the Chinese invasion means that my attempt to take the Book of Lore must be delayed. So be it. Immediate action is called for. Leaders respond wisely and readily to circumstances they cannot control. I can do that as well as create circumstances in which my plans thrive. The crest of the wave is not the only place a leader can swim!" He smiles with satisfaction at his own intelligence.

The wizard tries to remember what a cormorant looks like and fixes that picture into his mind. Rasputin watches as the wizard vanishes. In his place appears a strange, gooselike, glossy white-and-green-and-black water bird. Its thick bill is long, straight, and hooked viciously at the end. His webbed feet are on strong, short legs. It is equipped for both land and water. This bird is twice the size of the raven and looks to be a strong, powerful fighter.

Rasputin thinks, *This bird would be too big for me to tackle. I'm glad we're on the same side.* The raven has never seen a cormorant before and is not altogether sorry.

The bird has an unusually large bump on the back of its head, but it is the twitchy right eye that clearly identifies it as the wizard. The voice is gruff, almost a croak. "Let's be on our way, Rasputin." The bigger bird suits the action to his words, lumbers into the air, and beats down with his wings as hard and as fast as he can.

Rasputin, quicker into the air and more accustomed to wings, rises with him.

They head north to Goblin Castle and the horde of invisible Chinese.

THE FOREST

Scayper leads Bimbo and Bollin north from the Black Forest. Behind him, seventeen horses trot without attempting to pull away from the ropes he holds lightly in his hand. Count Fyrdwald's castle is well behind, and there is no sign of any pursuit. He searches for a hard, solid section of the forest track where the departure of three horses will not show hoof prints. At last, he finds something that will do just as well. A small tributary stream flows into the main river that runs into the castle lake. It crosses the track in a shallow cobblestone ford. He reins in, dismounts, and hands the reins of his horse and the seventeen others to Bimbo to hold.

"I want to go investigate the area to the east." He doesn't need to go far and is soon back. "Wait here for me. I'll be back in a few moments. I'm going to take the extra horses and release them into the forest."

He leaps into the saddle of one of the recent cavalry horses, clicks his tongue, digs his heels into the horse, and splashes through the ford followed by the loosely roped riderless horses. The stream makes a bend, and Scayper is soon out of sight.

A few moments pass before he is back on foot, carrying the two coils of rope. Bimbo leads Scayper's horse into the water, and Scayper mounts it from his side of the ford without getting his feet wet. "There was someone in the distance coming along the main track, walking, a long way away. Just one man. Probably a farmer. I've sent all the horses off one by one on a side track to the east. He'll not see them at all, though he will see their tracks and probably wonder what the goblin cavalry is doing in this area. We'll go down the bed of this stream. Follow me. We'll stay in the water as long as we can. We should be able to make good time now."

Scayper knows the area well and recognizes landmarks, although it is not clear whether he knows this particular small stream. They ride west beneath green overhanging arches and duck to avoid twigs and branches.

Haymun is sore from being so long in the saddle or, rather, being perched on part of a saddle. *I wish they had thought to allow me to ride on one of the horses they just released. Somehow, I don't think any one of the three would take kindly to the suggestion. These three are as tough as chewing leather with little difference between them.*

They reach the river that flows on down into the lake at Goblin Castle and then farther on to become Gibbins Brook once it is through the waterfall. The water is up to the knees of the horses. They travel downstream, heading south, until Scayper observes a track on the right bank. The river swings towards the east to the castle lake. Occasionally, in the distance, it is possible to glimpse, through the trees, the shimmering surface of lake water and, across it, the castle they left earlier. They have gone in a great semi-circular anti-clockwise arc to mislead the wizard. Scayper tells the boys, "It's time now to break away from the river and head southwest towards Blindhouse Wood."

An amazing change has come over Scayper. Little more than twelve hours ago, the two boys met him for the first time in the dungeon of the castle. He was a shackled, hairy bundle of a man— quiet and reserved, almost withdrawn—paying the punishment for trying to escape from the Wizard of Wozzle. Now he is alert, clear in his mind, sharp in his responses, a leader in his actions, and knowledgeable about the country they pass through. He is pleased the goblin king is captive with them. The fire in his belly from the Tabasco-laced rice has quieted down to a warm glow fit to toast marshmallows. He is willing to risk everything for these two young boys beside him. He believes that through them may come the deliverance of the kingdom and all the captives in the dungeon can be released. Thoughts, long dormant, rise once more within him. He turns to ask Bimbo a question.

Before he has a chance to ask, Bollin has his own question for the man slumped in front of him. "The wizard needs the raven to run his errands. Why is Rasputin here in Gyminge while the wizard is over on the Brook?"

Haymun has no useful lies to benefit his answer. "The wizard doesn't know that Rasputin is here. He thinks he was lost in the fighting at the farmhouse when Rasputin had charge of the teros who were supposed to break the kitchen window. When the bird didn't return, the wizard decided to close all the holes through the curtain to protect Gyminge. It meant that Rasputin wasn't able to get back to the Brook."

The king is glad for the opportunity to speak and volunteers more information. "The wizard can't close the toad tunnel, so he is implementing controls in order to check everyone who passes through. That is what Colonel Tyfuss is engaged in. All the Gyminge troops that could be spared are down there working on it."

Bollin has another question. "What is the wizard planning to do now? Why hasn't he come back earlier to take care of things in Gyminge? Things are in a bad way for the wizard here."

"I don't know, but I'm sure he is plotting something or other on the Brook. He keeps his ideas to himself. He hinted there will be one last attack on the Twith that cannot possibly fail. I don't know what it is. All I know is that the wizard plans to return to Gyminge on Sunday to inspect the fort Colonel Tyfuss is building. He will check on things at the castle then, I'm sure."

Scayper has a personal question. "How are we going to get over the border onto the Brook with so many of the wizard's forces at the border?"

Bimbo responds to Scayper's question. "I don't know, but I'm sure we will find a way. We might have to wait until after nightfall." He is conscious that the goblin king is listening to and remembering their conversation and will share it with the wizard as soon as he has an opportunity to do so.

Haymun asks, "What do you plan to do to me?"

Bimbo speaks openly. "You have been an evil enemy of your own people. You were once a trusted Twith seer. You betrayed them for your own benefit. You have not hesitated to oppress them. You saw them changed into goblins, these lovely people who once were free. You did that in order to gain power for yourself. Then you abused them as soldiers in your army. You are the one that the wizard relies on to maintain his power over your people. You will one day answer to them, and I fear there is little hope for you.

"My brother and I are not your judges, and we do not desire to be your judges. We shall not harm you unless you try to escape or do mischief. We might even release you when we know you are unable to prevent us reaching the Brook. We do not want you. However, our friend Scayper has suffered under you for hundreds of years. There are surely others like him that you have treated brutally and without concern. He for certain sees things differently than we do. We shall ask his advice about what to do with you when the time comes for a decision."

They make good progress riding along a narrow but well-worn trail bearing south. They are on the west side of the river, and probably by now, they have passed from the Dark Forest to the northern fringes of Blindhouse Wood. They intend to continue until they are through the trees. Then they will rest until nightfall so that a patrolling Rasputin will not see them. One of them will stay awake, guarding the king. The other two will sleep.

Scayper turns in the saddle with a question. "Bollin, in the dungeon, you mentioned someone called…" He does not have time to complete his question. Ahead of them along the path, a tree creaks and begins to fall. An arrow whistles through the air and sticks into a tree trunk just ahead of him, and then another. He reins up sharply, and so also do his two companions behind him.

A voice, harsh and grating, calls out, "Drop your reins. Put your hands high in the air. Do not move. We are more than you, and each of you is the target of one of our arrows. One false move and we fire!"

THE ROBBER GANG

Out from behind an oak tree in front of Scayper steps a man dressed in rough green-and-brown clothing. He holds a raised bow with an arrow at the string, aimed at Scayper's body. Another man, heavily bearded, large and powerfully built, steps through the undergrowth. He looks as strong as an ox and is the one who pushed over the tree that he previously almost cut through. He carries an axe in his hand with a bow slung over his back and a quiver of arrows at his side.

Scayper, taken by total surprise, drops his reins and begins to raise his arms.

At the rear, Bimbo realizes what is happening ahead. He jams his heels into the sides of his horse, pulls on his left rein, and yells, "Do your worst!"

The horse half rears, swings, and turns in its tracks. It bounds towards a similarly dressed man now standing on the forest path. After the three horses went by, he stepped out from the trees armed with a loaded bow to cut off their retreat. He fires at Bimbo. The boy catches the arrow on the king's shield he carries on his forearm. The archer, without time to reload, dives into the bushes to avoid the horse coming at him. Arrows whistle after Bimbo crouched low and urging the galloping horse to greater speed. One hits the saddle beneath Bimbo. The horse neighs with fright and fear, bucks once, and then continues its wild gallop.

This diversion is enough for Scayper. The man ahead of him has fired his arrow at Bimbo and is reloading. Scayper drives his heels in. The man accosting him dives for his life. The axeman beside swings his axe in vain before also diving. The great horse clears the fallen tree with ease and is into a wild charge with her rider bending low into her body. She gallops along the path with great racing strides until, around several bends, Scayper, looking back and seeing no pursuit, reins her slowly in and pats her shoulder.

There is no time to waste. He is not going to abandon the other two boys. He reaches down and slides out Bollin's broadsword he has tucked into his saddle.

"Right, Black Beauty. Let's get back over to the tree again, and then we'll see what needs to be done. If they want a fight, they are going to get one." He wheels the horse around and digs his heels into the horse's sides, urging the horse to racing speed with his knees and his body. "Go, Beauty! Go!"

The horse gathers speed.

Scayper screams the Twith war cry. Around the bend is the fallen tree. "Up, up. Up, Beauty! Up!"

The horse soars. The jump is clean.

There is no one on the path. *Where are they? What's happened? The robbers*—for that is what Scayper guesses they are—*must have taken the captives back along the path we already traveled.*

Scayper continues the gallop. He is now a long way back up the path with no sign of a fork from the path that the robbers could have taken. Suddenly, from the left-hand side of the path just ahead, he hears a shrill whistle. He pulls his horse to a halt and looks around. *I didn't imagine it. That was a whistle.* There is movement in the bushes. Someone is pushing through. He raises his sword and then lowers it. It is Bimbo!

"My horse is tethered over here. Come on through. It's well hidden, and there is a small clearing. What's happened?"

As the two share their experiences, it is clear there was no way Bollin's horse could have jumped the tree with two riders on its back in an attempt to follow Scayper. The robbers have obviously taken Bollin and King Haymun captive and have quickly disappeared into the woods with them. The king, easily recognizable by his crown, is a huge prize for them.

Bimbo has removed the arrow from the horse's saddle. Fortunately, it is not tipped with metal or stone and has only a pointed tip. Scayper checks the horse. There is only a minor skin wound that should heal naturally.

Bimbo is concerned about his brother. "We must start a search for them at the tree. It will be too dangerous for us to search on horseback. The horses will attract attention."

Scayper still has Corporal Pimple's ropes. Each horse is tethered with a long line to the oak tree on one side of the clearing. He does this with one of the ropes. There is good, thick grazing in the clearing, so the horses should be alright for some while without further attention. He will take the other rope with him.

Bimbo holds up the Royal Shield and the Royal Sword. "Should I hide these for safety? I have to be certain they get taken back to the Brook. But that would only give us the small broadsword and the dirk for weapons."

Scayper tells him, "I have been trained in swordsmanship. My brother and I were two of the best swordsmen north of the forest."

"Okay. You take the king's sword and shield as well. And keep your dirk. Give me the small broadsword."

As they walk back along the path towards the fallen tree, they say little. They look for hoof prints other than the ones their own horses made but don't see evidence of any at all. It is eerily quiet for a midsummer day in the forest. There is absolutely no birdsong. They move more slowly as soon as the fallen tree comes into sight. Each is on one side of the track, looking for hoof prints. If they should find any they do not recognize, it means that by now, the robbers could be far away. Occasionally, in soft spots on the track, they see a fresh footprint. Scayper finds an arrow and picks it up and studies it. "This fletching is made from chicken feathers."

They look now for the hoof prints of Bollin's horse.

"They were probably forced to dismount and walk, unless the state of King Haymun's feet brought forth an act of kindness and he was allowed to ride. If the robbers are on foot, it is unlikely their camp will be far away."

Scayper spots the hoof prints first. Only hoof prints of one horse lead from the fallen tree due west. Sunlight and shadow through the tree trunks give them their direction. There are still four or five hours of daylight left.

Bimbo is worried. "The robbers will be pleased with their capture of the king and with thoughts of a high ransom. They will not value Bollin as highly. They might feel he has no value as a captive because it will become clear to them he is a foreigner. They might well expect us to regroup and follow tracks, so we need to be careful. There could well be guards and archers with arrows at the ready lurking in hiding ahead. We must be quiet and stay alert."

Scayper, with the king's shield to guard him, will go first, and Bimbo will follow about ten paces behind. Every so often, when the growth is clear, Scayper waits until Bimbo catches up and they discuss the next step.

They have been walking steadily for some time. Suddenly, Scayper spots something on the ground ahead. It is deep red. It is a dress. They know it well. It is the cover of the king's sword that was stuffed in the pannier of Bollin's horse. They wonder why it is there.

"Was it thrown away by the robbers who have no use for it? Or did Bollin drop it as a clue?" They wonder whether the robbers are goblins broken free from the army or Twith never subdued by the wizard. "How will they deal with the goblin king?" They hang the dress over the branch of a tree and carry on.

Ahead is a pond. They push through the undergrowth, nettles, and scrub between the trees and then follow the tracks around the pond's southern edge. Studying the moist earth, it is easier now to make a guess as to how many men were walking. Probably not a dozen; more likely seven or eight. Bimbo looks for signs of the irregular footprints King Haymun would leave but doesn't see any. With the teething ring on his toe, he is probably still on the horse. The grass has only been lightly worn down by traffic. A barely visible trace of a track wanders off southwest into the deep forest. The robber party's prints continue due west.

Scayper pauses. They need to continue pursuing the robber party, but he feels led to choose a different path. It is some kind of instinct talking to him, as when an animal, whiskers twitching, senses unseen danger up ahead. Bimbo catches up. Scayper shares what he is feeling.

Bimbo is anxious to catch up with his brother, but he knows all too well that it is wise to trust the instincts of a Twith. They have senses Beyonders don't have. Maybe archers are in wait up ahead and this small path is a way around them. He nods his head in agreement. They can always cut north if they are getting nowhere and pick up the tracks again. That will not be difficult with so many in the kidnap party.

They are several hundred paces down the narrow, rarely trodden path when Scayper pauses. In the distance ahead, and still far through the thicket of trees, is a small cottage. They hurry towards it. It is a poor hut in need of repairs and a fresh coat of whitewash. It is a cob-walled, thatched cottage. A lazy wisp of smoke from the chimney curls in the clear blue sky.

Scayper looks into the small single window as Bimbo draws up alongside him. He sees a few simple furnishings. Flickering light on the wall confirms that there is someone within and a fire is burning. They see no one but hear the sound of a dog growling followed by barking.

Scayper knocks urgently at the door. "Is anyone there?"

The barking grows more insistent. A call comes from inside, a woman's voice. "Come on in!"

Cautiously, watching for a ferocious dog, they lift the timber latch and enter.

PRU AND NETTIE

Bimbo opens the conversation, standing at the door and trying to make out who is within. He is naturally courteous and does not want to frighten either of the two elderly women he sees sitting in front of a large fireplace. Both have turned to see who is standing at the front door. The woman nearest to him has her brown hair gathered into a bun on top of her head. She has a warm, friendly smile as she restrains a great brown-and-tan dog that looks more like a wolf than a dog. It looks a lot like Lupus.

"Excuse me. We do not wish to disturb you, but we wonder whether you could assist us with some directions."

Her voice sounds musical as she talks. "Well then, come on in, boy, and bring your friend in also. Pull the door shut behind you. We don't stand on ceremony here. We are not frightened. If you are robbers, we have had too many visits to pay much attention to that. They have already taken all they want from us, and they know we don't have any more, so they leave us alone. But you don't look or sound like robbers. Where are you from, boy? You are not from here!"

Bimbo still hasn't moved farther than the doorway. "I'm from the Beyond. I'm only visiting Gyminge, but this is my friend, Scayper. He does live here. My name is Bimbo."

"Just come right on in, lads, and make yourselves at home. Do you need a bite or so to eat? Nettie will get you something, won't you, my dear? There's some soup that's warm and can be hotter, and the bread is freshly baked. You can call me Pru, by the way. That's what my mother used to call me. My full name is Prudence, of course."

"Thank you very much, but we are in a hurry. We are traveling south towards the border. There are four of us. We were attacked by robbers, set upon by armed bowmen just an hour or so ago on the main path to the east of here. We think there were about eight of them. We two escaped. We wondered whether you might know anything about these men and where they live and if it's going to be possible to rescue our friends."

Pru, ignoring Bimbo's refusal, moves the pot of soup over the fire to reheat. "The answers to your three questions are yes, yes, and perhaps. Pull up that bench close. That's big enough for both of you. Sit yourselves down. Now listen carefully.

"We know of these men. You are right. They are a gang of robbers. They are notorious throughout southern Gyminge. All the local people are afraid of them. They are a good way away from here. They live due north, deep in the woods. It's about an hour's walk at the pace that you can walk. We'll send our dog, Loopy, along with you. She'll take you right to them so you won't need to bother yourselves about finding your way. They have horses when they choose to go further afield, but nearer to home, their usual custom is to walk on foot. There are altogether about a dozen of them. Their leader's name is Hardrada. He took the name from an eleventh-century Norwegian king who was so called because he was a Hard-Ruler.

"Nettie here was their cook for many years after they captured her. Eventually, they got tired of her cooking because they kept getting sick. They told her she could go, just turned her out one day without even a thank you. They had captured one of the cooks from the castle and thought he would serve them better. The poor fellow stopped by here when they got rid of him. He said that they all got sick with his cooking too. I don't know who they have for a cook now. I suppose it is one of their own men. Nettie found her way here after she was turned out, dropped in just as you have dropped in. We got on well together and have enjoyed each other's company ever since. It's good to have someone to talk to."

Bimbo and Scayper listen intently. "Is their camp in caves or in a clearing in the forest?"

It is Nettie who answers. Her cheery voice puts them at ease. "The camp is in the forest, in an open clearing. It is a large clearing. A stream runs along the west edge of it. That provides ample water for them, so it is a good location for their camp."

Scayper has another question. "Can you tell us anything about the guards they have around their camp?"

"They feel they are absolutely safe and do not post guards. They have a wicked reputation, and anyone with any sense stays away. The army from the castle never tried to tackle them. Hardrada lives in a tree house by himself. There is a great oak on the northwest edge of the clearing. There is no mistaking it, and the limbs have conveniently spread out in all four directions at about the same height. They support the platform the house is built on and curve up around the walls and roof. There is a fixed wooden ladder from the ground, but sometimes his men swing onto the platform from ropes hanging from the oak limbs or from smaller trees nearby.

"The men—some have womenfolk and children—live in huts around the edge of the clearing. They live by the sun. They are up at dawn, and when the light fails, they are soon asleep. There is a stable on the south side of the clearing, at the edge of the stream. A goblin who used to work in the stable at the castle takes care of the horses. He is their prisoner and is so terrified of them that he will be of no use to you. He is allowed to sleep with the horses, although next to the stable is a special hut where they keep prisoners. They have no need for guards on the prisoners. The walls are two inches of solid oak. Outside the door of the hut is a fenced area where the biggest dog I have ever seen is kept half starved. I never knew anyone to succeed in escaping."

Bimbo tries to remember all the details of what Nettie tells them. He is impressed with both women. They appear wise and have a sense of inner calm that will not easily be disturbed. "What is your counsel for us then?"

Pru smiles and thinks a while. She murmurs to Nettie, and her companion nods. "Go to the larder, young man, that door over there. Bring out the meat and potato pie on the lower shelf."

Bimbo strides to the pantry, easily locates the pie, and returns with an earthenware platter.

"Good. Set it down here."

He puts the pie down where Pru indicates, on the bench beside her chair.

The large, freshly baked, crusty pie smells delicious. It makes him realize that he really is hungry. So is Scayper.

Pru notices the boys eyeing the pie and asks, "Now will you go fetch that fresh loaf of bread from the upper shelf?"

Bimbo retrieves that and hands it to Pru.

Breaking it into two pieces, she gives one to each of her two guests. "Eat that now. I can see you are hungry. I don't want you eating the pie on the way."

Although pleasingly plump, Nettie springs from her chair to ladle out soup into bowls. Each of the boys is given a generous bowl of lentil soup.

They both eat the tasty soup hungrily. The bread is delicious. The crust is crisp and crunchy.

Nettie reaches up to the mantel shelf and carefully selects a container from among a whole row of similar containers. Her long, silvery hair cascades down her back like a waterfall shimmering in the sunlight. Her eyes twinkle with mischief as she lifts the lid off the pastry and sprinkles a generous coating of brown powder all over the filling. She steps back and admires her work and decides to give it another heavy dose. She looks over at Pru, who shakes her head.

She is not satisfied. "The dog is big, and the men are strong. Add a little more."

Nettie sprinkles a lot more powder onto the upper layer of the pie and replaces the pastry crust. She puts a kitchen knife on the platter beside the pie. Placing the platter in the center of a tea towel, she pulls the towel up and knots the corners.

Pru smiles. "The men at the camp didn't get sick because of Nettie's bad cooking but because of her good cooking. Nettie knows the herbs of the forest better than she knows the back of her hand. It was only a matter of time before they were always sick, even though the food was appetizing and cooked perfectly."

Nettie now begins her instructions and advice. She is as alert as Pru. The two women match each other. "You will, if you hurry, get to the camp before the light is done. Approach the camp from the southwest side, along the bank of the stream. Loopy will lead you to the right place. You can talk to her. She understands well. She is a dog that thinks. Choose your time. Feed the guard dog some of this pie, maybe a quarter of it. In a few minutes, it will be asleep. Leave the pie where the men can find it. Cut it into small pieces so that one or two greedy ones don't get all of it. Whoever eats it will soon be asleep. It won't cause them any long-term harm; just knock them out for a few hours.

"If you can, get into the stable and release the horses. Loopy will send them on their way and scatter them so that there can be no pursuit. If you need shelter or food, come back here. Loopy will stay with you until you dismiss her to come back home. Travel well, and be careful of that pie. Don't even lick your fingers if a little should happen to get on them."

Loopy is up and at the door, ready to go. It is amazing how much she resembles Lupus. Pru calls her back and talks to her, giving her clear instructions. "You stay with the boys until your help is no longer needed."

The dog barks twice, excitedly. Life has been quiet recently. She is anxious to be on her way.

SETTING OFF FOR THE RESCUE

The two rescuers are on their way. They are not anxious to wait for cover of darkness, although they might have to if they want to avoid taking on the entire robber gang. Scayper is not as fit yet as Bimbo. After running about three hundred paces, he is ready to slow to a quick walk. Bimbo carries the rope and the king's sword and shield to relieve some of Scayper's load. Scayper carries the lighter broadsword and the meat pie.

Loopy, content to slow down, lopes along just ahead of them. When they reach the main path where Scayper turned back, she moves farther ahead. Now progress is faster. She does not bark, merely pauses without a sound to turn her head and wait until they catch up. At the point of ambush, the tree across the path has been pulled to one side to allow other travelers to pass by.

Loopy knows where to go but waits until the boys point her north. She continues along the path with her nose close to the ground. When the dog smells the boys' horses, she does not approach them but waits near the clearing where they are tethered. She also smells something else. Crouching low to the ground, completely alert, she stays perfectly still. When the boys catch up, she does not move a muscle.

Scayper is also alert. Without a word, he prepares for a fight. He hands his sword, the rope, and the pie to Bimbo and reaches for the king's sword and shield. He whispers to Bimbo, "Remain near the path. Guard your back by standing against a tree." He hasn't forgotten the arrows of the ambush. Slowly, very slowly, he edges towards the clearing.

Loopy doesn't stir.

Scayper notices and stops. *That's odd.* He returns to the dog and kneels beside her. She raises her nose towards the trees ahead but still does not move. Scayper, and Bimbo behind him, search the trees with their eyes.

Bimbo is the first to spot the man high in one of the trees ahead. He can barely see him, but he is, without doubt, an archer. His bow is clearly visible. Bimbo slips close to Scayper and points. The man is motionless, with his head and most of his body hidden behind the trunk of the tree. From where he is hiding, he cannot see the boys. The two search the other trees. They see another and yet another. Three or four archers are spread high in the trees around the edge of the clearing. They are obviously waiting for the boys to come back and reclaim their horses.

Scayper smiles. "Let them stay there in the trees. There will be that many less in the camp. We'll take horses from there instead. Loopy, over to you. Show us the way around them."

Bimbo and Scayper exchange loads again to lighten the burden Scayper has to carry. Loopy is alert to the change of plans and runs off back down the main path past the ambush tree and keeps on running. She runs confidently. The two followers jog along comfortably behind her. Beyond the point where Scayper turned back at the time of the ambush, Loopy finds a small path to her right and halts. It goes well south of the direct route to the robber camp, and it means they will have to travel farther. They start running along it. Scayper will try to keep up with his healthy young friend. He has a strong will and is not going to fall behind if he can avoid it. There are no noises behind them to suggest they are being followed.

They make best progress by running three hundred paces and then walking briskly the same distance. Loopy adjusts to this and keeps looking back to check how they are doing. The path threads its way across a meadow that slopes slightly downhill, filled with a golden mass of buttercups with a few daisies scattered amongst them. The strong light throws longer shadows as afternoon merges into evening. As the slope turns upwards beyond them, Loopy slows and then stops. A small stream wanders lazily through the meadow and across their path. She drinks thirstily.

To each side of the meadow are woods, thick with deciduous trees. Either side of the stream a narrow path is lightly worn by foot travelers. Loopy turns north without crossing the stream. As soon as she enters the woods, she stops. Slinking low to the ground, she sniffs the path ahead as she creeps slowly along.

The boys realize, *We must be really near the robber camp.*

Fortunately, the light summer breeze is from the northeast. Loopy picks up a scent. The foliage overhead is thick, and the full, unbroken light only makes its way through as sunbeams. The dog stops dead in her tracks and sinks to the ground. Scayper and Bimbo hide behind trees.

Children are playing ahead. Their voices, raised in excitement, ripple with shouts and laughter. All through time, streams of flowing water have been a favorite playground for children. The world of newts, sticklebacks, lizards, stepping stones, wet shoes, and muddy knees has been a recipe for happiness and memories carried into old age. A mother's voice calls, followed by others. The children voice reluctance, but gradually, that fades to nothing.

Loopy cautiously resumes her forward journey. They pass the place where the children were playing. A pair of child's shoes, soaked right through, rests forgotten on the bank of the stream. Someone might soon be back for those. Ahead is a brown wooden building, the smell betraying its use. It is a stable.

Bimbo beckons Loopy and Scayper to come close. "Before we get Bollin, we should prepare our escape. Let's first capture the stable boy. Pru says he is unlikely to be a problem. Then we can saddle four horses. We might only need three, but we'll give Haymun his choice to come with us if he wishes. He could prove useful to us for getting through to the cave-tunnel. If he doesn't want to come, we'll find some other way; it doesn't really matter too much now. It is Bollin we have to rescue. Nettie reminded us to release the other horses when we make our getaway, and Loopy will chase them well away. As soon as the horses are ready, we'll cut the pie. I will try to drop a quarter of it to the guard dog. I might need to get some clothes from the stable boy to do so.

"Scayper, suppose you go around to the east side of the compound and drop the rest of the meat pie somewhere where it can be found.

"Loopy, you can start barking over on that side as soon as I have fed the guard dog. Maybe you can howl like a wolf. Can you do that? That will distract attention from this side and help the robbers find the pie. Be sure you stay downwind until we have dealt with the guard dog; we don't want him setting off barking when he smells a strange dog in his territory. Come on, Scayper."

Bimbo climbs down the bank into the stream. Bending low, below the level of the bank, he paddles up beside the end of the stable. They are in the shade with the sun to the west, throwing shadows towards the center of the large clearing. Ahead of them, farther up the stream, is the great oak. Mostly hidden within its foliage is Hardrada's tree house. A little more than a man's height above the ground, reached by a ladder, is the wooden platform that forms both outside patio and the floor for the dwelling. The patio is empty.

Scayper is right behind him, armed with the king's sword and shield. Slowly, they raise their heads.

The Robber Camp

Bimbo and Scayper are very conscious of the danger they face from arrows. It is one thing to beat a man in a swordfight. That is man-to-man fighting. Archers pose a much greater problem. Arrows are a long-distance weapon. King Harold at Hastings discovered that!

Nettie said that guards are not posted because they feel themselves safe. The clearing has two children playing hop, skip, and jump over on the far side, but neither is looking towards them. The stable door is immediately beside the tiny brook. Bimbo, seeing the lay of the land, changes his plans. Hidden from the clearing, he reaches up and bangs three times with the broadsword against the side of the stable. He waits. Nothing happens. Scayper, needing no instruction, moves upstream well ahead of him and turns around. Crouching tight against the bank, he is ready to move back to assist when needed. Bimbo knocks again, the same three times. Again, nothing. He makes a last try, this time with the hilt of the broadsword.

The stable door creaks open.

Steps approach Bimbo, who lies twisted on the bank of the stream at the back of the stable. His head is hidden. He groans. "Help!"

The goblin groom leans over to have a better look. He cannot recognize which of the robbers it is. Once more, he hears the pitiful cry, more of a croak this time.

"Help!"

He hates them all, but he doesn't dare to not help them if they need help. They will make him pay. He leans farther forward before he ventures into the brook.

He doesn't know what is happening to him. His feet are jerked out from under him. As he falls, a hand grabs his shirt and pulls him forward into the water.

• Scayper catches him before he hits the water. Bimbo leaps forward and clamps his hand across the goblin's mouth.

"Arrgh!" The goblin is scared half to death. He is surrounded by wild men he does not recognize and a wolf with an ugly growl! He tries to work out what is happening.

Bimbo warns the shaking goblin, "Don't you dare make a noise or you have made your last sound. Where is the king?" He removes his hand from the boy's mouth but keeps it close in case the lad decides to get brave and shout for help.

The goblin does not answer immediately. He is assessing the situation. When he speaks, his voice is unusually high-pitched. "The king is next door with the ginger-haired boy. They are tied up. If you have come to get them, take me with you please. I'm a prisoner here too. I'll help you if you take me with you."

Bimbo is quick. "We'll see how much you help us. We'll take you with us if we think you help us enough. If you betray us, we'll catch you and punish you. How many men are here?"

"Don't fear about that. I hate these people. There are ten of them here just now. Hardrada is up in his tree house, alone. He's not married. They are probably all having their evening meals. What do you want me to do? I'll do whatever you want."

"Do you have any spare clothes in the stable?"

"Yes. I have my overalls."

"Bring them right away. Can you do that?"

The goblin nods. "My name is Skweejee."

He is stalling as he hungrily eyes the pie that Scayper is cutting so he can feed a quarter of it to the guard dog.

Bimbo gives him a shove. "Quickly. We need them right away."

Skweejee is more than pleased to cooperate and is soon back with the overalls.

Scayper is already dressed as a goblin from his adventures in the castle dungeon, so it is Bimbo who pulls on the overalls. He gives further orders. "Now go back into the stable. How many horses do you have?"

"There are usually six, but they captured three more today, black ones. Two have only just arrived. I was brushing them down when I heard your banging."

"Right. Saddle the three new horses for us and the best two of your old horses for the king and yourself. Hurry! Waste no time. We are going to come up into the stable and leave from there. Come back here as soon as you have the horses ready."

Scayper is clad much as Skweejee is clad. Their hair is much the same color. This can help.

Once the groom is back into the stable, Scayper leaves his weapons with Bimbo. Carrying only his dirk, he climbs up the bank, yawns, and stretches in full view of whoever might be watching. He imitates the way the goblin walks as he strolls into the stable. Scayper is well accustomed to horses. The goblin is not playing any tricks. He is busy preparing the horses just as fast as he can work. The new horses recognize Scayper and whinny. He pats Black Beauty. The two men work together, standing on opposite sides of the horses as they place the saddles and tighten them. Soon, the horses are ready.

It is safer for Skweejee to move around than Scayper so Scayper remains with the horses and sends the goblin back to Bimbo. He whispers to Bimbo that the horses are ready and once again eyes the luscious looking pie. The other three quarters of the pie has been cut into twelve equal portions. Bimbo removes the quarter being reserved for the guard dog and hands over the plate with the remaining pie to the goblin.

"Place this plate of pie on the platform of Hardrada's house. Don't you dare eat any of it yourself. Do you hear? It's important. Not even a tiny bite or a single crumb. We'll know if you do. Then come back here for the next errand."

As the goblin climbs the bank, he looks longingly at the pie. There are twelve slices of the most beautiful meat pie that he has ever seen. His mother was a wonderful meat-and-potato-pie maker, but even she never produced a pie of this perfection. The pastry is a delicate brown, cooked to a T. Walking towards the tree house, he raises the plate to his nostrils. The wonderful smell is overpowering! Roses and hyacinths combined could not produce such an irresistible smell. He slips a look back at Bimbo. The boy has turned to talk to Loopy. Any resolve he may have had slips away. *After all, even Hardrada couldn't possibly eat all these pieces.* A slice of pie quickly disappears into his mouth. The goblin reassures himself. "He'll never notice the difference." By the time he turns around from the steps below Hardrada's house to leave, there are not even eleven slices, only ten. Not a crumb is showing around his mouth, but in his stomach, there is a most delightful sensation. It is childhood restored, music and bells and dancing. He yawns. Life has suddenly taken an immense turn for the better. He walks back to Bimbo.

Bimbo gives him final instructions. "Give this piece of pie to the guard dog. Don't take any of it for yourself! Come back as soon as the dog is sleeping, and let me know. After that, you stay back in the stable until we are ready to leave."

Skweejee thinks, *You can't possibly waste a pie like this on a dog. Even a prize-winning dog doesn't deserve a pie like this, at least not all of it.* He is well acquainted with the guard dog. After all, they are neighbors if not friends. He leans over the fence and shares the pie with the dog. They share and share alike except for the last bite, which the dog snatches out of his hand before Skweejee can raise it to his own mouth.

The last bite fixes the dog. He falls on his back, sticks his four legs straight up into the air, and goes fast asleep. *Zonk!* Over the fence, Skweejee does the same, except that he only has two legs and they are both stretched out straight along the ground beside the fence.

THE PRISONER'S HUT

Bimbo does not waste any time. Any second, they could be discovered. It is unusual that there has been so little activity in the clearing with children and families around. Across on the far side, the two children, a boy and a girl, are still playing hopscotch. Bimbo climbs up the bank, shuffles slowly into the stable, and nods to Scayper, standing alert at the door with his dirk drawn. He whispers, "I left the two swords and the shield just below the edge of the bank by the stable door. Loopy has run around to the far side to start a wolf howl diversion as soon as it seems wise to do so. When that happens, even earlier if possible, you should recover the weapons and get them into the stable."

Bimbo borrows Scayper's dirk. He slips from the stable, sees Skweejee stretched out flat, and removes the hat off the snoring goblin's head. He pulls it down over his eyes and casually saunters over to the fence around the prisoners' hut. Beyond are the robber cabins around the edge of the clearing. A metal loop over the gate post fastens the gate closed. He lifts it and enters the small yard usually patrolled by the guard dog. He is glad it is sleeping. The animal is one of the largest dogs he has ever seen. Even in sleep, with its four legs sticking straight up into the air, it looks mean enough to give a crocodile nightmares.

There is a loose rope laying in the yard. To play safe before anything else happens, Bimbo lashes the front and hind legs of the dog together, tight. The dog does not move or even know that anything has happened.

There is no padlock securing the hut to prevent anyone escaping. With such a dog, it is not needed. Bimbo lifts the outside latch securing the prisoners' door and slips inside. He pulls the door almost closed behind him. There is no window in the hut. It is almost pitch dark except for the thin sliver of light where the door is ajar. He can't make out much of anything. Bimbo has his dirk in front of him ready to use. "Are you here, Bollin?"

A groan comes from the far end of the cabin. "Over here. My hands are tied to the wall, and my feet are tied together. I can't move. My, am I glad you've come!"

Bimbo is relieved to hear his brother's voice, although it is twisted with pain. He moves over carefully to where Bollin is tied to the wall by ropes attached to wall rings. He is upright against the wall and facing it, his arms outspread. Bimbo holds the dirk in his mouth. He feels for and fumbles with the knotted ropes securing his brother's wrists. The knots are tied tightly. Bimbo steadily persists pulling at the knots. He doesn't want to try and cut the ropes off because he doesn't want to risk cutting his brother. The knot finally gives, and Bimbo carefully lowers Bollin's cramped arm to his side.

Bollin groans as restored circulation causes discomfort. The knot on the other wrist is just as tight and difficult, but it too gives after much tugging and pulling. Again, Bimbo lowers his brother's arm. He whispers his intentions as he holds his brother's shoulders and lowers him backward onto the straw on the floor. Bollin groans again with the pain of moving his upper limbs.

Now Bimbo cuts the rope binding his brother's feet together and pulls him to his feet.

Bollin, grateful for a helping hand, scrambles awkwardly to his feet and starts stamping his legs and waving his arms to restore circulation, wincing with pain as he does so.

"Bollin, Scayper and I and a wolf-dog like Lupus are here. Sorry we took so long. We need to get away as soon as we can. The horses are saddled and waiting next door in the stable. Keep moving your arms and legs. Can you ride, or shall I take you on my horse?"

Colin twists his upper body from side to side. "I think I should be able to ride after a few more minutes' exercise."

"Where is King Haymun? Is he here?"

"No. I'm here by myself. The chief of the gang, someone called Hardrada, he is huge, took him up to the tree house to interview him. He is holding him for ransom. Haymun is really scared for his life. He has heard of this gang of robbers before. They will stop at nothing to get what they want. The king will do anything he is told to save his life. He is not sure they will spare him even if the ransom is paid.

"Do you think King Haymun will want to come with us, or will he want to stay here?"

"Oh, there's no doubt about that one. He might be our prisoner too, but to be with us will feel like freedom to him. Give him a chance and he'll come with us."

"Bollin, listen carefully. Keep exercising your arms and legs until your limbs are working properly. We have taken care of the dog outside; he'll be no trouble to you. Watch what happens through the chink in the door while you're stretching and restoring circulation to your arms and legs. Five horses are saddled and ready in the stable. Scayper is there, waiting. When you are able to move, get over there and take care of the horses so that Scayper can help me. Go across slowly, as though you belong here. We'll try to get Haymun."

"It's okay, Bimbo. I'll follow you now. Off you go. I can make it."

There is not a second to waste before the alarm will be raised as the activity at the stable and Hardrada's is spotted. Bollin rests an arm on Bimbo's shoulder for support. The two brothers avoid running but walk briskly to the stable, hoping to put off the moment of alarm for a short while. Scayper has dragged the sleeping body of the stable boy over by the stable door, and the two boys step over him.

Bimbo returns the dirk to Scayper. "We are going after Haymun. He is with Hardrada in the tree house. Bollin will hold the horses. Come on."

Now they throw caution to the winds. Scayper grabs the weapons from the brook side and passes the smaller sword to Bimbo as they run around the edge of the clearing to the oak tree and the tree house. He pushes the boy gently to one side as they reach the steps. "I'll go first. I have the shield, and I'm better with a sword."

From behind them, across the clearing, as they scramble up the steps comes the first of a long, drawn-out series of howls that strikes fear into the hearts of all who hear. Loopy, racing from place to place, is howling high and howling low. A pack of wolves thinks she is signaling that there's a meal ahead. Each of their howls barely ends before another wolf answers from somewhere else. The robber camp is surrounded by a wolf pack about to go on the rampage.

The two children playing hopscotch, stricken with terror, look around desperately but are too scared to move.

A mother and a father dash out. Each grabs up a child and scuttles back into one of the huts.

Scayper notices that Nettie's pie plate is missing from the platform where it had been placed but wastes no time puzzling about it. He flings open the door of the tree house, his left arm shielded and the sword in his right hand, ready to strike the first blow.

THE TREE HOUSE

The inside of Hardrada's house is one large room, as large as the spread of the supporting oak limbs will permit. There are windows towards the clearing and towards the sunset. There are no windows towards the stable or on the opposite side, to the north. Earlier, he was questioning his royal captive when he heard a noise outside, but various robber wives provide the huge chief with food when he is not eating with his men, so he was not alarmed. He looked out towards the clearing but didn't see any woman returning to her hut, only the goblin stableman and the two children of his chief lieutenant playing hopscotch. The robber chief went out to see what might have caused the noise he heard.

King Haymun is bound by ropes to a caned wicker chair. They are not very tight. There is really little need to tie him up, but Hardrada sometimes has to leave his tree cabin in a hurry. He doesn't want to be concerned about what his guest has been doing while he is away.

While Hardrada is out of the room, Haymun mutters quietly to himself. "Where did things start going wrong? How on earth have I, the king of Gyminge, ended up as the prisoner of the dreaded robber baron, Hardrada? The man could crush stones to dust between two of his fingers. It probably started with crossing the bog on the back of the old woman's cat. But the beginning of my present series of misfortunes was the attack on me by that awful barn owl from the farmhouse. I hate owls! No, that's not when it really started. It goes back even earlier, years ago, in fact. The real beginning of my troubles began when the wizard heard that a group of escaped Twith was living on the Brook. It might have been better if he had just left them alone. There has been nothing but trouble ever since."

When Hardrada comes in from outside, he brings a plate holding more than half a meat pie. The pie is simply perfection. It could only be more perfect if it were a complete pie rather than three eighths of a pie.

King Haymun realizes how hungry he is. *When did I last eat? I missed breakfast and lunch, so I haven't eaten for twenty-four hours!* He quickly counts the number of slices of pie. Ten slices! *This meat pie has a smell such as I have not smelled since I last visited my grandmother.* His mother had been no great shakes as a cook beyond liver sausage and boiled eggs. She even got the boiled eggs wrong sometimes. The king watches, and waits, and hopes. *Even kidnap victims get hungry. Doesn't Hardrada understand that a prisoner dead from starvation has little commercial value?*

Hardrada uses the first two slices of meat pie merely as appetizers. He licks his lips after each bite. *I didn't catch sight of which of the wives presented me with the wonderful meat pie, but I will have to find out in order to make sure she prepares me another.*

He had been discussing how much the wizard will be prepared to give to secure the release of the king. King Haymun doubts whether the wizard will place as high a value on him as the robber chief appears to think. As Hardrada eats, he continues sorting out the details of the ransom delivery and collection while the king answers questions and keeps his eyes focused hungrily on the disappearing pie. Because the robber chief is so huge, it takes no less than four slices of pie to put him to sleep. But, when they do take effect, it is *Zonk!* His speech suddenly slurs and falters. His hands rest on the table. His head nods a while and droops onto his hands. He begins to snore. The volume of the snore fits the size of the man.

Haymun doubts whether the robber chief counted the pieces of pie as he has. *If I am asked, I will just say there was one less to begin with.* He begins to work his way forward. His bonds are loose. It is not difficult to wriggle one hand free. He does not wish to disturb the ropes because he will replace the hand after it has served the present purpose. He reaches across the table towards the pie in front of Hardrada. *Oh! I'm not quite close enough.* He rises to his feet. The chair rises with him. He takes two or three tiny, tottering steps towards the pie. He is still not quite near enough. The snoring increases. He reaches forward for one last stretch. His fingers reach the pie plate, but as they do, his chair, balancing on its two front legs, slips. There is a crash of collapsing furniture. Haymun, the pie, and the plate all end up in a tangle on the floor. He feels even greater pain in his left toe than before. As he cracks his forehead on the near leg of the table, he sees a bright light, and then slumber for the king is without the benefit of the pie to help him. His earlier bump in the cave-tunnel was on the left-hand side of his forehead. Now, a new bump is developing on the right side of his head.

Hardrada does not stir, even when the door opens and Scayper and Bimbo burst in upon them.

Scayper recognizes the sleeping robber chief as the man who felled the tree across the path earlier in the afternoon. He wastes no time looking around or trying to fathom what has happened before he flung the door open. He drags King Haymun out from under the table by his legs. Bimbo, crowding behind him, unravels the rope to free the king.

Scayper keeps an eye on what is happening in the clearing below. They have been seen mounting the steps to the tree house. Men begin to emerge from their houses. They gather on the far side of the clearing, pointing towards the oak tree. Scayper goes out onto the platform. There are several hanging ropes suspended from the extended limbs of the oak above, and one from a neighboring sycamore. They are obviously used by the robber chief when he doesn't want to take the time to climb down the ladder.

Scayper returns to Bimbo. "Help me get Hardrada out onto the porch, where he can be seen."

The man is still fast asleep. They drag him out by hands under his armpits.

The king still lies on the floor, recovering from his accident. As he comes to his senses, he spots the broken pie plate and the pieces of pie that still remain on the floor. One piece is quite undamaged apart from any dust that it might have acquired from a floor not frequently swept.

Bimbo returns to the room and sees Haymun taking his first bite of pie. The boy simultaneously knocks the pie out of the king's hands and slaps him on the back so that he almost chokes. He doesn't even have time to swallow for the food shoots out of his mouth as though propelled by a rocket.

Bimbo is irate. "Don't you dare eat that pie or we'll just leave you behind here for this gang to deal with you. Can't you see what happened to Hardrada? We have enough on our hands without you. Come on!"

When the boys dragged Hardrada onto the porch, they laid him over the railings near the ladder. He leans forward, fast asleep, his shaggy hair hanging loose. Over his head, clearly in view of the observers, Scayper holds his dirk high. He can see Bollin standing ready for action in the stable.

Across the clearing, the men are armed with bows loaded with arrows aimed at the tree house. They stay grouped together and do not move forward. They are all focused on the tree house, and none of them looks across at the stable.

Scayper bellows out at the top of his commanding voice. "Bring your bows and arrows close in here, and drop them on the ground. Do it NOW!"

There is no movement. Scayper wastes no time. He reaches over and catches hold of Hardrada's hair, cuts off a handful, and scatters it into the air. He reaches over for a new handful and pulls the man's head up. "I'll soon run out of hair. Are you ready to move? MOVE!"

THE ESCAPE

At first, no one moves. They look at each other, questioning, wondering whether they dare risk their leader's safety. One of the taller men moves forward, and then other bowmen walk after him. They move forward in a group, slowly and deliberately. Below the platform of the tree house, they reluctantly drop their bows and arrows on the ground. They glare up at Scayper and walk back, regrouping where they stood previously. Their actions mean that they have made a silent bargain with their enemy. He will not harm Hardrada if they do as he says. Now they wait to see what he will do.

Outside some of the huts, women and children stand watching. The howling of the wolf-dog and the wolves continues at intervals.

Scayper turns to Bimbo. "Take the two swords and the shield. I'll need to travel light. Go down and get mounted and ready to move off. Be as quick as you can. After you have our horses out, whistle for Loopy. Release all the other horses inside the stable, and let Loopy guard the stable door. Bring Black Beauty and station her between here and the stable for me. I will use the rope to swing down onto her back. Try to get her as close as you can into the right place for me to land. I might not land softly. As soon as I am on the horse, charge the gang of robbers across the clearing. Beyond them is the main path to the north-south track. Keep together. Loopy will bring the loose horses behind you, and I will chase them far enough away that there will be no pursuit."

Bimbo nods. They are working at high risk and high speed and are quick to drop previous plans, make changes, and adapt. Working with Scayper is like working with Bollin. They plan one thing and do another. He takes the weapons, sticking them under one arm and keeping the other as free as possible. Fortunately, they haven't been needed in the tree house. He waits at the foot of the steps for Haymun to join him. Somewhere along the way, the king has lost his crown. Bimbo hasn't spotted it in Hardrada's room. It probably wouldn't fit now anyway.

Haymun is still groggy and holding his hand to his head. His toe hurts as much as his head but it is more awkward trying to hold that while going down a ladder. They hurry across to the stable.

At the stable door, Skweejee is still asleep. Nettie's herb is surely a powerful sedative. Bimbo wonders what to do with him. He looks as though he'll be asleep for a month, although Nettie said it was more temporary. But she wasn't expecting anyone to consume almost four pieces.

Bollin helps Bimbo put Haymun on one of the robber's horses, the best of the pair, and then, to Haymun's surprise, the two Shadow boys lift and drape the sleeping stable boy across his horse in front of him.

Now, Bollin mounts his horse. The horse knows him, but the boy is hardly agile and moves slowly into the saddle. He tucks the broadsword beneath the side of the saddle. Only Black Beauty and Bimbo's mount are left.

Before mounting his own horse, Bimbo goes back to the far end of the stable. He makes sure that every horse not being used by them—four of them remain—is facing towards the door and is free from all restraining ropes. It will be up to Loopy to get them out later.

Bimbo mounts his own horse, tucking the king's sword beneath the side of the saddle. Fixing the shield to his left arm, he takes hold of Black Beauty's reins, and whistles for Loopy. The dog appears promptly from near the stream rather than from across the clearing.

Bimbo explains their plans. "You are to guard the stable door when the saddled horses leave the stable. Scayper is going to swing down onto his horse. As soon as he is mounted, the rest of us are going to charge ahead. Then you get the four stable horses galloping after us, and Scayper will help you keep them moving until we are far enough off to be safe. We'll stop at a convenient place to sort things out. That might be the place where we'll part from you. We'll see."

Loopy is quite clear about what she is to do. She barks once. As she goes quiet, so also do the wolves. They do not smell anything to their liking and turn for home.

Bimbo turns to his brother. "Haymun will be right behind me. I will put Black Beauty a ways behind him. You wait the same distance behind her. We want to leave room for Scayper to land on Black Beauty. If he misses, he'll need some space to run around and get mounted."

Bimbo chooses the position for Black Beauty as carefully as he can. "Easy, girl. Stand as still as you can, and brace yourself. Scayper is going to try and land on you from that porch up there." He looks up to see whether Scayper approves where the horse is.

The horse stands perfectly still, not moving a muscle.

Scayper holds Hardrada's shoulder tight. He still has his dirk raised high. The robber chief is completely sunk in deep sleep. His hair is now very short. Scayper looks at the position of Black Beauty, stands back to check the line of his swing, and sticks up his thumb. He pulls Hardrada back from the low railing so that he will not fall over it and leans him against the door of his tree house. He places the handle of his dirk between his teeth. With both hands, he grasps hold of the swing rope and launches himself into space.

Scayper holds the rope higher than the mark that shows where Hardrada usually holds it. The robber, when he launches out, aims to land on the ground. Scayper is aiming higher, for the back of his horse. At the bottom of the swing, he is low to the ground and his legs are bent at knee and thigh. At the other side of the swing, at the point where he is no longer moving forward and about to move back, he releases the rope and drops onto the back of the waiting horse with scarcely a shock to the animal. Grabbing the reins, he steers the horse out of the way of those behind her.

Bimbo can be proud of the position he selected for the horse. The swing is perfect, and the position of Black Beauty could not have been better. He whistles a signal to Loopy to get the free horses out. Yelling, "Charge!" he digs his heels into the sides of his horse. The animal leaps forward. Now he yells the Twith war cry that he learned from Jock. It strikes fear into the hearts of the listening robbers.

The group of robbers dives for their lives in all directions as horses charge through. They will wait for a safe moment and then run like the wind to the sides of the clearing.

Bimbo is away to the edge of the clearing. King Haymun is next. He can't respond as quickly as Bimbo, although he is not slow. The king has an extra passenger to contend with. Skweejee sleeps on, not conscious of the jolting and the bouncing as the king tries to catch up.

Bollin has two horses to handle. Fortunately, the riderless horse knows the drill. It too has once been a cavalry horse and knows it must keep up so the reins stay slack.

Loopy has everything under control. She starts howling like a wolf at the far end of the stable. The howl rises higher. No horse can hear a sound like that without wanting to run for its life, away from it. All four horses gallop pell-mell as they come out of the stable, nostrils flared back. Stricken with panic, they soon gain on the horses ahead of them. Galloping behind them is Scayper on Black Beauty and alongside him is a very satisfied half-wolf female dog that has enjoyed her best afternoon's outing for many a long month.

Bimbo is going like the clappers down the forest trail to the east. When he reaches the path leading south, he pulls up to wait for the others. They will not need to ride so fast from here. The stable horses passed him long ago, racing north towards Goblin Castle.

NIGHTFALL

Approaching the cave-tunnel at a steady canter from the north are four horsemen, intending to arrive there at nightfall. Bollin has somewhat recovered his agility. He has been filling in the story of his misadventures with the robbers and concludes with, "They are a gang of desperate men. We are fortunate to have escaped from their clutches."

On the southwest edge of Blindhouse Wood, Bimbo pulls to a stop. "We need to decide what to do about our captives. Shall we take them with us or leave them here?"

The sleeping goblin is not able to make a choice. King Haymun makes the choice for him. "This man should be left here. Tether his horse to that tree over there. Put him down on the grass to sleep the night through…and however much longer he needs. It might well be days. For myself, I will accept the offer of an escort and accompany you to the fort at the border. I hope I can be of service to you there before bidding you farewell." By putting it this way, he hopes they will understand that he does not consider himself a prisoner.

Bimbo makes no response but assists Scayper to unload the goblin who has not once opened his eyes since they left the robber camp. The tethered horse will have all the grazing it needs and will not be far away when the goblin finally does wake up. King Haymun is probably right. Skweejee looks as though he is going to be out for days.

Loopy is going to miss her new friends. Her errand, however, is finished, and she is ready to work her way back home to Pru and Nettie. It will take less than an hour. The three adventurers each give her a big hug. They give her messages for Pru and Nettie and stand waving as the dog runs back up the trail they just traveled.

As Loopy is about to enter the trees, she stops, turns, and barks twice. Then she turns and is lost to sight.

The four now move into a steady canter, Scayper leading. The rising moon is only half full. They ride almost due east, heading for the toad trail that goes between the cave-tunnel and the woods. Then they will turn south.

All three search the sky ahead, looking for any sight of a bird in flight. If it is not Rasputin, then it will be the wizard disguised as a bird.

Scayper begins to sing. The song has a chorus. The two brothers join in the chorus and occasionally add a new verse themselves. Even King Haymun is humming. He doesn't know the wizard is already back in Gyminge and looking for someone to vent his wrath on.

As night falls and darkness deepens, another group prepares to head for the border of Gyminge. Waiting at the entrance to Mole Hall near Squidgy's cottage on the Brook are the first of the goblin troops, ready to go.

Sergeant Major Aga checks that his troops are, indeed, ready. "Do you all have your mess tins?"

A unanimous, "Yes, sir!" rings out.

"Do you all have your water bottles?"

Again, they say, "Yes, sir!"

"Men, I know you have few weapons. But remember, you must be prepared for hard fighting all the way. The wizard warned us to expect the Chinese to use entirely new tactics. They are inscrutable. Watch their eyes! They won't blink! They will use surprise tactics out of the blue! Even invisibility!"

Aga inspects all the barrack rooms for tidiness and falls in behind his troops.

On the wizard's direct orders, the other officers reluctantly lead the goblins, hundreds of them. They fear the new tactics used by the Chinese will be a head-on attack. How do you fight an invisible enemy? An officer's place is in the middle of the troops, encouraging them, not at the front, remote from the men behind. What will the men do without officers to give them orders? They might well break and run! They are not going to run forward but back to their barracks! They won't care about the ones ahead of them they are deserting, the cowards!

The half-moon struggles to make its presence known and slowly gains strength over the fading sunlight. The sun is already below the horizon.

Cajjer, after being threatened by Mrs. Squidge, agrees to lead the goblins to the croc' pond. However, he downright refuses to go any farther and swishes his sore tail around as if that were reason enough. He meows his readiness to move off. The cat moves slowly along the path. Goblins are small and have difficulty keeping up.

The SnuggleWump wonders whether he should turn his eyes red and decides on amber as a halfway stage.

Overhead, Tuwhit peers down, trying to make out what is happening.

At the camp by the border, darkness has fallen. It is near midnight and there is virtual silence. A candle splutters a faint light. After his exertions getting his whole garrison on their way back to the castle, Colonel Tyfuss is resting on his tummy. His construction force of goblins should be well into Blindhouse Wood if they continued jogging at the same pace as when they left. There has been some grumbling. They were force-marched to get here to start work and hardly got started when they are force-marched back.

A stump of rotted blackthorn was moved to make way for the colonel's tent. He watches a colony of woodlouses trying to reorganize their home. They are diligent and obviously respond willingly to their leader's orders. There appears to be no rebellion in the ranks. The creatures move around busily, though it is hard to spot if they know what they are doing. They are more industrious than the woodlouses the ex-doctor is accustomed to. Those were farther north, and he wonders if it is due to the change of climate or that this particular leader is a better organizer.

Two cooks—neither of which is Rasputin's former guide through the tunnel—begin boiling the porridge in the cookhouse tent. They too have candles. Every cooking pot they have is filled with porridge. They have been told there will be a continuing arrival of up to seven hundred and fifty goblins from the Brook beginning forty minutes after nightfall. The goblins will be carrying their own mess tins. Anyone without a mess tin will be served hot porridge straight into his cupped hands. If the goblin needs to add sugar or the porridge is too hot, too bad! He should have remembered to bring his mess tin! There will be no nonsense and no time wasted.

THE DOCTOR

As they ride, Bimbo thinks of what lies ahead. He is anxious to get back to the farmhouse with their trophies and with Scayper. So far, they have been more successful than they might have hoped. He drops back to talk to Bollin, who is still following the king. "I'm undecided what to do about King Haymun once we arrive at the border. I doubt whether he'll be anything more than a nuisance as a prisoner. Jock probably won't want him around. I would just as soon leave him with Dr. Tyfuss if we can get through to the waterfall without using him as a hostage. What do you think, Bollin?"

"I think you're right. Jock won't have any use for him, and he'd just be more trouble than he's worth. Let's just turn him loose. He can find his way back to the castle, and we'll be long gone before he gets there to warn the wizard."

Haymun's presence with them as they ride means they have done little talking about things it is unwise for the king to overhear. Bimbo speaks to Bollin in Urdu, "I would like to spend some time before we get to the Brook telling Scayper about the Twith he's going to meet. And about Jock's plans for the Return, and Dayko's Rime, and the Shadow children, and the Real children, and...oh, so many things!"

Bollin laughs, "Well, we don't know anything much about Scayper either...what his real name is, where he comes from, and what he would like to be doing in the days to come. When he fully recovers his strength, there's one thing for sure: with his fine qualities, he'll be a great addition to the free Twith. From seven, they have grown to nine, and now they will be ten. They are getting stronger all the time."

Ahead, as they move down the toad trail towards the silhouetted trees in the hedge at the cave-tunnel, Bollin spots a small light. "Look, Bimbo. It must be the goblin camp at the border."

They rein in and are silent. There are few noises disturbing the silence of the night sky. They are unable to hear the crows over on the Brook, returning late to their nests.

Bimbo does not want Haymun bursting ahead of them and spreading the alarm among the goblin garrison. He makes sure his own horse blocks King Haymun's way. "Bollin, will you go ahead on foot and check whether it is okay for us to go on into the camp? We'll pull off the trail into the meadow so that the horses can graze."

In Urdu, he tells his brother, "See if Dr. Tyfuss is there. Tell him very little, but say the king is with us. Find out from him how things stand. Scayper and I will make sure the king does not go forward until we are ready for him to do so. Ask Vyruss what he feels we should do with the king, and, for that matter, the horses as well. See if there is going to be any difficulty getting through the cave-tunnel. When you report back, be sure you don't betray to the king that Vyruss is now working with us. Okay?"

Bollin nods. He dismounts and hands the reins of his horse to his brother. He is ready for this last part of their adventure. Earlier, he heard the king's explanation that Dr. Tyfuss is now a colonel supervising the construction of a fort or immigration center. He also saw the raven flying south as they crossed the lake early in the morning. There has been more than enough time for the bird and the wizard to get back into Gyminge. They could both be with Dr. Tyfuss for all he knows.

Bollin moves forward stealthily. His ears and eyes are finely tuned. He circles to the west. A mouse scuttles in the grass before him. He slips forward from the shelter of a bush to a point in the hedge bordering the bog on the other side. The curtain will be ahead of him and to his right, but he is not concerned about that.

There are tents to his left, but all is silent there, and there are no noises to suggest occupants.

Strange! Where is everybody? There are no guards. This smells like an ambush! There must be guards somewhere. He begins to get a tight, cold feeling in the pit of his stomach.

Bollin lost the dagger when he was captured by the robbers, but Scayper has given him the dirk. He draws it from its sheath and holds it half raised in his right hand as he cautiously tiptoes forward towards the single one of the lights ahead, a candle flame to the right of the other two lights. There are voices from near the pair of lights, goblin voices. *That doesn't sound like an ambush. What is going on?* As he eases nearer, he sees the body of a man crouched on the ground. *Is he poised to leap?*

The man moves, but only to place the candle in a better position. He is behaving strangely rather than warily. He is silent, hearing nothing around him, intent only upon something on the ground in front of him.

Bollin suddenly recognizes who it is and drops on the ground beside him with a warning press of his hand on the man's shoulder. "What are you doing, Vyruss?"

The doctor is pleased as he recognizes the boy, although Bollin feels the pleasure rather than sees it. Vyruss turns his face away from his observation to look directly at Bollin. "I'm watching how the woodlouses build their nests. It's fascinating. I have watched them before. One day, I think I shall write a book about it. I'm hoping to use some of their ideas on this camp, unless you want me to come back with you. What's your news? What do you want me to do?"

"Listen, Vyruss. We are on our way back to the farmhouse. We want you to stay here and try to make sure the way isn't blocked when we are ready to come back through later on. We have King Haymun with us. He can tell you his own news if he stays behind here. Will we need to take him with us to get through to the waterfall and the curtain? If we don't, we'll happily leave him here with you. We haven't discussed you with him at all. He doesn't even know we know you. You can let him talk, but don't believe everything you hear. We have horses. What should we do with them? What's going on here?"

Colonel Tyfuss scrambles to his feet hurriedly. He is agitated. Time is short. "You have to hurry. Waste no time at all! How far away are the others? Just turn the horses loose. If you are going through the tunnel, you had better run. There are seven hundred and fifty goblin soldiers, the whole garrison from the Brook, coming through within the next half hour. It will take hours for all of them to get through, maybe until tomorrow daylight. The wizard has ordered everybody back. They are probably already crossing the Brook. Gyminge has been invaded by Chinese, and they are in control of the castle. The wizard and Rasputin have already gone through here on their way back. My whole garrison, except for my meager kitchen staff and myself, is making a forced march back to the castle. We are supposed to feed all the goblins when they come through from the Brook; otherwise, we too would be gone."

Enough said! The boy wastes no time on farewells. He runs off into the darkness as fast as he can run. He speaks in Urdu in hurried tones to Bimbo. "Seven hundred and fifty goblins are on their way across the bog to the waterfall. There is no one this side to be afraid of. You and Scayper gallop for the cave-tunnel and get to the waterfall before the goblins do. You can stop them there. Remember, you won't have any weight once you go through the curtain. Take everything with you. Leave your horses at the tunnel entrance. I'll get rid of them and my own. I'll see to King Haymun, and then I'll come through as quickly as I can after you. Don't forget to duck your heads. Hurry! Hurry!"

TO THE WATERFALL

Scayper has never been through the cave-tunnel. Bimbo calls back to him to keep his head down as they work their way through. Bimbo has been through five times previously and can manage without light to help. He knows when to expect the dip in the roof. They hurry as fast as they dare. Bimbo carries both the king's sword and the king's shield. The shield is on his left arm, and its upper edge alerts him to the height of the roof ahead. There is a faint smell of hyacinths in the following breeze. The splashing of the waterfall ahead, reflecting the recent rainfall, is more noisy than at other times.

To Scayper, the air smells differently. As they near the waterfall, he begins to hear noises he has not heard since the fall of Gyminge. *Surely that can't be an owl I'm hearing? It sounds just like the call that Tuwhit used to make those many, many years ago when Gyminge was free.*

Bimbo calls out to him, "Beware the edge of the bank ahead. Find the path to the right." Looking through the sheet of falling water ahead, there appears to be a series of bright yellow lights spread along the surface of the bog. Bimbo can hear sounds, strange, rhythmic sounds! He yells, "I'm going ahead!" He leaves Scayper to work out his own way down the bank. Bimbo is through the waterfall and calls out, "Come on through, but stay off the bog. If you can't get down, I'll come back for you as soon as I can." Stepping through the curtain, he raises the king's sword as he jumps out onto the bog.

The sounds he hears are mainly the background noise of toad choirs, multiple choirs, rehearsing *The Bachelor's Lament* for a wedding. The burping of the toads in their thousands and the slow sucking sounds of squelching bog activated by the simultaneous downbeat of toad feet assist each other like echoes. The bog itself is pulsing. Above those unexpected sounds, he hears the additional noise of voices. Goblin caution has been thrown to the winds. No one is going to be able to hear the wizard's men crossing the bog with that heavy booming background beating the very air into shreds. The leading officers call back to and fro to each other.

Bimbo is only just in time, a matter of seconds rather than minutes. The goblins are very near! The first of them is only a few steps from the curtain. There are others in a long line behind him. Bimbo lets out the Twith war cry at the top of his voice. Scayper, on his way down the side path, hears and responds with not only the Twith war cry but other war yells he remembers or manufactures. Their shouts are amplified and echoed by the waterfall and the hollow space between it and the bank of the field.

Bimbo feels his weightlessness returning. He jumps towards the first of the parsnip lamps in front of him without knowing what kind of light it is. He kicks it over into the bog. The light shines downwards. The steady, deep beat of the toad music stirs him up. He is getting excited. He continues screaming war cries and throws in verses from the psalms in Punjabi.

This strikes panic into the goblins. They catch glints of light from the whirling sword blade. They recognize the words immediately as Mandarin Chinese sung by hordes of invisible soldiers descending onto the bog because Gyminge is not big enough to hold them all. The beat of feet stirring the bog is straight from the Chinese mainland. The wizard was right after all!

Bimbo swings at the first goblin as he kicks at the next lamp and then another.

At the close of the failed attempt on the farmhouse, Taymar deprived the goblins of their belts, their boots, and their weapons. Of the three, the one loss most easily rectified is the belt. Not a single goblin is marching clad only in his underpants; all have trousers. The trousers are held up with string or rope. In a few cases only, those with exceptional foresight have used bootlaces. One way or another, they have each coped with the problem. The goblins who were in sick bay during the attack, had their belts and boots stolen by their friends. Friendship only goes so far.

Many of the goblins march in slippers. These are okay on leafy paths through the woods, but not so hot in a bog, steadily pulsing up and down. If they don't get the rhythm right, the bog sucks down as they lift up, and the slipper is likely to follow the force of gravity. In the long term, it might well be that the ones marching barefoot are better off, except for the mud between their toes. At least they are not going to lose their slippers.

Hardly a goblin has weapons. No one has tried to steal the swords, the pikes, the lances, or the bows and arrows of the goblins who were in sick bay. If they should happen to meet an enemy during the night march, they know who the enemy will go against first. Not the man who flings up his empty arms in despair and yells, "Fainitz!" No. The enemy is no coward. He is going to head straight for the goblin with a weapon in his hand, and his target must face a desperate fighter determined to spill blood. They are better off without weapons. Especially those who are loving fathers. They don't wish to have orphaned children.

The goblin that Bimbo swings at as he launches his attack is an officer of junior rank. He has been forced to lead by officers of senior rank behind him. He is a man of undoubted courage, as long as there is no enemy ahead of him to call him to account. Faced by invisible Chinese ahead of him and his fellow officers behind him, there is no doubt he knows who his friends are. He recalls his father's advice when he first joined the army. "Dead heroes have only a short life!" He turns on his heel at the same time as he swings his tummy out of the way of the sword flashing in the limited light. The turn catches him off balance, for he is only just on balance when he is standing flat on his two feet. As he falls, he twists to his left, towards the second man who is more agile than he is. He misses and does a belly flop into the bog. He stays in that position, listening anxiously to the glug-glug-glugging of the bog around him, and wonders, *What next?*

The goblins have had problems before when they lined up close one behind the other. It happens again. The first man in the whole column of seven hundred and fifty had either refused or been unable to move forward. In fact, his reverse movements backwards have only failed because his companions did not cooperate. Nevertheless, chaos ensues. The goblins dare not step out of line because beyond the edge of the toad trail on the bog is the bog itself, which will suck them down, and they will be lost forever.

Although goblins are not overly intelligent, the difficulties experienced earlier by King Haymun floundering in the bog, let alone the previous battle at the waterfall by Sergeant Aga and his pursuit party, have not passed unnoticed.

Where does a man, number 277 in the column, go when the neighbor ahead, number 276 in the column, does not go forward because number 275 has left no space into which he can move? Add to that problem two other problems. A weightless Shadow boy hands over the king's sword and shield to a warrior Twith bellowing strange oaths. With the sword held high, he stands like a steam railway train at a station, ready to charge down the tracks towards them.

The Shadow boy starts dancing in and out amongst them like a butterfly, unconcerned about the bog's powers. To their horror, he runs along the toad path, kicking over the lamps that alone keep them on the safe path across the bog.

The other problem is the owl. Scayper does not know yet, but it is the same Tuwhit he knew from long ago. The bird is enjoying a night out. Recognizing the war cries from Scayper and Bimbo, he joins in the fun. He knocks out, one by one, the lights from the far end. Tuwhit is careful to not have too long of a contact with any parsnip. Once burned, twice shy!

In his nest, Crusty hears, above the toad rehearsals, the screams from an excited owl and noises that suggest at least one of the recent passengers that he dropped at the waterfall is back. He takes flight and circles lazily, watching the action but not joining in. Everything seems well out of control.

Roughly one third of the goblins are already flat in the bog. That exceeds two hundred in number. More keep falling, helpless to remain standing. They are in bumps and clumps, all anxiously trying to clamber to their feet and quite willing to use their neighbors as stepping stones in the process. As they do so, they bring others, who are still standing, down to their level. They shout and yell.

Bimbo happily adds to the confusion. He is enjoying his weightlessness. Kept close to the surface only by the weight of his clothes and the broadsword, he yells out snatches of Urdu and Punjabi. In addition, as he skips between lamps, he yells out encouragements to his victims. "Remember Shanghai! We are betrayed! Run for your lives! Dive! We'll never make it! We are ambushed! Chiang Kai Shek! They are more than us! We can't see them! Mao Tse Tung! Help! Back to Squidgy's! Stay on the trail! Hong Kong or bust! Chop suey and chopsticks!"

Bollin now arrives after dealing with King Haymun. He slides past Scayper and jumps down onto the bog to join his brother. Although he has only a dirk to wave, he contributes to the confusion by his yells. He sees Bimbo has matters well under control near the waterfall and joins in creating diversions farther along the line from his brother. They are a team working together.

The retreating goblins, attacked from all directions, are past caring about anything except eventually touching ground that doesn't give way with each step forward. Panic begins to spread amongst the goblins and quickly turns into terror. They cannot go forward. There is no swordsman amongst them who dares try to tackle that terrible figure waiting at the waterfall for their champion to come forward. The skills of Chinese two-handed swordsmen are famous worldwide. Even worse, there are two other of the enemy wreaking destruction among them. They cannot go backwards because there are no lights left to show them the way. They cannot go to either left or right, for that way is the unexplored bog itself. Their enemies are immune to the dangers the goblins face. The fight is unequal!

Slowly, the lights on the bog go out. As the last of the parsnip lights disappears, Tuwhit looks forward to something even better than a dozen birthday parties all at once. He alone is well equipped to go at goblins in the darkness, and he goes to town against them. He makes broad, low swoops over the tangled, twisted, screaming, yelling column. It is unfair that some shall still be on their feet while their companions are on their backs or their knees or their tummies. From the croc' pond, his low, gliding dive seems almost to brush his wing feathers into the bog itself. After his third pass, there is not a goblin left standing.

Sergeant Major Aga begins to crawl his way back to the croc' pond. He feels how firm the surface ahead of him is before he moves a knee forward. Behind him, a long, long line of muddy, weaponless goblins begins to crawl after him. Each one hopes that he doesn't make a mistake and lose his way back. The main interest of each is the heels of the goblin crawling ahead. They are going to swing neither to the left nor to the right. While the one in front is slowly moving, the ones behind will keep on crawling also in the same hand and knee marks.

Tuwhit swoops in to the hawthorn drooping over the waterfall. Amid his laughter, he croaks "Anyone want a ride? Ho-ho-ho-ho. Ho-ho-ho-ho! What a night! What a night! I can't remember when I last enjoyed myself so much!"

Bimbo and Bollin smile at each other as they help Scayper onto Tuwhit's back for the journey to the farmhouse. Ahead might be new adventures, but this one at last is over. They forget they are tired and that it is already Saturday morning. They are too excited.

"Jock will be so pleased that our secret quest has been such a success. We not only recovered the sword but found the shield as well."

Scayper is looking forward to meeting the free Twith on the Brook. *I'm not familiar with the name Jock. But Cymbeline...could it be?*